# GUILT EDGED

*A Selection of Recent Titles by Judith Cutler*

*The Lina Townend Series*

DRAWING THE LINE
SILVER GUILT *
RING OF GUILT *
GUILTY PLEASURES *
GUILT TRIP *
GUILT EDGED *

*The Josie Welford Series*

THE FOOD DETECTIVE
THE CHINESE TAKEOUT

*The Frances Harman Series*

LIFE SENTENCE
COLD PURSUIT
STILL WATERS
BURYING THE PAST *

* *available from Severn House*

C0052 91659

This ᵇ
rene
autho

# GUILT EDGED

Judith Cutler

**Severn House Large Print**
London & New York

This first large print edition published 2016
in Great Britain and the USA by
SEVERN HOUSE PUBLISHERS LTD of
19 Cedar Road, Sutton, Surrey, England, SM2 5DA.
First world regular print edition published 2013 by
Severn House Publishers Ltd., London and New York.

British Library Cataloguing in Publication Data
*A CIP catalogue record for this title is available from the British Library.*

ISBN-13: 9780727894120

Severn House Publishers support the Forest Stewardship Council™
[FSC™], the leading international forest certification organisation. All
our titles that are printed on FSC certified paper carry the FSC logo.

MIX
Paper from
responsible sources
FSC
www.fsc.org    FSC® C013056

Typeset by Palimpsest Book Production Ltd.,
Falkirk, Stirlingshire, Scotland.
Printed and bound in Great Britain by
T J International, Padstow, Cornwall.

*To my dear son Jon,*
*and the unemployed army of talented*
*young men and women desperate to do a*
*fair day's work for a fair day's pay*

# ACKNOWLEDGMENTS

This novel could not have been written without the generous and inspiring help of Philip Allwood, auctioneer and raconteur extraordinaire, who took me behind the scenes at Moore, Allen, Cirencester, and freely shared his expertise and love of antiques. It goes without saying that he and his team are nothing at all like Brian and Helen Baker's completely fictitious firm.

Lina and I both found invaluable information in *The Portrait Minature in England* by Katherine Coombs (V and A Publications, 1998), for which we are truly grateful.

# One

'Talk to me about a horse? What do you mean, someone wants to talk about a horse?' Tearing my eyes from the blank computer screen they'd been glued to for heaven knows how long, I turned to Mary Walker. She might technically have been just an employee of Tripp and Townend, Antique Dealers, of Bredeham, but she ran the shop part of the firm as if it were an outlet of Harrods, at the very least. Why should she imagine I'd want a horse, especially just at this moment? For goodness' sake, didn't I have enough to worry about?

Then another thought struck me. 'I didn't run it over or something, did I? Or make it jump or bolt or whatever horses do?' I could have done. My mind hadn't exactly been on my driving last night.

'It's not a real horse,' Mary Walker said gently. She'd been alternately bracing and soothing ever since she'd arrived for work, trying to work out what tone to adopt. Her smile was apologetic. 'China. A model horse.'

She nodded as I repeated the words, my throat as dry as my lips. 'We don't have any model horses,' I managed to whisper.

'The lady doesn't want to buy. She wants to sell. I've told her it's outside my remit, and that you might not be available, of course.'

1

'But you think I ought to be?' Swallowing hard, I surrendered to Mary Walker's kind pressure on my shoulder and got up. After all, I wasn't making much progress with Internet trade, and in my current state, I'd do more harm than good if I tried to do my usual job, which was the restoration of precious china. Grabbing the home phone handset, just in case, I followed her to the shop. And why not? I reminded myself that wherever Griff was, however he was, I needed to keep our business ticking over, even if all I wanted to do was cower under the duvet with Tim the Bear, Griff's best ever present, for company. I was an antiques dealer, I told myself firmly, and that meant dealing: buying as well as selling.

But I'm also what we call in the trade a divvy – someone with a nose for good things amongst a pile of dross. Or – occasionally – a nose for bad things. And this was the nose that, despite everything, was twitching now.

'It's china,' the woman said softly. 'A horse, like I told your boss.'

I let that pass.

Aged about fifty, she was discreetly made-up and quietly dressed – just the sort of person you'd run into in an M and S Foodhall. Her smile was both gentle and polite. In fact, I could see nothing to justify my immediate surge of suspicion. I wished I could: I never knew if I simply had a weird instinct, or if my eyes picked up things my brain didn't have time to process quickly enough, so I was in fact unconsciously drawing on knowledge. Certainly, last week's dowsing for dross in the homes of the Best People in France had been

2

based on good, solid book-learning, underpinned by Griff's patient teaching. And yet – and yet . . . Griff would sometimes quote Hamlet's comment that there were more things in heaven and earth than could be explained by simple science.

Responding to my nod of encouragement, she swallowed and fished her horse, thickly quilted in bubble-wrap, from her basket, a good old-fashioned wickerwork one I took an immediate fancy to. 'I understand it's a collector's item,' she said; it sounded more a declaration than a simple statement. 'My mother-in-law used to like models, especially of horses. I hate to part with it, but you know what it's like these days – redundancy . . . debts . . .'

Thank God I didn't. Our shop trade might be poor, but the Internet kept us going very nicely, and the recession had actually helped me by sending items for restoration my way that would once have been dealt with by in-house museum restorers. There was even the prospect of some work for my boyfriend Morris's aristo contacts in Paris. Though I wasn't at all sure today whether I wanted to trade on that relationship. Assuming it still was a relationship.

Without speaking, I laid on the counter the sheet of green baize we keep to protect both the glass itself and any item the customer wants to look at. Or – very rarely – wants us to look at. Why on earth had she chosen us? We did very little buying like this, our stock coming from sales and fairs, and some trading with mates. *Buy cheap and sell dear* was Griff's motto, and had,

3

naturally, become mine. And how could you buy cheap from a woman reduced to selling a cherished heirloom?

'She said it reminded her of her own horse,' the woman continued, with something of a catch in her throat. 'A countrywoman – mad about them. Of course, all her horses are long gone now.' She sighed deeply.

Mistake. If you want to tug my heart strings don't go for *the privileged past now reduced to penury* story. Look around our cottage and the shop and you'd see comfortable middle-class writ large. But that was Griff's doing. My background, after my mother's death, was an endless succession of foster and care homes; privileged I was not. I had come into Griff's life because my last foster mother decided that Griff needed someone to look after him – or maybe that he needed someone to look after. Whichever it was, if it hadn't been for Griff's endless love and patience, I'd probably be in jail by now. Or dead. Dirty needles and unprotected sex, that sort of existence.

It really wasn't a very good idea to be thinking about Griff, was it? But I think she took my teary sniff as a sign of sympathy.

'So this is the one we hung on to longest. Poor Puck – I hope you'll go to a good home.' She sniffed too.

I think I was supposed to ask what had happened to the original horse, the one that this Beswick model resembled. But what if I got the answer, 'Glue factory'?

Beswick model horses come in all shapes and

colours and sizes and are like Marmite: you like them – or not. My pa quite liked gee gees, at least those running races on Channel Four, so perhaps he'd have appreciated this white jobbie more than I did. Griff, a townie to his fingertips despite having lived in the same Kentish village for years, would not. Once I'd ventured to describe a model foal as cute – which it was. Griff had sniffed, audibly, and told me I was damning it with faint praise. To tell the truth, Griff thought horses were terrifying creatures, with sharp bits on five corners, and incontinent to boot. I had no strong feelings either way, never having been through the pony stage when I was a child.

'They're quite rare, these white ones, aren't they?' the woman prompted me. 'Collector's items,' she repeated.

They might well be. I could have been honest and told her I didn't have a clue. We specialized in middle to upper range Victorian china, and though we were venturing more and more into the twentieth century, as the taste for Art Deco grew, this definitely did not include twentieth century model animals. But Griff had told me that admitting ignorance was never a good move: it was better to play for time. And it wasn't just his advice that made me say, 'We'd need to do some research before we could even think of making an offer. Can you leave it with us?'

'There was one on TV that fetched six hundred pounds,' she said, which didn't seem to be an answer to anything.

Perhaps I should have told her point-blank that

5

even if we bought it, it wouldn't be for the retail price – we had to be able to make a profit on it. Instead, I said mildly, 'A preliminary investigation won't take long. Can you wait a few minutes? There's a nice tea room halfway down the village street.'

'Leave something that valuable? With you?' Her tone was decidedly less pleasant.

I didn't tell her I dealt with items worth ten times that on a daily basis. And sometimes a hundred times more.

'I don't like to let it out of my sight,' she grumbled.

But as I reached regretfully for the basket and the bubble-wrap, she said, 'Oh, very well. Just ten minutes, maybe.' She looked round for a chair, and plonked herself on it. She rose quickly, because Mrs Walker had placed a teasel on it, a hangover from when she'd worked in Bossingham Hall where they wanted to prevent just such an assault on a valuable item of furniture. Whether it was such a good idea in a shop – we wanted to sell the chair, after all, and a customer might want to see if it was comfortable, or at very least would bear his or her weight – I wasn't so sure.

Leaving Mrs Walker to soothe ruffled feelings, I gathered up – what was the animal called? Puck? – and headed to my work room, to check for flaws under the bright lights I need for restoration work. The glaze was absolutely perfect. Puck had obviously been well looked after. On the off-chance that a restorer as good as me had been at work, I blacked out the room and applied the ultraviolet lamp. No, no signs of repair.

Restoring the room to daylight again, I left Puck where he was, basking in the sun, and nipped into the office to see if the Internet could help.

Yes and no. Mrs Thingy was right. White horses of this size in this particular pose were rare, and did fetch six hundred pounds, sometimes more, when perfect. But . . . but . . . but . . .

On impulse, I phoned an old friend of mine, Titus Oates. Ninety-nine per cent of what he sold was spot on. The other one per cent was cunningly forged by people like my father. Griff cordially loathed him; on the other hand, I knew I could trust him to have the latest information about any dodgy deals going – all of which he disapproved of, as it happened. That one per cent apart, he was the most law-abiding man I knew.

'White Beswick horses?' I asked, getting through first ring. Titus didn't like preliminaries. He didn't like phones at all, actually, but accepted that sometimes there had to be an alternative to a muttered hole-in-corner conversation during an antiques fair.

'Not your line, doll.'

'Quite. So why should someone want to sell me one?'

'What's the old geezer say? Hey? What's up? You still there, doll?'

'Sorry.' I sniffed, then sobbed, 'Griff's bad, Titus. Heart. Arteries.'

'Shit. Heart not good. Arteries not so bad. They can do bypasses. Ask your dad. All that TV he watches, he's an expert.' When I said nothing, he prompted me: 'Needs an op?'

'Today,' I sobbed. 'Oh, Titus, he's in the

operating theatre now,' I managed, the words coming out in a rush. 'Now, this minute.'

'Jesus, doll, and you're worrying about sodding china nags? Actually, best thing you can do – take your mind off things. This here Beswick. Got a name for the seller? Not like you. Anyway, so much as a sniff it might be dodgy, put them off. I'll talk to people. Right? Let me know how the old man goes, OK?'

He was right. I was in no state to make rational decisions. Missing the chance to make the odd hundred pounds wouldn't ruin our business, but selling anything that wasn't right might well. Griff had spent years building up a reputation for absolute honesty; hadn't he dinned into me that provenance was all? And here I was thinking of going against all the instincts that told me to avoid this item.

Back in my work room, I took photos from every angle and peered closely just once more. No, I couldn't fault it. But that didn't mean there wasn't a fault.

Rewrapping Puck carefully – breaking him now I was about to return him to his owner wouldn't be a good move – I went back to the shop.

'I hoped I'd be able to speak to the senior partner,' I lied, 'but he's not available just now.' That was true at least. 'I'm sorry to disappoint you, but until he's back in the office, I can't make a decision. As you say, six hundred pounds is a lot of money.'

Slightly to my surprise, she stripped the bubble wrap back and peered closely at the animal with narrowed, even hostile, eyes. Presumably, she thought I might have chipped it or worse. Actually, the way my hands were shaking again she had a point. 'And when will that be?' she asked Mrs Walker – as the boss, no doubt.

Mary stepped forward. Presumably, she'd been able to explain away the teasel. 'Mr Tripp's going to be tied up for the next few days, Mrs Fielding. Why don't you take our card and phone us before you come back? I'd hate you to have another wasted journey.'

'There are other antique shops.' As if that was a threat, not a statement.

Mary actually took a step backwards, but then produced a pacifying smile. 'So there are. But you'll quite understand why Lina – she's only the restorer, you see, Mrs Fielding – can't make such decisions.'

Any other day it would have been an effort to keep my face straight. *Only the restorer!* What with my hands and with my divvy's nose, these days I was actually the major earner in the partnership. Not that that mattered a jot. Griff was the boss.

I didn't wait to hear the rest of the conversation. Usually Mrs Walker – and I! – would have talked up my role in the partnership. Today she'd played the winning card for me and was now milking the situation for every drop of sympathy she could. But if I laughed I knew that I'd quickly succumb to hysterical tears.

'She's very young, isn't she?' Mrs Fielding observed without waiting for me to get completely out of earshot. 'Has she just had a row with her boyfriend or something?'

9

Actually, though I'd not exactly had a row with Morris, my boyfriend, Mrs Fielding wasn't far out. Morris – he only ever used his surname because his first name, Reginald, wasn't exactly cool – had disappeared off the face of the earth. OK. Exaggeration. But despite knowing Griff was ill and that I needed him, he'd not responded to my texts, my phone messages or even my emails.

Perhaps he wouldn't call on the house phone anyway; perhaps he was even now trying my mobile, which I'd put down somewhere. God knows where.

What should I do now? It was as if something huge and heavy – a giant version of those earthenware pots Griff used to force rhubarb – was sitting over me. All I felt was one huge enveloping wordless dread, that Griff might not . . . that he would . . . I knew dimly that there were things I should have done – quite urgent things – but couldn't recall what they were, let alone why they might be urgent.

When would it be two o'clock, and I could phone to find how he was?

I wandered back into the shop. The phone rang. I pounced. Just the usual hum to show the line wasn't in use. So it wasn't the phone. It was the shop doorbell. These days we didn't leave the door open, even when Mrs Walker was accompanied by her fiancé, who liked to sit and write poetry in a far corner. Anyone wanting to come in had to wait while we checked that the security cameras had a nice snap before buzzing him or her in. This time it wasn't a customer, but the

10

fiancé himself, Paul Banner. Mary, who said nothing about my strange mistake, gave a little coo of delight at the sight of Paul, hugged him, and swept off. He gave me a hesitant smile and then a tentative hug. Why Griff and I should always call him Paul, while addressing his future wife, whom we'd known for so much longer, more formally, I could never work out. Today my brain didn't even bother to try or to ask why he was here – Tuesday was his golf day, wasn't it? Griff had speculated that golf was a hangover from his accounting days since it didn't seem to sit well with poetry.

Mary returned before we could do much more than agree that the weather was fine, carrying a tray, complete with lace cloth, teapot, cups, saucers and plates. She and Griff were as one in the belief that mugs were an invention of the devil.

'There,' she declared, 'green tea just as you like it. Of course you like it, Paul: it's so good for you,' she insisted as he pulled a face. He was really a builder's tea and two sugars man. 'Scones in my basket there. We've just had such a weird woman – quite gave me the creeps. I really wished you were here – though she'd have thought you were the boss, wouldn't she, Lina?' She didn't bother to explain, but continued, 'Since you're here, darling, would you mind if Lina and I did girlie things for a few moments? She's been to Paris, remember, and I haven't seen what she bought there. I know it was a working visit, but I can't imagine dear Griff not insisting she bought some clothes. And shoes, if I know Griff – such good taste, Paul!'

'Good enough to pick out your wedding dress,' Paul agreed, helping himself to a scone. 'What about you, Lina? Has he organized your bridesmaid's outfit yet?'

I was just about to wail, when Mrs Walker took my arm. 'No need to worry about that. Pop a scone on your saucer, and we'll go and look at your Paris booty,' she declared, scooping me out of the shop and back into the cottage.

The chic bags still lay haphazardly in a corner of my bedroom, their contents languishing in the tissue Griff had swathed them in before we'd left France. So much had happened, nasty dangerous stuff, since we'd got home, that they'd simply slipped my mind. At least I remembered shoving our dirty clothes in the machine, but I couldn't remember for the life of me if I'd ever switched it on. Probably I hadn't – and Griff would be tutting with frustration if I didn't get the benefit of a lovely drying day. Explaining briefly, I trotted downstairs and set the machine off, only to find that I was clutching Tim the Bear.

By the time I got back, Mrs Walker had transformed my room. Clothes, now on hangers, were festooned from the wardrobe doors, and pairs of shoes nestled like glossy birds in the now lidless boxes. She'd even collapsed and flattened the bags into their original folds.

She was actually stroking one of the dresses. 'So he did think of the wedding, bless the dear man. Oh, Lina, this colour will go perfectly with the dress he made me buy. Not quite white, not quite cream, not quite grey – oh, it's a gem. Like a pearl, against the opalescent greeny-blues and mauves of mine.' This was delicate Italian painted silk, just right for a lady in her sixties, and she was right: the two outfits would complement each other beautifully.

Actually, though I'd never tell her, Griff had picked out my dress for me to wear for a formal evening in French society, where it had acquitted itself very well amongst all the top of the range gear the other women were wearing. It had gone further: it had reminded me that though I came from what my father mysteriously called the wrong side of the blanket, I was actually an aristocrat's daughter. *Noblesse* had never *obliged* my pa to do anything, such as take an interest in any of his illegitimate children, and no one would pick him out as a lord; indeed, his closest mate was the decidedly shady pleb Titus. But that evening, his daughter carried herself as if she was in the habit of sporting aristocratic ermine. Griff had played a superb supporting role, of course, as dapper and worldly as he knew how.

'And these shoes, Lina – just the right height for you and for the dress,' Mary was saying. 'Wonderful colour, a bit more definite than nude. But if the weather's unkind, you'll need a little stole or something – you won't get away with wearing thermal undies under something as sheer as this. Any undies, come to think of it.'

I made my mouth say, 'I'm sure the sun will shine for you.' And I really hoped it would. For their sake, not mine.

'But it'll be *autumn* sun . . . You know, I'm sure a little retro fur stole – better still, a cape – is the answer. You and Griff must know some specialized clothing dealers, Lina, who'd help. Why don't you check through your address book and email a few people? You could always send them a photo of the dress.'

If only she'd stop yapping. I might scream if she didn't. But even as I tried to work out an excuse to get rid of her, it dawned on me that all she was trying to do was to take my mind off Griff. 'That's a good idea,' I croaked. 'Let's move the other clothes into the wardrobe so that I can get a good shot of the dress without a lot of clutter.'

Miraculously, the room returned to nice tidy normality, as if Griff hadn't maxed out his credit card on a loving legacy. No, I didn't like that word at all. Not legacy. Gift.

If he didn't pull through, would I ever be able to touch them, let alone wear them?

'You know,' Mrs Walker declared, head on one side, 'the best way to give a proper impression of the dress would be for you to be wearing it. But first you'll need to run a comb through your hair, and maybe put on a little make-up. I wonder why Griff calls it slap? It must be his theatrical background. And he's taught you to apply it so well – there, just a bit more lippie, as he will call it. Now, I suggest we put a tea-towel or something over your head so you won't get anything on the fabric when you pull it on. Or do you step in? Of course. Let me just – oh, my goodness – real buttons! I thought they were just for decoration, and there'd be a hidden zip. Good job my hands are warm.' As she talked, she worked her way up my back. 'It's usually the bride who needs

14

help getting dressed, not the bridesmaid! Promise you'll help me with the make-up, Lina?'

'Griff'll do that,' I said firmly. But she was right about the cape; even on a day like this I was dithering with cold.

She squeezed my hand. 'Of course he will.' She turned me round to face the mirror. 'There. Who wouldn't sell you a fur cape to go with that? Now, where's your mobile? Or your camera? Is that it there? Beside those posh teddy bears? Thanks. Stand a bit straighter. Good. And if you don't feel like smiling, how about looking meaningfully into the distance? No, that makes you look as if you're about to start an aria. Not Wagner, you're much too slender for that. Though they are encouraging opera stars to lose weight and look like normal human beings. Chin down a little? Excellent. And one more?' She showed me what she'd done.

Heavens, she was good with the camera, wasn't she? All this time she'd worked for us, and, always irritated by her constant chatter, I'd never recalled she had talents beyond talking customers into parting with their money. But she had a degree and was a qualified teacher, for heaven's sake. It was just that life had given her a couple of really nasty kicks which had taken away her confidence. It seemed that a combination of working with Griff and the prospect of marrying a really nice guy had brought it back.

Just now she was checking a list of people who might help out, and we were sending them texts and the pictures via the phone. She might have kept up a constant commentary, but her hands

15

and brain worked regardless. The phone still in my hand, somehow I found myself heading back to the shop with her, telling Paul how she'd organized everything.

'Once a teacher always a teacher,' he said with an affectionate smile.

'Quite. Sometimes I can even remember how to be in two places at once,' she said. 'But if Lina hadn't stepped in when the Bossingham Hall administrators sacked me—'

'I still think you should have gone for unfair dismissal,' Paul growled.

'Hard to do that when I was only a volunteer!'

They exchanged a look. It was as if he was asking her if she'd done something; hers in reply told him to shut up. All very clever. And they weren't even married yet.

The little silence held.

My mobile broke it. Mary and Paul melted out of the shop.

'Hi, Lina. Lina? Are you OK?'

Morris! 'I hardly recognized your voice.' It wasn't the warmest of greetings, but he sounded as if he was talking through cotton wool.

'I just wanted to know how Griff is.'

Hadn't he read anything that I'd sent him? 'He's in surgery now. Right now. At this moment.'

'Never! I thought he was just having a spot of angina.' Morris wasn't telling the whole truth. Two days ago he'd been sufficiently worried about Griff to take him straight to A and E in Ashford's William Harvey hospital; he'd even seen him safe into the cardiac unit. But he'd not waited for me there, just left a note, saying he

16

had to return to France for a vital meeting. It seemed he had time to talk to Europe's top policemen but not to his girlfriend. He'd told Griff he thought he'd got the flu coming on and didn't want to pass it on to me. Personally, at that moment I'd have swapped a kind hug for a few germs. One day I'd tell him that.

Not now.

'I told you in my texts – and there are a couple of voicemail messages . . .'

'Sorry – flat battery. Anyway, you can tell me now.'

'The angina was so serious he needed immediate surgery. A triple bypass. I can phone at two to find out how he is.' As if he needed to know that. Or even wanted to.

He coughed and sneezed convincingly. Perhaps he did have the flu. 'Jesus!' he croaked. 'Let me know if I can do anything, won't you?' he said in the same tone as people who say, 'We must do lunch sometime,' knowing you never will. 'Got to fly – another bloody meeting.'

'But . . . OK.' I cut the call. Why didn't I feel anything? Anything at all? I was sure I ought to.

I'm not sure how long I glared resentfully at the undeserving phone, but my reverie was interrupted by Mary and Paul, who looked as if they had continued their silent conversation out loud and weren't too happy with the result.

Coughing, Paul spoke first, punctuating what he said with sideways, challenging looks at Mary. 'In the circumstances, with Griff . . . so . . . poorly . . .' He leant confidentially forward on to the counter, speaking in the sort of hushed

17

voice people use in church and trailing to an embarrassed halt. Finally, he took a deep breath and continued, 'Mary and I wonder if we should postpone the wedding.'

Postpone the wedding! If I showed how touched I was I'd burst into tears. But I mustn't Give Way, as Griff himself would have put it.

'No need at all,' I declared briskly, probably as surprised as they were by my positive tone. 'Griff's promised to lead Mary up the aisle, and lead her up the aisle he will.'

'Yes, of course he will,' she declared. 'Paul was just wondering how long he'd be convalescent, weren't you, dear?' She shot Paul a sideways look.

He nodded, but I had the feeling he wanted to say more. He did: 'We'll leave you to be the judge of . . . If you think he needs a few extra weeks, that's all.'

I took a gulp of air. 'If anything will speed his recovery, the thought of the wedding will. Not just the champagne, either.' But they were right to worry. How long would he be ill? Everything had happened so quickly that I'd simply no idea how long he'd be an invalid or what sort of care he'd need.

His long-term lover, Aidan, had enough money to throw squads of private nurses our way until he was fit enough to travel, and then would certainly want to whizz him off somewhere luxurious to recuperate. But my place was at his side, as long as he needed me there.

Mary patted my hand, and then pushed a tissue into the other one. I hadn't even realized I was

18

crying. 'It's all so sudden, isn't it?' she said, in her usual gossipy voice. 'We realized this summer when he had all those tests that he had health problems. Of course, he wouldn't speak about them – as if ignoring them would make them go away, bless him. We knew it'd only end one way – with an operation, I mean,' she explained hastily. 'I didn't say anything to you, Lina, not because I didn't want to but because – well, it wasn't my place to. And it was so much better for you to hear it from Griff. It made you closer than ever, didn't it? But now it's all happened in such a rush.' She did something she'd never done before – she put her arms round me and hugged me. She must have felt the sob rising. 'Now, Lina, I really do think you should sit down and let me make us all a nice cup of tea. That's what Griff would want. And you should certainly eat: there are still plenty of scones, and I can't have Paul finishing them off – he'll never get into his wedding trousers.'

# Two

Two o'clock approached. I could hardly breathe. Literally. My God, what was Griff going through?

The phone rang. I pounced. An Asian voice asked me about our loft insulation. I snarled – shouldn't have done so really, since she was probably paid less than a pittance. And then it rang again. A phone survey. No thanks. And then I won a bloody holiday in Florida.

All I wanted was clear phone lines. Just in case the hospital wanted to call me. Please God, let it be two o'clock soon.

All the time this invisible band tightened round my chest. All I could think about was how I'd felt his pain when he'd had the bad attack that had kept him in hospital. Was this really *his* chest that was hurting?

The phone again.

'Yes?' It came out halfway between a snarl and a gasp.

'Only me!' sang a voice.

Big help, when I was almost deafened by the whooshing in my ears.

'Just phoning about Griff—'

Robin, my clergyman friend. Last time I'd seen him he'd just given Communion to a man dying in the very hospital where Griff was being treated. And now – he'd phoned to break the news, hadn't he?

I started to sob, scream, whatever.

'Is he still in hospital?' I heard at last.

'You've not phoned to tell me he's dead? Please tell me you've not!'

'I think the hospital would call you,' he said matter-of-factly. 'Or get the police to come. No, I was just on my way to the maternity unit at Pembury to see Freya and thought I might drop in to see you. Why should Griff be dead?' he asked. 'He's in hospital, for goodness' sake.'

'So was that guy you gave Communion too. And he died.'

'So you've been putting two and two together and making about forty-three. Oh, Lina.'

'He's in the operating theatre right now. Robin, get off the line. I need to phone. They said I could at two.'

'It's not mandatory. Five minutes won't hurt.'

'It'll hurt me! I need to know the minute I can.'

'Well, there's three minutes to go, if you're being literal. Perhaps it's not the time to ask, but I was wondering if I could tell Freya you might be dropping in to see her.'

He'd asked the same last time we'd met.

'I told you then: if God brings Griff through safely, then maybe I'll forgive Freya.'

'And I told you, God doesn't work like that.' For Robin, that was pretty stroppy. 'You need to forgive because—'

'Robin, it's bang on two, by my watch. I have to phone now, I really do.' End of call.

Time to call the hospital. Now.

Except I couldn't make my hands work. Fifty

21

thousand euros' worth of china repair might be coming my way – and I couldn't dial. After half a dozen attempts, I nearly smashed the phone. Then I remembered the number was on speed dial. And I got through after two rings.

And then I couldn't manage the words. At last the woman at the other end must have worked out I was in a state, because she told me quite sharply to slow down and take a deep breath. At last we established who I was and who I wanted to ask about.

'I'm afraid we only give information to patients' immediate families.'

I was just about to let rip when it dawned on me: of course, we have different surnames. 'I'm Griff's granddaughter,' I lied. But since we'd agreed this between us and I was down as his next of kin, I didn't even cross my fingers behind my back. Actually, they were tightly enough crossed, but for Griff.

'He's doing fine. We've just got him breathing on his own. A very routine operation, according to the surgeon. You'll be able to visit tomorrow.' She must have heard my sob. Her tone changed. I could even hear the smile softening her voice. 'Very well. Tonight. Just five minutes.'

If I had the ten minute long cry I wanted, Mary would fear the worst. So I dug as deep as I could, and made my legs run across the yard, and forced the voice to work. 'Griff's fine!'

Only a croak, but I managed a louder one as I opened the shop's back door. I wasn't sure why Mary came out to me, hugging me and having a bit of a weep too, until Paul emerged, grabbing her firmly by the shoulders and pushing her back in. He scooped me up and propelled me to the kitchen, where he set about making tea.

'Mary's just about managed to unload that hideous epergne – the one that got wished on you as part of an auction lot they wouldn't break up. So there's two good reasons for a cuppa – and a scone, I'd say,' he added, looking at me. 'There are still some left.'

I didn't argue. I drank and ate. And then I took a second cup and a second scone to the office. I had to tell a load of folk Griff was OK. People who didn't even know he was ill, some of them. But first of all would be Aidan, his long-term lover who was stuck down in New Zealand after his sister's death. He'd want to know the good news whatever time of night or day it was, just as I would.

Then I thought I'd better make my peace with Robin. That was the nice thing about old friends. Or at least the nice thing about him. Once the S word came out, he didn't try to lecture me or tell me not to behave so badly in future. He just said it was fine, and asked how Griff was and what I was going to do.

'And then I think I'll nip off to the church and have a word with God,' I ended.

'It works just as well where you are,' he said, sounding as if he was trying not to laugh.

'Look, if someone gives you a nice present, isn't it more polite to write a proper letter than to send a text? Well, then. I think God deserves

23

a bit of effort from me after the efforts He made for me, don't you?'

'Can't argue with that,' he said.

As the nurse had promised, I was allowed to see Griff in the evening. I'd never seen him so small and frail – old, in fact. He was in a vast space-age bed, with all tubes and dials and monitors everywhere, which Griff's nurse – one-to-one care even in these cash-strapped times was amazing – constantly checked. I spent five wonderful but terrifying minutes, just holding a hand and talking softly. As I tore myself away, she came over, smiling.

'I promise you he's doing well.'

I gaped and gestured.

'So well in fact that he won't need one-to-one nursing much longer. He'll be moved out of Intensive Care within forty-eight hours if he continues this way. To the next stage: High Dependency. One nurse to three patients.' She patted my arm. 'Honestly. Just go home and leave him to us. You wait – we'll have the roses back in his cheeks by the end of the week.' She gave me another look, both searching and sympathetic. 'Look, why don't you phone again, ten-ish, just to make sure. It's not a problem – the patient does better if he knows his family isn't worried. And you're all he's got, aren't you?'

'Yes,' I said, dismissing Aidan without a second thought. 'And he's all I've got, too.'

Paul, who'd insisted on driving me over, was waiting in the car park. Hospitals didn't suit him, he insisted.

'I could take you straight home,' he said, 'as I promised. But please come and have a bite with us. Mary won't admit it, but she's prepared a special spread. Actually, she'd love you to stay overnight with us too. She thinks the world of you, you know. Ever since you stood up for her against that lying bitch at your dad's place.'

'He doesn't own Bossingham Hall any more,' I pointed out. 'It was the woman the trustees employed that was the problem.'

He nodded patiently, pulling out on to the main road. 'Anyway, taking her part then, and then offering her a job with you – you saved her sanity if not her life, Lina. And feeding you and offering you the spare bed – she's trying to say thank you, in no matter how small a way.'

All my mind would register was the number of words ending in -*ing* he'd used. I fished desperately for something appropriate to say. 'Every time she takes a job off Griff's hands she does that. She's got a wonderful way with customers – as you must have seen, since you ride shotgun every day. Every day except Tuesdays, now I come to think of it, Paul – how come you were with us today?'

'Just in case – in case you had to get to the hospital quickly,' he admitted.

I nodded. 'Thank you. I'd have been a menace if I'd had to drive. And even with this wonderful news I keep getting these tears coming from nowhere. Paul – this sounds awful, I know – I'd love to eat with you, oh, yes, please, but I really can't stay over. It's a sort of touching wood, you know.' It was. 'But I shall have a taxi home to

Bredeham. I insist. Promise you won't argue? Oh, I know Mary will. But I want us all to raise a glass to Griff's health without you having to worry about staying sober. OK? Promise you understand and will make poor Mary understand? And I'd better take this call. It's Pa.'

'Brace yourself, then!' He was so obviously trying not to listen that I nearly laughed.

Pa tended to bark when he used his new phone, as if unconvinced that such a small object could do the work of a nice old-fashioned Bakelite one. 'That old queer of yours OK?' Hell, he was talking like Titus now, as well as working for him.

'He will be. They let me see him.' I burbled away about how soon he'd be moved into High Dependency.

'Only two days post-operative? They don't hang about, do they? Well done him.' Pa spoke, as Titus observed, as one who never missed a medical programme, fact or fiction, on TV. He never missed much else either, come to think of it. 'So what time shall I expect you? I think I've worked out a way to switch off the CCTV in the trustees' part of the Hall, so you can have a nice four-poster all to yourself. . . .'

He wasn't really supposed to enter the main house, except to use the library. Needless to say, he always chose the most circuitous route possible to get there, taking in the attics and the bedrooms where he'd begotten me and my thirty siblings. As for the CCTV, I reckon modern systems were out of Pa's class, and there was no way I'd try to sleep with a sinister silent eye watching me and recording every toss and turn.

'I'd love to, Pa,' I lied. 'But I've given the hospital the house number, not my mobile, so that's where I have to be. I'll pop in tomorrow to see you – on the way there or the way back, whichever is more convenient for you.'

Until a few weeks back, he'd done his illicit work in some corner of his wing he made damned sure I never entered. However, one of my police contacts had made it clear they were on to Titus, so now every last incriminating item was – wherever. I didn't know, and I certainly didn't want to know. This meant that for the first time since I'd known him, I could no longer assume he'd be in whenever I dropped by.

'Ah. Let me see . . . What time did you say you could see old Tripp? Afternoon visiting, and then again in the evening, if I know you. So, morning. Ten-ish. We could go to a supermarket. I need some more shampoo.' The expensive sort he would drink, not use on his hair. Why could he never simply call it champagne? But that was Pa for you. 'We could even have lunch. Early, of course. So you won't be late for visiting hours.'

'Great. It's a date.' But the fact he wanted me out of the house for such a long period worried me. 'Pa, you're breaking up – see you in the morning.'

Mobile coverage was very poor in parts of Kent, but this was just an excuse to cut the call. If he said any more I'd have to worry more, and I'd got an idea I didn't have any worry juice left in me.

Paul and Mary lived alternately in each other's houses, week by week. Tonight we were in

27

Mary's cottage in a hamlet called Bossingham, which gave its name to Pa's place, Bossingham Hall. But if I'd declined an invitation to stay with her, there was no way I could accept one from Pa, even if I'd wanted to. And I really did just want to curl up in my own bed, knowing Griff was safe in someone else's hands.

But I could at least turn round my excuse when I recovered from Mary's huge enveloping hug. 'I can't stay,' I said, 'in case I drop it out to Pa and really upset him.'

She seemed to accept what I said at face value, topping up my glass with champagne. Mistake. It went straight to my head, more particularly to my eyelids, and equally to my knees. In no time I found myself on the sofa, parking the glass with exaggerated care on an occasional table and blinking very hard. And very slowly.

When I surfaced, they'd adjourned to the kitchen, their voices occasionally reaching me through this haze of tiredness.

Mostly, I couldn't be bothered to listen. Then I heard Mary's voice, sharper than usual.

'Of course the poor dear child wants to go home,' she said, with a hint of exasperated sadness in her voice, 'and call a taxi we can. But it's not because of her pa or even the fear the hospital will call her at the cottage. It's because she's hoping against hope that no-good boyfriend of hers will turn up. I'd love for her sake to think he will, but I'm not holding my breath – and I hope she isn't either, poor lamb.'

Five years ago I'd have been on my feet, smashing the glass into her face for talking like that. Even now I was so busy stuffing my hands in my mouth to stop myself yelling at her that I didn't catch Paul's rumble of a response.

I ought to interrupt them. It was rude to eavesdrop. Rude and scary. But my legs were still rubbery, and I couldn't trust my mouth to be much better.

'He's good-looking enough, I grant you, but a man of his age? Forty if he's a day, and her not yet twenty-four. And what sort of life is it dancing attendance on his little daughter, when she ought to be having fun with people her own age?'

Another rumble.

'He lets her down time and again and seems to think he can make everything better by sending her yet another Steiff bear. She doesn't even like them, you know – they're too expensive and too stiff to cuddle. No, she prefers that teddy Griff gave her. Loves it, as if she were a child.'

It struck me quite hard that she was right about that. What if she was right about the other things too?

Paul said something else I missed.

'I'll bet there's another Steiff on its way as we speak – as if that would make up for him not being there at the hospital when the police had finished with her on Sunday. Skipping off to France, as if some police meeting was more important than comforting your girlfriend. I mean, it wasn't just Griff who was ill – she'd been assaulted herself! Could have been killed!'

I suppose I could have been. Some rich lowlife had decided to kidnap me and douse me in petrol, and that was just for starters. However, all that had faded into insignificance when I'd found that

29

Griff had been admitted to hospital with acute angina.[1]

Another rumble – I think that this time Paul was telling her they'd been through all this before.

'I'm sorry. Of course we have. Now, is that rice ready?'

'Almost. But I think we could all manage a drop more bubbly first, don't you?'

And that was the last I heard for a bit. Perhaps it was just the thought of Tim, but I fell asleep again. It was only the delicate striking of a pretty clock Griff had found for them as an engagement present that woke me. Even as I opened my eyes I realized the snooze was useful for two reasons: I felt much better, for one thing, and more to the point it implied I'd not been busy listening in to their private conversation. Thank goodness I hadn't slept so long I ruined the meal, which became very jolly indeed – so jolly I found I was a minute late phoning the hospital.

'He's still very well, Lina. Even better, actually. His vital signs are improving by the minute. Griff, it's your granddaughter!' I heard Griff's nurse call. 'Can I give her a message? He's sending you his love, Lina.'

'Tell him I love him. Now, may I give you a different number – just in case?' I dictated it. 'Tell Griff I've been kidnapped by Mary and Paul.'

I heard her relay the information. 'He's giving a big thumbs up.'

Of course he was: I'd bet a pound he and Mary

1 See *Guilt Trip*

30

had planned the whole kidnapping in advance, not for today – there'd been no time – but for any time there might be an emergency. So instead of leaping up and demanding a taxi, I smiled humbly and asked if I could change my mind about the spare bed. The look she and Paul exchanged confirmed my suspicions. So it didn't surprise me at all to find my nightie on her spare bed. Or Tim the Bear sitting on the pillow, arms outstretched.

# Three

I was in the shower when my phone rang. My God! It was only six forty-five, too early for me to ring the hospital. What if—?

I flew to pick it up, falling over umpteen things I'd forgotten were in Mary's spare room.

'Yes?' I screamed at last.

'Goodness me, sweet one, such volume at this unconscionable hour.'

Griff. Griff himself. I sat down hard on the bed, only to realize I was squashing Tim the Bear.

His voice might have been a bit weaker than usual, and he scared me to death when he said he couldn't remember either my being with him last night or my phone call – and then saved the day by saying his new nurse was telling him he'd probably lost all of yesterday.

'New?'

'Oh yes. Veronica. I have to share the dear girl with two others now I'm no longer in ITU—'

'Not in ITU?' Pa would have made more of it than I did, but I twigged it was important. 'I thought they said forty-eight hours? You're that well already? Wow and double wow.'

'My darling child, that is such a feeble expression. But after all you've been through these last few days, I shall forgive you.' *Me* going through things, not *him*! I swallowed a sob. 'The truth is they needed the bed for someone else, and I was nearest the door . . . Now, my precious one, could I ask you to bring me a few things I forgot to ask for the other night? Do you have a pencil handy . . .?'

'*Middlemarch*?' Pa chuntered as we left Waterstones. 'That's a damned thick book for an invalid. You should get him one of those electronic jobbies – save the poor old bugger's wrists. What else does he need? Slippers? Surely you took him slippers!'

Pa was always miffed if I had to spend time and effort on Griff: they were horribly jealous of each other. But we eventually ran to earth the sort Griff wanted – soft, heelless slip-ons he wouldn't have to bend to put on. Clearly, Pa disapproved, as if they were a sign of total degeneracy.

Then I made things worse by dawdling outside a newly-opened shop. An antiques shop.

'Heavens, Lina – don't you see enough of other folk's rubbish?' As if I didn't keep him in food and champagne by selling his or his trustees' cast-offs. Not that the trustees knew, as it happens.

'I do. Have them up to here.' I sawed the air three inches above my head. 'But there's something in there that interests me.' There was. Eight hundred pounds' worth of white Beswick horse, according to the absolutely transparent code on the label round its neck. Eight hundred? Well, Canterbury is a tourist magnet, with appropriate prices. 'Look, Pa, you were talking about getting yourself a new cap – why not pop into the gents' outfitters there and I'll look at that china horse.

Then I'll come and find you – three minutes max?' He had a clear choice. Follow me or do something that suited him. He took himself off in a huff a two year old would be proud of.

If I'd hoped the dealer would be an old mate whose brain I could pick I was disappointed. Behind the counter there was a highly decorative female of about thirty who looked alert when the shop bell pinged, took one look at me, and then drooped back to her copy of a celebrity mag.

'Can you tell me anything about that horse?' I'd have preferred a more subtle approach, but didn't want to irritate poor Pa any more than I had to.

She reached it roughly out of the window, putting it and everything else in its path at risk of injury. 'Cash: eight hundred and fifty pounds,' she announced with a dazzling smile. So she was ripping off her employer, was she? Or maybe she was just dim and couldn't recall the code. I'd reserve judgement.

'Can you tell me anything else about it?'

Not without peering at its base, she couldn't. 'Beswick.'

'Oh. May I look?' I didn't wait for an answer, but examined the poor beast as closely as I could in the subdued lighting that was all the shop offered. The glaze was perfect, just as Puck's had been. Perhaps this was Puck, come to think of it. Perhaps Mrs Thingy had found another buyer – and hadn't wasted much time doing so. Perhaps I'd made a mistake turning it down. Or had I? I made a regretful excuse and left, to find Pa just leaving the outfitters, sporting a very fetching cap set at a rakish angle. Rakish? Well, that was my pa to a T.

'And after all that you didn't buy the bloody nag?'

'I don't think Titus would have let me,' I said, touching the side of my nose.

He harrumphed and stomped off in silence.

It took a big shop at Sainsbury's, including three cases of excellent champagne, courtesy of some silver I'd managed to sell for him, to restore him to comparative good humour, and he did actually stand me lunch – a sandwich, all we'd got time for. And then, back at his place, as I unloaded the goodies he'd bought, he shocked me so much I almost dropped a box of eggs.

He patted one of the cases still lurking in the boot. 'That's for Griff. He may not be allowed any booze for a bit, but when he is, he needs decent stuff. With my compliments, tell him.'

I was so touched I actually kissed his cheek.

Paul and Mary had told me not to think of trying to drive back to Bredeham between afternoon and evening visiting. They'd mind the shop, and if there were any tricky Internet orders, one of them would phone me for a decision. Meanwhile, I was so elated at the sight of Griff's newly pink cheeks and his ability to knock off two crosswords before lunch that I decided to head into Ashford itself for a spot of retail therapy, which was altogether easier without a grumpy toddler in his seventies in tow.

Pa had been so tetchy that I'd forgotten to buy anything for my supper – and it was Paul and

Mary's ballroom dance class night tonight, so they'd consented to let me go home. M and S was the obvious answer. Then I just drifted. Despite my dreamless sleep the previous night, I felt as if my legs were made of toffee. And I didn't really want to buy anything. I wasn't ready for autumn clothes yet. But it was too soon to go back to the car or the hospital, so I let my feet take me to the older part of the town, where there were still some small individual shops, including Rob Sampson's Antiques Emporium. I vaguely knew Rob from sales and fairs. We weren't rivals – he functioned at a slightly lower part of the market than we did, with bits of memorabilia to compensate for his stock's general lack of age.

Although it was only about four thirty, the shop was closed. Maybe he was off at a sale – I remembered with a pang there was a house-clearance auction Griff and I had meant to go to over on the Isle of Oxney.

Rob didn't have the luxury of a Mary Walker to give his windows a regular polish. Or maybe the accumulated dirt was supposed to give an air of mystery to the unprepossessing items on display. Coronation plates; a pair of Charles-Diana wedding commemorative thimbles; a very ugly Portmeirion mug celebrating the Moon Landing. A Beswick horse. White. Puck's brother, no doubt about that. Same size, same height, same stance, with its tail in exactly the same position relative to the legs as Puck's. A clone.

Scratching my head, I drifted back for a cup

of coffee – but all I wanted was more time with Griff, of course.

He'd sounded and looked so perky I decided I must celebrate somehow, even though I was on my own. I dropped the shopping on the kitchen table, and although I meant to return Tim the Bear, still slightly rumpled after a day safe in the depths of my bag, to his rightful place, he insisted on keeping me company downstairs, ensconced on a couple of cushions. But he'd be on his own for a bit: I dived back into the village, to the best takeaway in the world. I bought a very unhealthy option – chicken tikka in a huge fluffy naan – with a nod at healthy eating in the form of a portion of salad almost as big as the portion of chips. Afzal, who'd come round the counter to hug me when I gave him the good news about Griff, always gave me extra greenery, reasoning that some folk wouldn't have any at all.

Blowing him a kiss, I took my fragrant bundle and headed home. The M and S meals, basking in their balanced nutrition, glared at me until I stowed them in the freezer. Also glaring at me was a large parcel, which a neighbour had taken in for me and now dropped off as he headed to the pub. It looked the right size for a bear. Let it wait. I'd not been as hungry as this since I was a kid, and nothing was going to keep me from all those unhealthy carbs and evil cholesterol.

At last, so full I could hardly move, I reached for some red wine – known, after all, for its health-giving properties – and a knife with which to attack the cardboard box. Even without Mary's dire predictions the previous evening, I'd have suspected it was a teddy. However, Tim (ready to glower) and I were both mistaken. It was an exotic bouquet, already arranged in its own tightly-bound reservoir of water. Surprised – even taken aback – I fished out the printed note.

> *Dearest Lina*
> *I hear on the grapevine that Griff is unwell. My thoughts and prayers for you both.*
> *Harvey*

Harvey was a fellow dealer, much higher up the food chain, who had once been smitten with me – and I with him, truth to tell, until I realized he was married. I put the arrangement in a corner near the standard lamp, where it glowed. So did the answerphone, pulsing frantically away. *Eighteen* messages? I didn't know the thing would hold that many. But they'd all have to wait till I'd phoned Aidan, down in New Zealand.

And then there were the emails. Sixty-odd, and more coming in. Personal ones, wishing us both well, and offering help. Many were in response to my messages, but clearly a friendly network had spread the information to the US, to South Africa and even to China. All were concerned about Griff; the vast majority were full of concern for me too.

There was a knock at the door. Surely this time . . .? But I forced myself to walk downstairs and check the CCTV before I flung open the door to welcome Morris.

Not Morris. A bunch of flowers. Two, possibly. And the neighbour from the cottage the other side waving at the camera.

It turned out to be three bunches, plus a box of the neighbour's home-made flapjack, oozing butter and golden syrup. Not ideal for Griff, but since it also oozed kindness I just smiled and tried to hold back tears.

The cottage now looking and smelling like a florist's, it was time for me and Tim to head for bed. But not until I'd taken this text. A text? From Titus? Had he really reached the twenty-first century? I was so gobsmacked that I sat on the stairs to read it – or that might have been because of the extra glass of red wine, come to think of it. It looked more like an eye-chart than a message: he'd obviously not got the hang of the delete button. The gist of it was that I should look at the local auctioneer's website for details of Friday's sale.

I did. Guess what? Amidst a whole lot of other items, household and otherwise, were teams of Beswick horses. And viewing was at ten thirty tomorrow morning.

# Four

I wasn't in the shower when Griff phoned the next morning – worse, I was still in bed. He tried – half-heartedly – to put me off visiting in the afternoon, but we both knew I'd be there, even if I wasn't allowed to take any of the flowers meant for him. Today he was going to start walking again. No lazing around for today's patients, he grumbled mildly, not like in the old days when they had weeks of bed rest.

As for me, I had a quick breakfast before dealing with all the email and Internet enquiries. As I sent off one message, another pinged in. And another. There was even one from an actor who'd briefly been a leading lady; she declared that she and Griff had once been very close, and that she would drop everything to come and nurse him. Over Aidan's dead body – and mine, of course. How close had she been, if she thought he'd ever welcome her attentions? Or, to be fair, any woman's.

Putting aside such speculations, I welcomed Mary and Paul to the shop with the news of Griff. I also pressed on them some of today's delivery of flowers: four bouquets from friends in Australia and Canada, and a couple of house plants, so far. They said they'd love some for the shop, but I insisted they should take some for their living room. Oh, and why not their kitchen and bedroom!

Griff could spare them, after all. I took a photo of each bunch and accompanying card so that he could see how highly people valued him. Loved him.

'None of these is from anyone who'd rather you kept them yourself?' Mary asked hesitantly.

I just shook my head. Since I wasn't supposed to have heard their conversation about Morris I could hardly respond with a wry smile and a shrug and admit that he'd not yet sent a bear. Perhaps he really was ill, and I should be alarmed rather than angry that I hadn't heard from him. Perhaps he'd expected me to phone to ask how he was. Perhaps I should have done.

Maybe I'd have time later. Meanwhile, I'd leave my friends in charge and nip down to see what the auction had to offer.

Baker's had moved from an expensive spot in Tunbridge Wells, now under some new executive residences, to a former farmyard, complete with milking parlour – ripe for conversion, of course – on the edge of the village. There was still a decided whiff of manure. I pulled up in a cleanish-looking corner, where the other three or four cars had parked.

The yard itself was old, but Brian Baker had had a new barn built, with an entirely new – and dung-free – floor. It was full of items for the next day's general auction. In one corner was a stack of pictures; I could only see the first in line, a pretty enough Victorian watercolour. In another was a pretty weird mixture of Elvis Presley memorabilia. Bookshelves, ancient and modern, lined the longest wall. Furniture occupied most of the centre; it ranged from last year's IKEA to some excellent antiques, including some genuine-looking Jacobean chairs. Except, when I had a close peep, I had a feeling that they were more 'looking' than 'genuine'. Then there was a clump of furniture that was just depressingly old. Some easy-chairs in particular looked so sad that you could almost imagine their owners taking their very last nap in them – and not waking up. Even in these cash-strapped times, when more and more people were buying second-hand (going green, they'd call it, if they were middle-class enough), I couldn't imagine anyone taking a wing chair in patchily balding green uncut moquette into their home. Some of the carpets should have been burned, surely: some had downright filthy patches, bringing a whiff of dog and urine to the area. The usual sad collection of unfinished whisky and brandy bottles stood on a small central table: it always made my heart turn, wondering why the owners hadn't gone wild and drained the lot before they turned up their toes. With Griff where he was they almost reduced me to tears.

Brian, his short ginger hair looking, as it always did, like a guard dog's hackles, greeted me in his usual brisk way, as if time was just about to run out on the opening bids and he was going to rap on a desk with his gavel. Like all his employees, he wore a magenta pinafore covered in a pattern of intertwined gavels and pound signs. He'd not heard about Griff's op, but spent a minute assuring me that everything would be fine – his father-in-law had had a bypass too and was still, at the age of eighty-one, playing tennis. He waved his wife, Helen, over to verify it, and zipped off to deal with a phone call. As if she had all the time in the world, she produced real coffee in real china mugs and asked me when Griff was due home. I goggled. Home? Of course he'd have to come home, without all those machines to keep an eye on him. No nurses, either. Although that was what I wanted more than anything else, I suddenly found the prospect so terrifying that I sank, mouth wide open, on to a cardboard box. She patted my hand as she relieved me of the mug, declaring, 'You'll manage.'

Digging in her apron pocket for a pencil and pad, she drifted back to what she'd been doing before – checking the items up for sale tomorrow. She also seemed to be keeping an eye on the activities of a young man I'd not seen before, tall enough to make the standard Baker's apron look more like a pretty pinnie.

'Tristam, our intern,' Brian, who'd popped up behind me, said into my ear. 'A Fine Arts graduate from Reading.' He sounded drily impressed when he said it; he must have meant the university, not just the town. 'All book-learning yet, but we'll kit him out with the practical knowledge.'

It was the opposite with me, of course – I'd barely read a book till Griff came on the scene.

'Does he have book-learning about Beswick horses?' I asked. 'Or would that be your and Helen's practical knowledge?'

Not surprisingly he pulled a face. 'You? Beswick horses? Bit of a departure for Tripp and Townend, isn't it?' He walked me over to another box – not the one I'd sat on. He dipped his hands in and came up with horse after horse. As he plonked them on a table he said, 'What you need to remember is that quantity isn't the same as quality. The lady wanting us to sell this lot – well, she's acquired a lot of models with no rarity value at all. It's like Ty Beanies versus Steiff bears,' he said, still delving and coming up with more. 'There are some rare models, and some very rare, which would turn in a nice little profit – but alas, she hasn't got any of those. Just these common or garden ones. Are you looking for anything in particular? Because these have to go as one lot.' It sounded like a threat.

'I'm not so much looking to buy as looking for a reason not to buy one brought to our shop the other day.' I showed him the photos of Puck. 'The person wanting to sell him told me he was a collector's item, and all I could do was nod, I'm afraid.'

'How much did she want?'

'She said she'd seen them going for at least six hundred – I didn't get as far as telling her we'd offer less so we could make our profit. Actually, I saw one for a couple of hundred more in Canterbury.'

He tapped my phone. 'I'd say she was about right – they've sold for that here. So what's the problem? And do you mind if Tristam listens in? Because it's all grist to his mill,' he added.

What girl in her right mind would object to having Tristam join in? He'd got nice broad shoulders to go with his height, and a really lovely bum. Hell, what was I doing eyeing up a bloke

44

when I'd already got a boyfriend? Even if he wasn't much in evidence at the moment.

Tristam wiped his hands on his apron before he shook mine, a gesture that made me think of some Hardy character I'd read about with Griff. He had a gentle, half-diffident smile revealing lovely teeth. 'Tristam Collingwood.'

'Lina Townend.'

'What do you know about Beswick horses, Tristam?' Brian asked.

'The old ones made by Royal Doulton or those made by John Sinclair from Sheffield?' He sounded awfully posh, but ducked his head like a schoolboy as he spoke. Public schoolboy, no doubt.

'Doulton,' I said.

Tristam nodded as if I'd said the right thing. 'You want to look for those sculpted by Arthur Gredington.'

Brian smiled approvingly. 'And if you wanted to go for broke?'

'Oh, you'd look for the *Spirit of Whitfield*.'

'Would you?' I prompted, not having a clue.

'Yup. There was a pit pony called Kruger who retired from some coal mine in Staffordshire or wherever.' I didn't know a lot about mines myself, or about the Midlands, but I wouldn't have sounded quite so dismissive. 'Anyway, this horse – the model, I mean – fetched nine thousand five hundred pounds. As I say, a record.'

A lot of book-learning there.

'Colour?' Brian prompted.

'Forget brown. They're all over the place. You'd want the rarer colours.'

45

'Such as white,' I mused. 'Which was what I was offered the other day.' I showed him the photos too. 'Trouble is,' I said, mainly to Brian, 'I smelt a rat.'

He rolled his eyes. 'Not you and your nose again!'

Tristam peered. 'It's a very pretty nose.' Then he, not I, blushed.

'Her divvy's nose, Tris,' Brian said tartly. 'Sometimes you'll find some old codger swearing he can pick out a bargain at a hundred paces. Well, Lina's a young codger. Thing is,' he added, with narrow eyes, as if resenting the admission, 'as often as not she's right. You might want to talk to her about how she does it – but not until you've finished with those boxes,' he added firmly.

'My nose doesn't know anything about these.' I pointed at the collection on the table. 'But the funny thing is, that one over there is the first cousin of the one this woman brought to us.' I picked it up and cradled it. 'Yes. Same height, same stance, everything.'

'Yes. Brown fifty, white six to eight hundred. What's the problem, Lina?'

I pulled a face, touching my nose. 'This. And the fact I keep seeing them. Some white, some brown.' I pointed to his batch.

Helen called him over to deal with some query. But he said over his shoulder, 'Keep seeing them? Now that's more interesting. Worrying, even. Especially as you can go for months without seeing a white one.'

But I'd only seen three, hadn't I? And one of

46

the two in the antiques shops could have been the one I rejected. Maybe I was simply imagining a problem.

Since I was here, I might as well cast my eyes over the other lots before I said a proper goodbye, so I mooched quietly round, almost listening for something interesting to summon me.

Would I call Tristam something interesting? Possibly – though I was never sure about guys with public school accents. Maybe I was afraid that at bottom they'd be like my aristo dad. Anyway, he waved as I approached a stack of pictures in dauntingly heavy frames. Not a goodbye sort of wave. So I drifted over, not least because he was unpacking more pictures, little domestic portraits, by and large – mostly amateur, in the worst sense. On the table beside him, though, were not just small pictures but proper miniatures – to judge by the sitters' clothes, one or two Elizabethan, others later.

I knew even less about miniatures than I did about Beswick horses, but I liked them much more, to be honest. Not just because they're sometimes exquisite works of art in their own right, but because they're so personal in scale. You could imagine some guy having his likeness done for a woman he fancied – or maybe it was all arranged, dynastic marriages when the trend for miniatures started, way back in Tudor times. Just don't ask me which Tudor.

In fact, rather than return Tristam's smile, I pounced on one – not literally, because handling something like this ought to be a cotton glove job. Set within a little gold frame, against a background of stunning blue, was this smiling, devil-may-care face. Heavens, a young man, probably my own age, with eyes like that, and that lovely curling hair – yes, he'd make your heart beat faster. But you'd never know where you were with him.

Any more than I did with Morris, a sour voice told me. Of course, that was because he was so tied up with work. And his daughter, of course.

And possibly the flu.

I mustn't start crying. Not over a man. I focused on the picture. 'Hilliard?' I breathed, rather hoarsely, but at least without a sob.

'Do you really think so? I suppose the vellum is right, and so is the playing card backing.' Pulling on gloves, he turned it to show me. 'But others are more inclined to think it's more like an Isaac Oliver.' For *others* read *I*. 'And, to be honest, actually no more than school of. Someone's very first day at school, too,' he snorted. 'I mean, imagine something by a master turning up in the back woods like this.' So he didn't rate Kent any more highly than the Midlands.

'Hang on, didn't a missing Rembrandt turn up in the Cotswolds? Cirencester? Thanks to a really tenacious actioneer's research?'

'Chance in thousands,' he said.

'But this one's lovely – head and shoulders better than anything else you've got.' He looked so miffed that I added, 'Surely it won't be in the same sale as the Beswick beasties, anyway.'

'Hardly. Next week. Fine art. They're all one lot, by the way, since there's nothing any good in there. My God, call these fine?' he asked, with

48

a sweeping gesture. Without waiting for an answer, he continued, 'I'm just reviewing and noting their general condition before putting them in the strong room. Brian thought he'd make use of my expertise before I leave.' He clearly meant me to pursue what he was saying so I obliged. Should I go for *expertise* or *leave*?

I chose the second. 'Leave?'

'That's what interns do. They move on. Though actually I may stay a few more weeks than we agreed, because the guy they'd got lined up to come after me got a job. A real job.'

I nodded, hoping I looked as if I understood what he was on about. There'd been stuff in the media about interns. Weren't they young people who'd just left university working for politicians because they wanted a political career them-selves? So what was one doing picking up pictures and wearing a pinnie? It must just be a posh term for an apprentice. I played around with the idea; why, I could have been an intern myself, not just a hands-on apprentice! 'So where are you moving on to?' I asked at last, since he clearly wanted me to.

'Oh, Bonham's or Sotheby's,' he said carelessly.

Aiming high or what? 'Next?' I stopped myself squeaking. 'Still as an intern?'

He looked less certain. 'Maybe a few more auction houses down the road.'

Then I recalled something else about interns. Another term for what they were doing was work experience. And they worked for nothing. Some got expenses, but some didn't even get food or travel allowance. How could ordinary people afford to do that? People with student loans weighing them down?'

'Interns don't get paid, right?'

'Too bloody right. Not even expenses. So I work in a bar practically every evening. At least I'm lucky to have that.'

'So will you be here for the sale?' I asked, wishing I hadn't, as it might have sounded as if I wanted to see him again.

'It all depends. Tell me,' he continued, changing gear with a clunk, 'how does this divvying business work?'

'If I knew that,' I said coolly, 'I'd win the Lottery every week.'

'Can we try it out? See if you can pick up something good?'

I thought I just had.

'Or something dodgy? If it works on fakes, too?' he pursued. 'Though I'm sure there aren't any fakes round here,' he added quickly.

'You'd be surprised,' I said darkly. 'They're all over the place.' Hadn't I spent the best part of a week sniffing them out in high places? And getting assaulted for my pains? But I didn't want to tell him about that: it might seem like boasting, not simple pride in a job well-done. And then, as if one of the wretched things had kicked me, I realized what could be the problem with the white horses. My only excuse for being so dim – well, it was more a reason than an excuse – was Griff's illness. 'That Beswick model we were talking about earlier – what's the betting some-one's found a way of repainting the ordinary brown ones white and reglazing them?'

He looked at me in amazement. 'But even then they only fetch six hundred pounds. Eight, max.' What he did not need to say was, *eight hundred pounds is peanuts.*

I didn't point out that to some people it might be a lot of money. 'It depends how many white horses you fake. How many you can flog to antique dealers. How many you can shift at fairs. How many you can get reputable auction houses like this to sell for you. Say you shift ten. Think big and aim for a hundred. Right?' I checked my watch. 'Time I was off.' And I'd better have a word with Brian. When I twiddled my fingers to say goodbye he thought I was waving to him; in fact I was really bidding the handsome young man in the miniature farewell. Or adieu. I'd rather it was adieu.

Brian wasn't particularly impressed with my theory about White Puck but conceded it might be worth emailing some of his mates. 'Have you found anything else?' he asked, touching his nose.

Despite myself, I looked in the direction of Tristam, but in fact not at him. At the not-Hilliard. Or not-Isaac Oliver.

'Oh, our latest sales asset. Has all the old ladies eating out his hand. And you young ones too. If he opened his own place he'd make a mint. Kensington or somewhere. When he's learned his trade, that is,' he added grimly.

'He knows a lot. About some things,' I added, thinking about that miniature.

But Brian didn't pick up on the note of doubt. He gripped my arm. 'I can see what you're thinking. That I'm exploiting him. That I ought

51

to pay him. You know what, Lina, the moment he actually does some work instead of parroting off stuff I learnt years ago, I might.' Sensing I wasn't convinced, he added, 'He knows what he knows, but that isn't enough for an auctioneer. You have to back up with research. All the time. You look for anything that might not be quite what it says on the tin.'

'Provenance,' I said with a grin.

His grip tightened. 'Exactly. You don't just look at the front of a picture, say.'

'I know you have to look at the back of what he tells me is absolutely not a Hilliard!'

Brian shook his head. 'It's not, Lina. It's School of Isaac Oliver, as I'm sure he told you. The paperwork confirms it. Very good provenance with that, as it happens, with paperwork going back over a century – some eccentric guy's private collection. Warwickshire. Lord Somethingorother.'

Why didn't my pa collect things like that? 'But the front must be pretty important – brushwork and pigment and so on?'

'Sure it is. And so are the signatures, assuming they've got a name attached. But Hell's bells, how many John Constables would I be selling every month if I didn't check the rest? And David Coxes? Fakes are all over the place.'

I nodded. 'So lots of the swans that people's grannies have left them are just pretty miserable geese.'

'Quite. You look at the back: little scribbles, labels from shops or sales. You follow everything up. As you do, I should imagine?' Suddenly, I was propelled into his office.

Like the one at his old rooms, it was smaller than it should have been for a man of his size. One wall was lined with bookshelves, heaving with well-thumbed reference books. So far, so like Griff's office. But whereas we had tome upon tome about china and porcelain, this guy had books about everything from Japanese netsuke to Henry Moore sketches. Piles of magazines. And his old, filthy computer. His old office had had a layer of dust that made that Ashford antiques emporium look positively sterile. I suspected that this would soon be the same.

'Tristam just doesn't realize how much he doesn't know! He might check something online, but he ticks boxes, paints by numbers. You – you I could train.'

'I'd be hard work. Me and my nose.' I thought of the gorgeous miniature. 'I can tell you if I like something – like a portrait. But I don't know about the materials artists work in. The way they achieve texture, modelling on the faces . . .'

'Tristam would. And he'd be able to tell me. All the same, Lina, I reckon your instinct's worth twice his book learning any day. So I'd pay you double what I pay him.'

I was ready to take his bait, to tell him nothing would part me from Griff. And then I realized what twice zero made. Another big round zero.

# Five

Griff had been promoted to a chair, and there were fewer tubes in evidence, so I was walking on air after my afternoon visit. Killing time till the evening session, I headed back into Ashford, popping the Fiesta into the Vicarage Lane car park, not very far from Rob Sampson's Antiques Emporium. As I said, he wasn't a mate, but if he'd been landed with anything dodgy, he might want to know. I was jumping the gun a little, though, wasn't I? This might be a genuine white horse, worthy of the little label round his front hoof telling anyone who knew these things he was worth five hundred and fifty pounds. About right, given that Ashford wasn't a tourist Mecca.

First of all, however, as I'd not been able to find any books on miniatures on Griff's shelves, I popped into the library and found what seemed a nice, clearly-written guide. Then I headed for Rob's, trying to plan how to approach the subject of the horse. Not an idea worth having. So just I mooched in, catching him in mid-scratch. I wasn't sure I wanted to shake the hand he promptly removed from his crotch, however – but since I'd sloshed that hospital germ-killer liquid all over my hands before and after visiting Griff I supposed I could risk it. But it seemed he was happy to give the casual nod that was all Titus ever managed.

I nodded back. 'I've come to pick your brain, Rob.'

His eyebrows disappeared into what was left of his hair. 'You're the one who's supposed to be the bloody bee's knees.' His eyes took in the book on miniatures.

'Oh, I am,' I said with my sunniest smile. 'But only when I know about things. And that leaves plenty of gaps, believe me.' I patted the book. After all, ignorance wasn't a crime.

'And what gap would you want me to fill?' His words weren't encouraging, but at least he managed to respond with a smile of his own. Full of gaps.

I had to bite back what I wanted to say, which was that I happened to know that Ashford had a very good NHS dentist who'd work wonders with the ruin of Rob's teeth. But even NHS dentists had to charge something – and I had a sudden lurch of fear that Rob wasn't making enough money even for that. Even top-notch people like Harvey Sanditon were cutting back on expensive fairs like LAPADA ones, because what they could make wouldn't cover the cost of stall rental; people like Rob might be going to the wall. Was I about to make things worse?

'I don't know a thing about Beswick horses,' I said, 'and I had this woman trying to sell me one the other day.'

He frowned. 'Why you? You're Victorian, you and Griff.'

'Early twentieth century too, these days. People's tastes change. Anyway, stray punters might not know that people specialize. I sent her away, obviously, because she wanted six hundred quid and—'

'What did Griff say?'

'Ah! You haven't heard the news. He's down the road in the William Harvey getting over a heart op. So I couldn't ask him.'

'Sorry to hear that. Is he OK? Good.' Rob scratched again – behind his ear this time. 'Are you saying that she knew Griff was out of the way and was chancing her arm?'

I must have looked as taken aback as I felt. Then I shook my head. 'Even I didn't know till the day before that Griff was going to have surgery. And people might assume that I wouldn't make a decision without Griff.'

'Not people who've seen you in action at fairs or auctions. OK, so you turned this woman down. And you're here because—?'

'You've got the twin in the window, and I thought you might tell me about it.'

'Let's start with this,' he said, raising a finger like an umpire, and disappearing into his office. He returned clutching a tatty bit of paper. 'Original receipt, Lina. And I mean original, not just one from a fair last week. From a shop up in Birmingham. So anyone forking out their hard earned cash for that little fellow knows they're getting the real McCoy.'

My eyebrows shot up. Most antiques at this level didn't come with provenance. And why should they? When Auntie Flo gave her favourite niece a pretty ornament for Christmas, the last thing she'd want her to know was how much the present had cost.

Assuming I'd decoded the label correctly, Rob was selling for under the odds.

I risked a bit of cheek. 'Can I have a look at the real McCoy?'

Raising his eyes to heaven, he eased himself round the counter. 'There. Reason I'm not asking the full whack your punter wanted is that,' he said, pointing to a tiny chip on a rear hoof. He gave me a look I wasn't sure I liked. 'Hey, they say you did that repair job on that vase some idiot knocked over in a museum. Bet you could fix that so that no one'd know.'

As if I was interested, I looked the horse over from nose to tail. There was something about it that, chip and all, felt right. The glaze was just a tiny bit worn – someone had loved it enough to dust it and sometimes even wash it. Eventually, I tapped its nose gently. 'I wish I could make you better, Dobbin. But with Griff out of action and likely to be for quite a few weeks, I can't take on any more work – I've got a waiting list eight weeks' long, and someone'll buy you long before then.'

'I hope.'

'I hope so too, Rob. Times aren't good, are they?'

'You can say that a-bloody-gain.'

'Tell you what,' I said. 'Why don't you put a spotlight on him? Make him stand out a bit?'

'You'll be telling me how to arrange my window next!'

'Why not? Griff sent me on a course a couple of years back. And we start with some Windolene . . .'

\* \* \*

57

'You cleaned Rob Sampson's window for him? Dear child, the man's a scoundrel – goes round knocking on old ladies' doors and offering to take junk off their hands,' Griff, still in his chair, hissed – but not so loudly that any other patient or visitor might hear.

I almost hung my head. 'I felt sorry for him.' What a good job I hadn't mentioned Rob's hint that I might do an illicit repair for him – presumably splitting the profit.

'That's his stock-in-trade, sweet one – making dear old ladies feel they'd better sell him something cheap so he can feed his starving children . . . Oh, so long as you didn't buy anything – you didn't, did you?' he shot at me.

'No. But I learned something. About horses.' Taking his hand, I told him all about the visitor we'd had on Tuesday.

'And you reckon there's a plague of forgeries? You haven't much in the way of evidence, my love.'

'No. And I don't want any. You can hardly call it a plague, and even if it were it's nothing to do with Tripp and Townend. Not our area. Not our period. I've got better fish to fry. But what do I do if Mrs Thingy comes back?'

'Easy. Tell her you've spoken to your partner and in these trying financial times we can't help her. Tell her to try an auction house. She might get more than she asked you for – which we certainly wouldn't offer anyway, of course.'

'Quite.'

A nurse stopped in front of him. 'Griff, if I've told you once today about not crossing your legs

58

I've told you a dozen times. You. Must. Not. Nor when you get home. OK?' He nodded first at Griff and then at me. I writhed, as if I'd done something wrong myself.

As for Griff, he waited till the man's back was turned and pulled a naughty schoolboy's face. I could have done handsprings – this was the Griff I knew and loved.

After a much more sensible supper than the previous evening's, I had a long silent conversation with Tim the Bear. In the end, I shrugged; yes, I probably ought to phone Morris, oughtn't I? Griff had carefully not remarked on the fact that Morris's name didn't appear on any of the messages accompanying flowers or the get-well cards. All the time, however, the words *sin of omission* thumped oddly but ominously round my head.

I left a cheerful message on Morris's voicemail and texted him for good measure. What about an email? Between us we agreed to give Morris some time to respond. If I'd heard nothing by the morning, then, once I knew Griff was still making good progress, I might just email him.

Griff would be freed from more tubes today, he told me with a chuckle over the phone on Friday morning. There was even a rumour that he'd start climbing stairs when the physios were free. I could have sung and danced my way round the cottage. In fact, I did. So there was no reason not to contact Morris straightaway, except for some forty-odd emails popping into the in-box.

59

Most were work, so since it was only a few minutes past seven I could ignore them for another hour. One, however, was from Brian at Baker's Auction House, so simply because I was feeling nosy I opened it.

It was pretty short. Would I care to pop in for a coffee early next week, when there was a nice breathing space before the next sale?

Puzzled, I replied that I'd love to, but it was dependent on when Griff was released from hospital, when I'd be in a sort of purdah for a bit until he was well enough to be left alone.

My palms sweated: how much of an invalid would he be? I'd never nursed anyone and didn't want to get things wrong. Medication! I knew he'd have to take lots of tablets: what if I got them wrong? What if after all he'd been through I let him die on my watch? The bright sun was shut out as this blanket of responsibility fell on me.

This was something no amount of silent sympathy from Tim the Bear could help with.

Griff mustn't know, of course. So when he asked how I was getting on without him, I'd better have a list of things I'd done. And since we tried never to lie to each other, I'd better go and do them. Starting with the washing. That always felt good.

Then those emails. All of them.

I was halfway through when I remembered Morris. I brought up his address – no problem there. But what could I say? Should I be tender and concerned? Or furious? There must be some midway point. I was ready to hit myself in

60

frustration. Ready, but not actually doing it. I sat on my hands to stop myself.

And then, thank goodness, someone rang the front door bell. What if? Oh, what if? Please!

I flew downstairs. I almost opened the door before checking – but then I remembered the very least I should do was check the spyhole.

More flowers. I was beginning to hate the things.

When they were safe in the last of our vases, I returned to the computer, to find a message pinging in, but not from Morris. From Aidan, Griff's long-term lover.

He and I might not like each other but we both loved Griff (which was probably why we didn't like each other, of course). Griff hated to see us at each other's throats, so we had what you might call an armed truce. Ultra-smooth himself, he deplored my streetwise cockiness and wasn't impressed by my pa's ramshackle ways; I found him a pompous old git, whose saving grace was his beautiful Georgian house in Tenterden, filled with exquisite period furniture.

He'd been away from Kent for weeks, watching his New Zealand-based sister die; I'd made Griff brief him about what was happening here, and then I'd taken over myself, making sure he knew Griff had survived the operation and was now on the mend. He'd just arrived back in the UK, he said, and would spare me the trouble of visiting Griff this afternoon.

Would he indeed? I had to delete six or seven emails telling him what I thought of his idea. In the end I gave up and returned to the other tricky

61

one. This took me about ten minutes and fifteen tries (by which time the in-box had got even fuller), and all I came up with was a really stupid message:

*Long time no hear. Worried. All well?*
*XXX*

How about that for feeble? I messed around with things like *missing you lots*, and *can't wait to see you*. Finally, I settled on *Griff's op a success – he's making good progress*, popping it between the question mark and the XXXs.

There was nothing for it but to spend the rest of the morning tackling the rest of the in-box. I tried to ignore the irritating little voice observing that what I *really* wanted was to get any response from Morris as soon as it arrived, telling myself that since so much business was Internet-based, I needed to respond promptly to enquiries and orders. I still found that words required a lot of concentration, so when someone tapped on the office door I jumped out of my skin.

'Mary thought you'd need a cuppa,' Paul said, setting down a mug of green tea. After a few moments' hesitation, he pulled up the spare chair and coughed.

'Problem?' I prompted.

'Tell me to mind my own business if you want,' he said, waiting. But since I said nothing he coughed again and said, 'Tell me, Lina, does Griff have an accountant? And I'm not touting for business, since I don't practise any more; I'm just asking.'

'He's got someone he sends all his receipts and bills to every autumn: is that what you mean?'

He nodded, swallowed, and said nothing.

People don't just happen to ask about things like money, do they? Something was obviously worrying him. Had old Mr Westwood done a runner with all our money? I asked cautiously, 'Is there some problem? Something that can't wait till Griff gets home?'

'It's something that's been worrying Mary, too.'

Which didn't seem to be an answer to anything. I raised an eyebrow.

'We maybe should have mentioned it before Griff was taken ill. Before the op. But it seemed a bit . . . ghoulish. You see, we want to make sure you're financially safe . . . him being so much older than . . . Of course, we hope he lives another twenty years. But you share both his business and his cottage. This leaves you very vulnerable, financially.'

I took a deep breath. Half of me wanted to scream at him for his cheek; the other half wanted to hug him and Mary for worrying about me. So I took another breath and said, 'We've made wills – both of us, actually – so we're protected. Power of Attorney, too.'

'Wonderful. But the taxman has ways of getting his hands on bequests. And local authorities pounce if anyone needs long term care that even the most loving family can't provide. As I said, I just wonder . . . hope . . . but I daren't tread on anyone's professional toes.' He risked a laugh, though it sounded very tight. 'With your permission I would like to talk to Griff when he's completely better. I wish I could talk to your father, too,' he added with a big grin.

Anyone trying to talk finances with Pa would end up feeling like a guest at the Mad Hatter's tea party. 'Don't forget I'm what he always calls a bastard, Paul,' I said firmly. 'And I've got no more claim on him than any of his other children.'

Paul raised an eyebrow. 'Not according to what Griff says. He says you're the only one that ever goes near the old bugger. Pardon my French.'

'That's probably the only sexual practice he's never tried,' I quipped – quoting Griff, as it happens. 'Anyway, about Griff – I really don't know.' The deep breath hurt. 'I can't think about his dying, Paul, in case it somehow makes it happen.'

'Doesn't work like that, Lina. And we all have to die: you must know that, or you wouldn't have bothered with a will yourself, would you?'

'All the same . . .'

'I'll choose my moment, don't you worry. And I promise it won't be till the hospital has given him the all-clear. Now, Mary said she'd got enough lunch for the three of us, and since you'll want to dash off to go to see Griff, would you like to join us in the shop for our picnic?'

The words burst out. 'Griff's friend Aidan's back – he says he doesn't want me at the hospital this afternoon.'

Paul said nothing for so long that I wondered whether he'd heard what I said. Finally, he asked, with almost no expression in his voice, 'And how do you feel about that?'

Behind my tears, I gave a bark of laughter.

'That's what my counsellor always used to ask when I was in a mess.'

'I'm flattered! And you'd say to the counsellor?'

'Cheeky bastard. Not you: Aidan, of course. I was so mad I didn't reply. Here.' I brought it up on the screen and pointed.

'He might actually mean it – that you could do with the afternoon off.' He pointed at yet more unread messages. 'To read those for a start.'

Squashing the thought that maybe he was actually too jet-lagged to phrase things more subtly, I said, 'He could have asked, not told.'

He nodded. 'Quite. So zero marks for tact. Has he known Griff long?'

He was nudging me into a kinder stance, wasn't he? 'For ever. And I know in his position I'd want to see Griff straight away, without an audience. But I . . . What if the shock kills Griff?' I blurted.

'Come on, Lina, he'll be on so many drugs at the moment I don't suppose he'll even be able to raise an eyebrow. But you could phone Aidan and tell him you want to go along yourself just to warn Griff – that would make sense. And you know what, after your gallivanting round France and all that stuff happening to you last weekend, I think taking time off from dashing to Ashford wouldn't be a bad idea. Tell Aidan you can alternate. Better than both of you sitting beside Griff's bed competing for his attention – now that wouldn't do him any good at all.'

I nodded. 'I'll text him. And then I'll be down for our picnic.'

# Six

'I told you that there was no need for you to visit Griff this afternoon,' Aidan said tartly as he locked his car, coincidentally parked next to mine.

I wanted to yell at him that he had no right to tell me anything. But his weeks in New Zealand had transformed him from his usual sleek, debonair and possibly pampered self to a weary and battered old man. I knew that such an ordeal would have aged anyone. All the same, without raising my voice, or at least not very much, I said, 'As I said in my text, I'm anxious that the shock of seeing anyone he didn't expect wouldn't be good for Griff. I know how you feel, Aidan—'

'Indeed you do not!' Not just blazing eyes but a jab of his index finger, too.

Just as I'd started to feel sorry for him! 'Well, I know how I feel. And I just want to protect Griff.'

'I hardly think your concern is necessary.'

'Maybe it isn't. Maybe I'm just stressed out of my mind and I'm being totally unreasonable. Look, give me just five minutes with him, since I can't bear not seeing him at all today, and then he's all yours for both visiting sessions. And then we should work out a visiting rota.'

'When's he being discharged? I need to book nursing staff.'

'You'll have to ask him. But he may want to

66

come home to the cottage,' I pointed out. 'First of all, at least.' I willed a smile into place. 'I'm sure you're already working out some lovely place to take him to convalesce,' I added as he went puce with fury. 'Calm down, Aidan, or you'll end up in the next bed to him,' I said flippantly.

Then I realized there were tears in his eyes. Anger? Frustration? Love? I understood all three. 'Just go,' I said quietly. 'I'll see him for a couple of minutes at the end.' Retreating to the car, I couldn't stop the tears – hell, more of them! Hadn't I shed enough? – and even more annoyingly I couldn't work out what they were for.

Then a text arrived. A text? I was ready to tell it to wait till I saw it was from Aidan. They wouldn't let him in since he wasn't a relative. The buggers! I was halfway across the car park before I drew breath.

So in the end I'd done it my way, having informed the jobsworth trying to exclude Aidan that if anyone would make Griff better it was his oldest, dearest friend, who would be sharing the visiting with me, starting with now and continuing this evening. My success wouldn't endear me to Aidan, of course: he was the sort of man who liked to make things happen, not to have to wait for others to wave magic wands. But I'd bounced in to see Griff, hugged him – no tubes at all today! – and told him I was on my way because someone else was waiting to see him. He knew at once, of course – and I'd rather I hadn't seen his face light up.

So when out of the blue I had a phone call from Tristam – he must have got my number from Brian, I suppose – asking me if I fancied a drink, maybe a club afterwards, that evening, I responded saying a drink and some food would suit me better. I added that since he was trade and he could tell me about pictures, I could put him on expenses. I didn't really think I could, but at least I was earning. He didn't strike me as the sort of person who'd otherwise want to be paid for, on what he might (or, of course, might not) have meant as a date. If I felt a bit iffy about that, on account of my still officially being with Morris and not being sure if I even liked Tristam, then I spun myself the same tale – I'd be learning about pictures.

Tris could eat for England. We'd agreed to meet in the village pub, since I could safely and easily walk there and back and wouldn't have to worry about my alcohol intake – or be dependent on someone I hardly knew for a lift. Altogether safer. He had the pub's double burger in a bap and chips, while I managed the standard burger without bread and with salad, just as Griff had trained me to do. Oh, and chips, of course, but half of them ended up down Tristam's throat. As did a lot of beer.

None of this stopped him talking – mostly, of course, about himself. As the bar got fuller and noisier with Friday night boozers, mostly kids wearing the same sort of rugby shirt as him, I reasoned it was a good job he'd acquired that carrying public school tone or I'd hardly have heard him. No one else seemed to be listening, so I carried on as his audience. Mother running this company, father running that. Prep school the name of which I didn't recognize, which seemed to surprise him, and public school I did. And, of course, Reading University. I made a silly quip that he should have gone to St Andrews, to hobnob with Will and Kate, but apart from registering I knew that other places did Fine Arts degrees, he didn't make much of my joke. For quite some time I was tempted to drop into the conversation something about my father being a lord, because it would have been nice to see his face. But I couldn't be bothered.

Suddenly, however, he changed gear, and started asking about me and my past – questions I always responded to in the most general of terms. I didn't want to be pitied or patronized. Fast-forwarding to my life with Griff, I talked about an apprenticeship (why on earth didn't I have the sense to call it an internship?) to teach me my restoration skills – almost true, since I was taught by two old friends of Griff's. When he asked for whom I'd undertaken freelance work since then I was truthful: it was nice to see his eyebrows go rocketing up. But there was no way I was going to give him a demonstration of my divvying skills, which he edged towards. At last we got on to what most interested me – and, to do him justice, him: what he called representational art and I called pictures.

'Do you paint yourself?'

He pulled a face. 'Sunday painter,' he mumbled. 'No future in it, of course. No present, either, to be honest. I just don't have that – that edge.' He sighed, almost painfully. 'I'd have liked to do some postgrad research but you've no idea how much that costs . . . So the best option was this auction house thing. And I even do that for free,' he added bitterly.

'Presumably your parents can support you? Regard what you're doing as an investment?' I prompted, rather pleased with the term.

'Things aren't too good on the business front, in case you haven't noticed,' he said, necking the last of his beer. Waving away my offer of another, he leant across the table. 'These horses of yours. What's your problem with them? Isn't it a case of *caveat emptor*? I mean, used, old, second-hand – no one expects them to be perfect.'

'I think,' I said, trying to sound judicious, not pompous, 'there's a difference between my buying a horse because I like it and my buying a horse because someone tells me it's valuable. And by painting the horse white, you're certainly implying it's valuable, even if you don't actually use words. In other words, you're not being honest.'

'But who's honest in this life? And aren't all values relative? I mean, take a Cézanne being sold for enough money to refloat the Greek economy. Is it worth it?'

I had an idea you needed a university education to be able to discuss such things seriously. 'Isn't there a difference,' I ventured, 'between a fake and something simply overpriced? I admit they're both a sort of robbery . . .'

'Some fakers' work is now worth thousands in

its own right,' he said, going off at what seemed to be yet another tangent. Then he lurched back. 'Tell me, if you had a row of white horses, would you be able to tell which was kosher and which was dodgy? With this nose of yours?' He touched it lightly and smiled the sort of smile that would have had ducks flocking off the water.

I responded in kind, my head slightly to one side. 'How would I know? Line them up and I'll see.'

'How about if I lined them up and blindfolded you?'

There had been times, though I wasn't telling him (or anyone else, for that matter) about them, that I'd simply known – without any logic – that I had to go to a certain stall at a fair and I'd find something there. It was time for a mild counter-attack. 'As I said, line them up and I'll see. And line up some Isaac Olivers and School of Isaac Olivers too. I'd love to know how you tell them apart. Properly, I mean. Not just with my funny instinct.'

Before he could say anything, one of the loud crowd at the bar lurched our way. It seemed they'd known each other from school, and the newcomer wasn't going to let the small matter of Tris's being with me stand in the way of a long and liquid reunion. In fact it suited me fine to settle up at the bar and slide out.

Although I'd have preferred a bit of street-lighting (one of the parish councillors was an astronomer and vetoed every attempt to pollute his night sky) I didn't turn a hair about walking home alone. Bredeham was a village, for heaven's sake, where everyone looked out for everyone else. Someone walking behind me was just taking the same route. That was all.

So I crossed over the road, just to see what he'd do. He crossed too.

Maybe he wasn't simply taking the same route.

Time for a Plan B. I'd got a torch which would double in an emergency as a cosh. I'd learned to fight without any rules at all. I'd even learned to run like hell and get away from trouble. The cottage itself would be as secure as Fort Knox.

Tim the Bear would be waiting; Aidan would have left a message reporting back on Griff; and there was nothing in the world to keep me from a good night's sleep.

But it would take time to open up. And someone the size of the guy following me might just be able to push his way in after me. I did the obvious thing: adopted Plan C.

Which involved Afzal and his mates at the take-away. As soon as they heard about my problem, they gathered round me protectively, making it quite clear to any observer that I wasn't alone and unprotected; if that message didn't go home, Ahmed, Afzal's fast-bowler cousin, and another guy I'd never met, went outside and stared mean-ingfully around. Meaningfully and actually quite threateningly. To my great shame and embarrass-ment, the only person in sight was a woman, heading briskly towards the car park. All the same, the lads insisted I had a lift home with the next food delivery. This involved a nice bit of banter about cricket and a highly circuitous route. Just because we were enjoying ourselves.

But someone was in the cottage. Ahmed and I shared a rapid intake of breath.

Whoever it was wasn't furtive, surely wasn't a-burgling. Not with all the lights ablaze in Griff's bedroom and now in mine. It looked as if the TV set in the living room was on. My mind went blank. Could it possibly, possibly be that they'd sent Griff home already? A tiny corner of my mind congratulated myself on having totally stripped and remade his bed, so it was hospital clean. He'd be safe with me.

It wasn't Griff. Of course it wasn't. Not with that car parked outside.

It was Morris!

Telling Ahmed everything was fine, and not to bother with the baseball bat he kept handy, I hopped out and ran to the door, waving and letting myself in.

Yes, it was Morris, all right, and, judging by the howls and sobs from upstairs, Leda, his little daughter. His wife's daughter, at least. There was also an inescapable smell. Someone had thrown up.

'Where the hell have you been?' he greeted me, emerging from the kitchen with a glass of water.

'Out. What's the matter with Leda?' I was already heading upstairs.

'I thought she was over the bug, but it seems she isn't. So where were you?' He followed me. 'I phoned you, texted you – why didn't you respond?

Because – I don't know why I'd switched my phone off. I said nothing.

The howls were coming from my room. At least it was my bedclothes she'd been sick all over. So why was there a pile of bedlinen on the floor in Griff's room?

'Look who's here, sweetheart! It's Lina!' he called, in the soppy but desperate voice of a man who didn't know what to do next.

Leda showed her feelings about me pretty clearly. She threw up again – was this what they called projectile vomiting? – all over my duvet. And all over Tim the Bear.

I grabbed him. Leda howled more loudly. Morris yelled and tried to grab him back. I know I screamed. I flung words at him I'd not used since Griff had rescued me. I wasn't proud of them – I knew a sick toddler was more important than a sicked-on bear – but I was beyond reason.

'You deal with her,' I managed at last. 'I'll deal with Tim.'

My poor dear friend. My poor, much loved, increasingly battered friend. The friend who Griff had given me to deliver love and comfort at levels even he couldn't manage. He'd been wet before, but never covered in pink and yellow vomit. I carried him tenderly – if gingerly – to the kitchen and started work on him. When I thought he was ready, I bunged him in a pillowcase – didn't want his eyes scratched – and popped him in the machine for a short spin.

Only then did I return to the mess upstairs – suddenly and blessedly quiet, incidentally – where Morris was demanding more bedclothes.

'Airing cupboard,' I said, eyeing afresh the pile in Griff's room.

'I've used those.'

How many sets of bedclothes had they got through?

'And a couple of towels. Er – seems she's not dry through the night after all.'

'Whose bed did she wet?'

'I thought if I put her in Griff's bed, you and I—'

'You thought! You didn't think, seeing all those nice clean sheets, that I'd achieved the next best thing to a sterile bed for a man who's coming home after major surgery? Thanks a bunch. Now he'll have to go and stay at Aidan's,' I added bitterly.

'Well, it's the obvious thing. Can't imagine why you thought he might come back here.' He dug an even deeper pit for himself. 'Anyway, I'm sure you can turn the mattress. When it's dry.'

'You'd better get the bedclothes downstairs,' I said. I couldn't think of anything else polite or constructive. 'No! Wait! Tim's in the machine!'

By the time I got there, Morris was already yanking him out.

He applied a nose to Tim's fur, just as I've seen parents do to suspect nappies. 'Still stinks.'

'Hey, what are you doing?' I'd never moved so fast in my life.

'Binning it, of course. You don't need it – look over there,' he said, a silly, stupid, complacent grin all over his face.

In Griff's own favourite armchair, without even the benefit of a Steiff button in its ear, sat the ugliest teddy bear I'd ever seen in my life.

# Seven

Speaking quietly, so as not to wake Leda, Morris informed me that I was self-centred and imma-ture, unfeeling and unloving. Equally quietly, I responded that he was at best irresponsible, putting at risk the health of his daughter by drag-ging her all the way from Paris. Not to mention Griff's – a stomach bug would do a man in his state no good at all.

'Why on earth did you even think of coming over?' I asked bluntly.

He didn't seem to have a clear answer to that. There was something about a birthday party in London Leda wanted to go to (was someone not yet two even capable of making such a decision?), no alternative babysitting at home and – though he never actually spelt it out – a desire to have sex with me. It was clear he was on to a loser there, since my bed was occupied by a feverish child and Griff's was still wet, though the smell of urine was less detectable than the smell of vomit in my room and, of course, on Tim. There was also a problem with bedlinen, since Griff considered tumble-dryers unenvironmental. Some wet sheets were draped hopefully over radiators giving out the last of their evening's heat; others lurked in the laundry basket. Casting green considerations to the winds, I turned on the heating again.

On the grounds that he had to sleep somewhere, and ought to be near poor Leda if she was ill again, I dispatched him upstairs. Tim had another bath, this time with a tiny drop of lavender oil in the water, another rinse and then, declaring that enough was enough, he retired to the airing cupboard.

I slept, fitfully, on the sofa.

Next day Leda was a nice sunny toddler and reassuringly hungry. I had to nip down to the village Londis to find croissants that were clearly vastly inferior to the genuine French article. I rather hoped that by the time I'd got back Morris would have discovered the washing whirligig and the pegs to deal with the laundry basket's contents. He hadn't. I don't think he really expected me to accept his invitation to spend the weekend in London with them, so he wasn't disappointed.

As long as we kept the conversation neutral we maintained a polite front. I mentioned I was interested in the possibility of a scam involving Beswick horses. It was clear such lowly fraud – if fraud it was – was beneath him.

It was time for them to go.

Various social hugs and kisses were exchanged; Leda snuggled up to me asking for Tim; Tim declined to emerge from the airing cupboard; the big new bear stared impassively at the proceedings.

If Leda had shown a desperate desire for *him*, I'd have handed him over with pleasure, and any or all of the other collector's bears. All she wanted was Tim, however, but she accepted with surprisingly good grace my story that he was poorly and mustn't be woken up – it was Morris who glowered at my continued selfishness. At last we all waved each other goodbye. Not adieu, but farewell, I was sure.

If I was to make the cottage habitable again, I didn't have time to worry about my feelings. I'd better start with ordering new mattresses for both beds, hadn't I?

I hadn't meant to tell anyone about Morris's departure from my life, but Mary Walker was no fool and was clearly dying to ask about all the sheets everywhere. Actually, I was glad to confide in her – after all, I knew her views on Morris second-hand, as it were, and might as well get them fresh. It was all very therapeutic. As for Tim, he had to have yet another bath, but not until she'd sent me down to Londis again, this time for some fabric treatment she told me was guaranteed to get rid of pongs.

My mates at the takeaway knew a man plus van who didn't mind working at weekends, so he turned up about noon to take away the old mattresses. Actually, I didn't think they'd get as far as the tip. The stains apart, they were still usable – it was just that I wanted perfection for Griff and there was something symbolic about getting rid of mine, which I'd only ever shared with Morris. The bad news was that the earliest replacements I could get from anywhere wouldn't arrive till Tuesday. I could have got cheaper ones within twenty-four hours, but Griff didn't do cheap. Not when it came to supporting his back. But I didn't worry unduly. After all,

Wednesday or Thursday seemed likely release days.

How about some lunch? I was just about to raise the idea with Mary and Paul when my phone rang. It was the guy who organized the Sunday antiques fairs down in Folkestone: he wanted to check that Tripp and Townend were coming tomorrow. Our usual stand awaited us.

I never thought I'd say it, but thank God Aidan was back. Just to make sure, I called him: yes, he fully intended to honour his commitment to see Griff this afternoon, and would indeed be prepared to exchange tomorrow's slots with me so I could visit after the fair. Not much enthusiasm there, but who needed enthusiasm?

Fortunately, Griff and I had perfected a routine for fairs, so all I did was put it into operation: boxes, lights, display stands. Stock – mid-range for Folkestone, with some pretty lower-end items just in case. Some of the things I'd had in mind weren't where I expected. Mary insisted she'd told me she'd sold them earlier in the week, and I believed her. She could have told me she'd done a decent deal on the Crown Jewels and I'd not have registered it.

Just as I was standing back congratulating myself on being pretty well ready, I got a text. Morris. He was sorry about last night. Sorry about the mess. Sorry about the harsh words. Why didn't I catch the next train and we could sort things out?

I texted back that I was on my way in the opposite direction – to see Griff. Then I switched off the phone.

* * *

79

I only just made it to Ashford for the evening visiting hour. But Griff was happily reading – one of the electronic books Pa had suggested I buy for him. Sod Aidan. But I smiled and made Griff show me how it worked, and made one or two inspired guesses when he forgot the purpose of some function or other. I didn't think it was necessary to talk about Morris, not yet, and he seemed happy to accept that I'd spent the day making preparations for the fair tomorrow. Happy-ish – I caught him looking at me appraisingly once or twice.

'All this dashing backwards and forwards, my love – it can't be good for you.'

'I'm fine,' I insisted. And I would be, soon. From time to time what I'd done made me sick with horror. What was I doing, breaking up with a good, decent man, who was doing the right thing and putting his daughter first? Perhaps he was right – perhaps I should have gone to London and patched things up. After all, I should have been grateful that a handsome, well-educated man with a responsible job should have deigned to love me. Me! A child off the streets, whatever Griff had managed to transform me into. No one else would ever want me, even on the part-time basis that was all Morris and I managed.

'Of course you're fine,' Griff agreed doubtfully. 'But you've got so many plates spinning, my angel.'

'I've had to put the restoration work on hold,' I admitted. 'I've emailed everyone on the waiting list to warn them. And Mary and Paul have been heroic in the shop. Do you remember that hideous epergne we got landed with in the Cotswolds?'

80

'That Victorian silver-gilt confection? They never sold that!'

'They did – and the chair Mary had put the teasel on!'

But, upbeat as I tried to be, I was fairly sure I hadn't taken him in. Not my Griff.

At least I had plenty of news to tell him the following evening, after the Folkestone fair.

'Two white Beswick horses, my love? Never!'

'Absolutely. Squaring up to each other – or whatever horses do – across the main hall. You should have seen the expression on Davina and Mike's faces when they clocked each other's displays. And then they both moved the horses.'

'And did either tell you where they'd acquired their version?'

'Davina wouldn't tell her own mother where she'd been born, would she? But Mike muttered something about a private sale. Just some bloke, he said – fancied he'd got some sort of West Country accent. Not like the woman who tried to sell me the white horse.' At this point it dawned on me that throughout the conversation Griff had no idea why on earth I should be interested in white horses. I remembered telling him all about them – hadn't he told me off for cleaning Rob Sampson's shop window? – but clearly the original attempt to sell us a horse simply hadn't registered. And why should it? While I was worrying about white glaze, he was technically dead, his breathing and circulation done for him by complex machinery.

I explained, then continued: 'Apart from the

duplicate Beswick horses, there was something altogether more up my street. A high-fired Ruskin ginger jar. *Sang de boeuf.*'

'Ruskin ware? So far south? In Birmingham, my love, it's not unknown, of course, but here? None of the local dealers seem to know anything about it, alas.'

Early on in my career with Griff, I'd fallen in love with some pottery made in the early twentieth century, much of it specially for the export market, with a lot finding its way to the USA. Typically of that period, some of it was so ugly that you wondered why on earth anyone should have bothered designing it in the first place; other pieces, especially high-fired *sang de boeuf*, were so lovely that I couldn't understand why the world didn't fight over them. It was these that fetched high prices: in the thousands as opposed to the hundreds.

'Quite. But just as I was about to negotiate for it, I realized it had a twin. On a different stall.'

He frowned. 'Quite a coincidence. Did you get close enough to handle either of them?'

'One was already being wrapped up when I approached.'

'Didn't the punter buy the second? What a missed opportunity!' Griff narrowed his eyes. 'But it was unlike you not to snap up the poor relict yourself, my love. Wasn't it? Or are you trying to tell me something? You think there's something wrong with the horses: are you now suspecting something's amiss with the Ruskins?'

I nodded. 'I only got to handle the one, Griff, and there was nothing wrong with it. Perfect. A real gem. The impressed Ruskin mark bang on. Everything about it was right.'

'But something about it was wrong?'

'Only in my head, maybe.'

'My darling child, I trust that head implicitly. Think of the brilliant work it did in Paris – is it really only ten days ago? So much has happened since then. Are you over your injuries? You suffered so much – and yet it had gone clean out of my mind. Oh, Lina. Forgetting important things . . .'

'It's the anaesthetic, I should imagine,' I said bracingly. 'In any case, I don't think a few bruises and a bit of a rash caused by petrol are in the same league as what you've been through. I'm fine. Promise. But the police want to see me again tomorrow – to clarify a few points in my statement, they say. So I hope Aidan will be able to see you in the afternoon, and I'll tell you all about it in the evening.'

'An all day affair? That sounds pretty stressful. And will Morris be able to hold your hand?'

I looked him in the eye. 'You've guessed, haven't you?'

'I knew there was something amiss, and that you didn't want to worry me by telling me all about it.' He held open his arms ready for me to cry all over his shoulder. The wince gave him away. 'Nothing to worry about, Lina. They might have unzipped my chest, but they've zipped it up again. And stapled it, just to make sure it doesn't unzip. But there are a lot of bruises,' he conceded.

'The funny thing is, I don't need a shoulder to

83

cry on. I feel bad about not wanting to put Leda
first all the time, especially given my own childhood. I don't think anyone even thought about
my needs and wishes till you did,' I said, with a
rueful grin. 'So I feel ashamed of myself for
getting cross when she threw up all over Tim the
Bear. Not cross with her – cross with Morris for
putting her in my bed and giving her something
that wasn't his to give. And that was after she
wet your bed . . .'

He pulled a face. 'I think, sweet one, that you'd
better begin at the beginning.'

The sight of my tear-messed face caught the eye
of one of the nurses at the busy desk, a woman
not much younger than Mary Walker.

'Aren't you Griff's granddaughter?' she asked,
stowing a biro in her top pocket and grabbing a
fistful of tissue, which she pushed in my
direction.

I nodded. Best to continue with the lie, after
all.

'You should be on top of the world, the way
he's progressing.'

'Boyfriend trouble,' I muttered, taking a tissue,
and then remembering to smile. 'Thanks. But
what's this about progress?'

'We'll be getting rid of him any day now, I
wouldn't wonder. Will you be his primary carer?
That's government speak for the one who loves
him to bits and looks after him,' she added with
a grin.

'Yes,' I said, dismissing Aidan's claims with a
last dab of the tissue. 'And actually I'm scared

stiff. Tablets and food and dressing the wounds and . . . Oh, should we employ a nurse? We could just afford it.'

She shook her head firmly. 'Waste of money. All you need is common sense – and Griff tells me you've got plenty of that. Wounds don't need dressing, these days – and the stitches just disappear without any interference from anyone. Just keep an eye on things – and don't leave him on his own for a week or so just in case . . . well, in case. Obviously, if any of the sites looks hot and red, talk to your local health centre straightaway.'

For health centre read one-man surgery, but never mind.

'The most important thing, oddly enough, is exercise.'

'Exercise? But I thought . . . an invalid . . . bed rest . . .'

'The heart's just a muscle, Lina. And muscles need to be used or they stop working. So you must make sure that right from the start he moves. When he sits, no leg-crossing – and by the way, he needs to wear compression stockings all the time. They're a bugger to get on and off, but they're a lifeline. Make him walk a little every quarter of an hour, just a turn around the room, then a little further. If he's downstairs, he must use the upstairs loo and vice versa. If he feels sleepy, send him on a route march upstairs. Twice. Make him walk, a real, outside walk, twice or three times a day – and make the distance he walks double each day.' She raised a hand to silence my squeak of protest. 'Harden your own heart. Make him walk if it rains, if it snows, even. We'll give him a schedule of other things to do – and not do. But it's up to you. If you want him better, then you have to be a slave-driver. He drops his hanky – he picks it up. He leaves a book upstairs – he's the one that fetches it.'

'I'll try,' I said doubtfully.

'You'll succeed,' she said sharply. 'That way we won't see him on this ward again. Tell you what, though, Lina, when he treads the boards again I wouldn't mind some tickets.' Another grin. 'Notice I said *when*, not *if*! Feeling better now?' She patted my arm kindly, adding, as she sent me on my way, 'By the way, in my experience boyfriends who make you cry are best ditched. Right?'

'Right,' I agreed, hoping I meant it. But then, still taking in the marvellous news about Griff, I said it as though I did: 'Right!'

# Eight

The police, who interviewed me over in Maidstone, hadn't actually confiscated my phone but it was clear that they didn't want me to take any notice of the volley of texts hurtling at me. I could quite see why – it would have taken even longer to talk them through, in minute detail, all the action of the previous weekend, which seemed light years ago. As it was it all went on so long that I was afraid I might be late for evening visiting in Ashford, particularly as there'd been a pile-up on the M20 and I'd have to take to the back roads.

However, I checked my phone before I set out. Thank goodness I did. The early ones had come from Griff, telling me he'd walked twice the distance and climbed twice the minimum number of stairs the physios demanded of pre-release patients. Then another: his blood and other test results had come through spot on. Then there came the biggie: he was going to be allowed to leave hospital if the medics agreed.

Today.

Without me. Without a bed to sleep in. I think I groaned aloud.

Then came a series from Aidan. Yes, to summarize, Griff was out and safely installed at Aidan's house in Tenterden; would I kindly join them for supper and possibly – in the absence, he understood, of a mattress on my bed – stay the night with them? Then I could assess for myself the level of Griff's care.

There were times – quite a lot, actually – when I wished Aidan spoke English. What on earth did he mean by assessing the level of care?

Only one way to find out. I texted back that I'd join them as soon as I'd touched base and picked up nightclothes. I wanted to scream, believe me. I wanted to shout. I wanted to swear. But the important thing was that Griff was safe. And that the guy who was waiting to let me out of the car park was getting dead impatient.

Tim, fluffy and at last sweet-smelling, needed a good brushing, but once I'd retied his ribbon into a nice bow he accepted with good grace that there were other priorities. He reminded me that Griff kept changes of clothing at Aidan's, where there were also toiletries aplenty, so there was no need to pack anything for Griff; I, on the other hand, might itch to get out of the sober suit in which I'd bearded the police (who always seem more respectful towards me if I'm dressed formally) but should remember that Aidan had a dress code for meals that excluded the jeans I had ready in my hands. And it might be nice to take over some of the many bouquets and pot-plants. Tim would travel in the top of my over-night bag, but didn't fancy being zipped in and squashed, thank you very much. I suspect that this was so he could make what I was fairly sure was a highly inappropriate gesture to the bear I'd still not got round to moving from the living room. As we drove, he transformed it into a truly

regal wave to the rocking zebra currently residing on the roof of High Halden's famous rocking horse factory.

It was a good job that Aidan lived in a whopping great house because it seemed that the night nurse he'd employed – so much for that nice nurse's opinion, but I tended to side with Aidan on this one – had demanded her own bedroom. This seemed to me, and even, I suspect, to Aidan, a contradiction in terms. Shouldn't she have been flitting round Griff, keeping an eye on his every move, taking his pulse and generally nursing him? It seemed she regarded the baby alarm with which she connected the two adjoining rooms as quite sufficient. Aidan was most apologetic about relegating me to a room without an en suite bathroom, a little way down the corridor. I smiled and declared that so long as it came with a mattress on the bed I'd be happy.

You'd think that having the responsibility for Griff's welfare spirited away from me by a combination of Aidan's ego and wealth, in whichever order, and the Northern Irish nurse who managed somehow to speak without ever moving her upper lip, I'd sleep the sleep of the just. But – probably as a result of the day' questioning – I was suddenly getting flashback to the events the police were interested in. Wh if they cluttered up my dreams and I woke screaming? It was best to find some way clearing my brain before I let myself doze The thing that I was most interested in was d

china and pottery. White horses and Ruskin. If it really was all dodgy. Who would run a scam like that? Assuming it was a scam. Someone who knew his (or her) stuff, with technical ability, proper equipment and a working knowledge of the market.

I checked my watch. Was it too late to contact Titus? Not that I suspected him or Pa of involvement, not for one moment. They forged old maps, mainly, or the odd frontispiece allegedly from an historic book. But there was very little that other people got up to that Titus didn't know about, as much, I suspected, to protect his back as anything else. He knew the police were interested him: what better way to fend them off than to offer them a bigger scam run by a big operator, maybe with other criminal sidelines? To me this seemed no better than grassing someone up, but, as he virtuously pointed out, major crime often involved drugs and/or people trafficking. I still found Titus on his high horse almost a contradiction in terms, but never managed to out-argue him.

Whatever the hour, there was no reason not to text him anyway. Not quite to my surprise I got an immediate response. No Ruskin he knew of. But did I know why someone should be making little gold picture frames?

Of course I didn't: with the price of gold these days, it made more sense to be selling the gold for scrap.

It really was time to sleep. But before I did so I made a last visit to the bathroom, which took me past Griff's door. Wanting more than anythir

else just to see him, I pushed at the door, left slightly ajar. And there he was, trying in vain to reach his painkillers and the glass of water.

'Are you allowed any more of these?' I whispered.

'Took the last one after supper,' he assured me.

'Promise?' I checked the bubble-pack anyway. And then the printed sheet the hospital had sent him away with.

'Another half hour, I reckon,' I said firmly. 'You seem to have tipped over a bit – can I have a go at those pillows for you?' Feeling very professional, I linked arms with him as I'd seen the nurses do, and took his weight. 'There. Fancy some music?' Aidan had laid on a radio with earphones. 'Or shall I help you to the loo?'

'As far as the loo door. I may be an old man but I do have some dignity.'

His bed tidy, the lower sheet so taut you could have bounced pennies on it, I helped him settle down again, before perching on the side of the bed and holding his hand. He was in discomfort, I figured, not actual pain, so if he was distracted he might forget he needed medication until it was time to take it. So I asked him about the miniatures of Aidan's ancestors that covered one of the walls. Rows and rows of them in pretty frames: some gilt, some silver gilt, some padded velvet. I have to say there was little family resemblance, or that might have been because the artists were so weak at catching a likeness – or anything else, for that matter.

'As you can see,' he said with an apologetic

smile, 'most of them are painted by amateurs. In the pejorative sense, I have to say.'

'Which is why they're not downstairs with the big boys' paintings,' I observed cynically.

'Quite. But you put your finger on an interesting fact, my love. At the time those ladies over there painted, circa 1800, miniatures were considered pretty well the only respectable art form for a young lady, apart from a few wishy-washy watercolours and their fans. At one point it was almost *de rigueur* for young ladies to paint them – and I'm sure you'll recall references to the small pieces of ivory they were painted on in two of the books we read together.'

He exaggerated, of course: in those days I could scarcely read, let alone read aloud. So Griff had spent evening upon evening reading the classics to me, making them, with all his actorly skills, come to vivid life. He'd also devised little memory games for me, since most of my life had been spent trying to block things out, not remember them.

I shook my head. 'I know you read *Jane Eyre* to me, and at one point she talked about making a miniature portrait of some evil society cow. There was something about having a piece of ivory ready prepared in her paintbox. But I think you only told me about the other one, which you said every Jane Austen scholar referred to when people complained she only wrote about villages – the piece of ivory two inches wide. By the way . . .' I told him about Tristam and his not-Isaac Oliver and how, thanks to Ashford Library, I was hoping to mug up all I could about the genre.

'You're a credit to me, Lina – a real credit. Especially using and pronouncing the word correctly.'

I squeezed his hand. I could scarcely keep my own eyes open. He caught me out in a yawn.

'It's time you caught up on your beauty sleep, dear one.' He accepted the tablet I gave him, and we worked out he could have the next one at about breakfast time. Just to make sure he didn't take an extra, either because he was a little dozy or because the night-nurse thought it was time, I took the packet with me. And slept like the dead.

Raised voices woke me next morning. Griff and Aidan's. I wouldn't have wanted Griff over-hearing any row I might have had with Morris, so I pulled the pillow over my ears and checked my mobile. Some work stuff; one text from Tristam suggesting another drink. One from Brian reminding me about coffee. And one from Morris, pleading, imploring me to see him.

I was just about to reply when I saw the time. It was after eight! I knew Mary was quite capable of opening the shop (Tuesdays were Paul's golf days), but I didn't like to leave her on the prem-ises entirely on her own, particularly as the new mattresses were due for delivery today, so I threw my clothes on and yelled to Griff that I had to fly. At least that shut them up. Of course, I wouldn't have gone without kissing him goodbye, so I dived into his room, to find Griff sitting on the edge of the bed with one long white sock on. Aidan, red in the face, heaved himself off his knees as I came in. The other sock drooped from his hand.

I managed not to gasp at the scar running from Griff's knee to his ankle. I'd known that was where they'd taken some of the replacement artery from, but seeing the site was quite different. Should I offer to take Aidan's place? My head told me not to, and the reason it gave was that I didn't want to stir up the trouble between them. But truly, I didn't wish to risk hurting Griff by touching the poor sore flesh. In any case a text told me the mattress men would deliver within the next hour, so I had to scoot. Really scoot.

I didn't bother trying to look calm and serene as I greeted the driver and his mate: they knew I'd pulled up in front of the house a mere half minute before they did. I was just making them tea when I had a text from a valued museum client: if they couriered an item down could I prioritize it? Like do it today?

I texted back. What was the item?

Only a Worcester Barr, Flight and Barr vase!

Forget texts – it was time to speak to the curator in person. Since the vase wouldn't arrive till the afternoon, and I preferred to work in natural light, I couldn't do much today, I pointed out. But I'd devote the whole of Wednesday to it, and any of Thursday that was called for. Friday too – sometimes glues and colours needed more time. The call over, I found myself rubbing my hands with pleasure. At last I could return to a nice secure world that I was in charge of.

Though I made up the beds, I wouldn't press Griff to return, not until he was ready. Whatever the nice nurse had told me, surely it really was better to have some skilled caring for him. And only then did it dawn on me that showering him and putting those dratted stockings on were surely part of the night nurse's job. I'd have to grit my teeth and talk about it to Aidan when I joined them for supper tonight. Yes, I'd have to go back to Tenterden. In my haste this morning I'd left Tim in Aidan's guest room and there was no way he was spending a night there without me.

'So how far did you walk today?' I asked Griff, hunched in one of Aidan's overlarge wing chairs. 'And uncross your legs while you tell me.'

Furtive or what? I might have caught him nicking Aidan's better miniatures.

I stood over him, arms akimbo. 'You didn't go out at all, did you? Oh, Griff. And it was a nice day, too. Never mind, let's wrap you up and walk you as far as the main road and back.'

'I was about to offer a pre-dinner sherry,' Aidan declared. 'Don't you realize, my dear girl, he's had major surgery? He's a sick man.'

'These days it's almost routine surgery,' I retorted heartlessly, not caring that Aidan was probably still jet-lagged and in need of careful handling. 'And in any case, he'll be even sicker if he doesn't walk. Every day. Every single day. Once today, but twice tomorrow. And three times on Thursday. It's as important as wearing those socks and taking his pills. Didn't that night nurse of yours tell you?' I asked, over my shoulder, as

I helped Griff up. Why we'd talked about him as if he wasn't there I didn't know.

There was a silence I couldn't understand.

I didn't press Griff for an explanation, any more than he'd nagged me about Morris. Instead, we made stately progress as far as the end of the road, talking about my Worcester repair job and how long it would take.

'No sign of Morris?' he asked.

'Just a text. But I don't want to see him again, ever. I feel so bad about ditching him,' I added in a whisper.

'With all due respect, my love, I don't feel you should.'

'You think he ditched me!'

'I didn't say that. And I didn't mean it. That lovely Archbishop John Sentamu once said, I believe, that there are two types of people in the world, and I'm going to particularize what he said to lovers. There are radiators, who give off warmth, and drains, people who take it. I see you as the former, and Morris as the latter. And I don't blame him, but his job, which has to be put first at all times. Not to mention his unusual domestic circumstances. Leda is a charming baby, but she is demanding, it must be said. And there are only so many hours in the day, my love, for him as for you.' He allowed himself a sigh, but I compelled him to walk another twenty yards. 'And I simply fail to see why looking after some other woman's child should be part of your remit.' He paused, taking a deep breath.

'I wonder what became of that other young policeman who was interested in you. Will.'

I wondered too. But I didn't think there was any point in speculating. 'Probably married with a couple of kids. And someone said he'd left the police.'

I turned us gently back to Aidan's. 'So now you know you can get this far and still keep talking, you must go further tomorrow morning. And tomorrow afternoon. Promise me. Because if you won't, I shall have to take you away from all this luxury.'

'Home,' he added – wistfully, I'd swear.

# Nine

Griff knew I was leaving really early next morning and would try not to wake anyone in the process. I did peep into his room, but he was fast asleep, and that was the way I wanted to keep it, so I didn't put on even my trainers till I'd fought my way through Aidan's security system and got outside.

I'd already put a couple of hours' work in on the Barr, Flight and Barr vase before my usual breakfast time, leaving the adhesive to start drying while I dealt with the overnight emails. At last I headed off for some toast. Except the bread was mouldy. At least there were a couple of poor Leda's croissants lurking sadly in the bottom of the bin, squashed and dry but at least edible: they must have been stuffed to the brim with preservatives. Beginning a list of other things I was running out of, I wished I could do what Griff would have done: bake a couple of loaves. But I really had no time. Especially when the rumble of a huge truck down the street reminded me that today was bin day. Bins were usually Griff's preserve, but they'd be mine for several weeks yet.

Another near squeak. The wheelie bin reached the pavement just as the refuse truck arrived outside the cottage. I waved as the men, who seemed to run everywhere, jeered at me.

Dragging the emptied bin back into the yard, I realized at long last how interdependent Griff and I had become. Symbiotic was the word he'd taught me. Gradually, as I'd taken on more and more of the physical jobs as his health had deteriorated, he'd quietly made my life easier in other ways, by nipping off to the village whenever supplies ran short, and sometimes doing a supermarket run if I was really pressed for time. Now I was trying to dash up a down escalator, or so it seemed. Thank God once more for Mary and Paul, whose car was just drawing up. I let them in through the yard gates, locking up securely behind them.

Paul emerged looking particularly smug, retrieving a large jiffy bag from the rear footwell. 'Neigh!' he greeted me.

Mary smiled apologetically. 'Yes – another white horse. Though actually I think it's a red herring.'

'She thinks it's the wrong size,' he explained, over the cup of tea I made for us all, as Mary ran an experienced eye over my shopping list, crossing out from time to time and adding other items.

'I'm afraid she's right,' I said with a smile as she scribbled *loo rolls*. 'It's not as big as the controversial gee gees. But this might be controversial too.' I turned it over and over. 'Where did you get it?'

'Junk shop in Folkestone. My golf partner needed a lift to pick up his car, so I parked up and browsed round. He was lurking right at the back of the shop – in fact there wasn't even a price on him. We settled on twenty pounds. Can't argue with that.' He patted the little horse. Colt? Foal?

''Course you can't,' I agreed, stroking the glaze. Immaculate. Apart from—

Paul didn't miss much. 'What have you found?'

I pointed. 'What does that look like? Under the glaze, here?'

'A bit of a fingerprint. Quality items don't usually come with faults like that, do they?'

'Absolutely not. Not unless they're stamped *seconds* or someone scratches out the trademark. Weird.'

He laughed. 'I can almost see your brain working, Lina.'

'I can feel it. But it's missing a gear at the moment.' I stared at the wretched thing. And at the fingerprint. 'I'd like to look at it under the UV light,' I said. 'Do you want to see?'

'Don't be too long,' Mary told him. 'You've a spot of shopping to do. If you want to eat lunch, that is.'

And lunch was on Tristam's mind too. Before Paul and I had got as far as the stairs, the office phone was ringing.

'Just a sarnie?' he urged, when I turned him down flat.

'I've got a rush job on,' I said. 'Any other week – but I'm practically fed and watered by intravenous drip at the moment.'

'Tomorrow, then?'

Hadn't he heard what I said? But a thought struck me: Griff was safe at Aidan's – dare I take one evening off? 'How about after work tonight? Nine-ish?'

But he was busy with his bar job, of course. So that was that.

Back to Paul's horse.

He operated the UV lamp with a flourish, as if allowed to participate in some weird ritual. But twist and turn the horse as we might, it showed up no signs of repair. And when we checked on the office computer, we found it wasn't particularly rare anyway.

Paul peered over my shoulder: 'Seems I paid the right price too. That'll teach me to think I'm an expert!' He looked at me sideways. 'Any idea what I can do with it? Get Mary to sell it in the shop? You know she could sell transistors in Silicon Valley.'

I almost nodded. But then I said, 'Actually, don't. Something's wrong, I feel it in my water. And that fingerprint's part of it.'

There we were, the three of us, gathered at Aidan's, but happy families it was not.

We managed to keep something of a conversation going over dinner, which was not good. Aidan was the sort of man who needed not just a cleaning lady and a gardener, but a cook-housekeeper, probably complete with mob cap and chatelaine. How he could kill grilled salmon and vegetables was beyond me, but I gave him brownie points for the oily fish at least. While Aidan slipped out to get the dessert, I asked Griff if he'd kept his promise to walk.

'I did indeed,' he said proudly, pointing to his

101

feet. To my delight he'd abandoned the old man's slippers for a pair of new slip-on shoes. OK, they fastened with Velcro, but they were a start. 'I went out twice. And went further than last night. But I didn't venture on to the High Street. To tell you the truth I was terrified someone would jostle me.' His shudder looked genuine. As did another when Aidan produced a decanter of red wine, with three of his exquisite eighteenth century glasses. He explained, in a whisper as Aidan went off to bring cheese and biscuits, which I suspected were very low down the list of things Griff should be eating, 'It must be the tablets, or perhaps the anaesthetic. But alcohol seems to have lost its charm.'

'It had better find it again soon,' I said cheerfully. 'Red's really good for hearts, according to the Internet. Now, this here exercise – you haven't forgotten that you're walking Mary down the aisle in six weeks' time? They were talking about postponing the wedding.'

'Heaven forbid! My child, you have put steel in my spine. Three walks a day? It shall be four!'

'They can't possibly hold Griff to his promise in the circumstances,' Aidan declared, coming in at the wrong moment. 'Surely they can find someone else.'

'I'm sure they could,' Griff agreed. 'But in no circumstances will they have to. I shall be well enough. I shall.' He paused, looked at Aidan, and changed tone. 'Now, Lina, do grapes have to be turned into wine before they are good for one? Because I really do fancy some of those on Aidan's delicious-looking cheeseboard . . .'

* * *

102

Although he had every TV channel available, some not even in English, Aidan declared there was nothing worth watching, upsetting Griff, who'd spotted some Test cricket in Australia. I fancied a loud comedy, but clearly that was off the cards. So I did what the men did: I settled down with a book, in my case the one about miniatures, and a notebook and pencil. I wanted to squeak with pleasure and exclaim out loud, but didn't dare until Aidan left the room to take a phone call.

'Look! It says that *miniature* didn't always mean *small*! It's to do with colouring with red lead. And what's this about *painting* being called *limning*?'

'I think you'll find, loved one, that the *n* isn't pronounced. *Limming*. As in Port Lympne,' he added with a chuckle.

'Do you remember when I thought *misled* was pronounced *mizled*?'

Aidan, returning, clearly didn't think my ignorance amusing. Or perhaps he resented an intimacy that excluded him. He seemed even less amused when I mentioned I'd met a handsome young expert on miniatures. Really not amused at all. With a glance at Griff, I shut up. I continued to make the odd note – fancy Nicholas Hilliard being trained not as an artist but as a goldsmith! And imagine women becoming not just amateur miniaturists, but professionals, working at Henry the Eighth's court, in an age when I'd never imagined women leaving the home. Take Levina Teerlinc: even I couldn't consider her in the same league as Holbein, for instance, but I did feel a little glow, especially as I detected a tiny connection between our first names.

I must have exclaimed out loud. Aidan snorted, and Griff looked apprehensive. I put my head down and jotted fast. But another silly grin must have spread across my face when I learned that one of the first artists, possibly *the* first, to paint on ivory, as opposed to vellum, was a woman, Rosalba Carriera.

The temperature in the room fell to zero. I checked my watch – quite needlessly. But it gave me some reason to excuse myself, saying I'd got a couple of calls to make. The book and the notepad went with me. That was me for the evening. I gave a general, polite goodnight.

Why I should feel twelve again, with yet another bad mark against my name, I had no idea. I was weepy and angry and everything in between. Eventually, I unpacked my laptop and checked our emails, just to see if there was anything interesting, or if I'd missed anything while I was stressed out. Maybe a bit of disciplined calm would improve my mood. Or something to look forward to.

As I cleaned my teeth, it dawned on me that the problem might not involve me at all, except that Aidan really wasn't happy I even existed. Aidan was probably still jet-lagged. And grieving, of course, for his sister. And worried about Griff, whom he thought I was forcing to do things he shouldn't. And Griff had had major – if routine! – surgery, and probably felt tetchy too. Perhaps the trouble lay between them and was nothing to do with me.

'That's all very well,' I told myself, reaching for Tim, 'but I'd rather not be here at all. Bloody great mausoleum. I want to go home. Now.'

Tim stared. Firstly, I'd always coveted the elegant house. Secondly, if I went home this evening there'd be a row, and that wouldn't do Griff any good at all. Head down, early night. Invent something to do tomorrow. Maybe organize the coffee Brian suggested. Allow yourself lunch with Tristam and tell Griff you've got to work late. Anything. I emailed Brian. Coffee at eleven thirty would be good.

Because I was slow to take things in, even though I'd made notes to help, I was rereading the book when Griff came up to bed. I'd nicked the radio and earphones that were supposed to be for his use, and retreated to my own world. I might even have dropped off. But I came to with a jolt when I realized I hadn't kissed Griff goodnight.

I found him sitting up in bed with his electronic book. There was a vaguely smug air about him, but he was clearly too engaged with the book to want to do more than bid me his usual fond goodnight, until I told him that I'd again be going back to Bredeham very early.

'You know, I might just try out my new mattress tomorrow night,' I said. 'I'm so behind with my restoration work, I could do with the extra time. And,' I added, because I knew it would be unanswerable, 'there's just the sniff of a date. That guy Tristam who's working for Brian Baker. For free,' I reminded him.

'Capitalists' charter, internships,' he declared,

surprising me. Then he snorted. 'At least he won't be having a Lewinsky moment with Brian.'

Griff, in his dressing-gown and those heelless slippers, was pottering round the kitchen when I slipped downstairs ready to leave. I was taken aback. Much as I applauded his brilliant progress, I did think someone his age was entitled to have his first cup of tea of the day while he was still in bed. As I took the tea he'd made with a smile and a kiss, I asked, 'So what's with the night nurse? Isn't this her job?'

He looked round furtively. 'There don't seem to be many things that are her job,' he said. He dropped his voice conspiratorially. 'What I really want to do is come home, but I don't want to be a burden to you.' He put a finger to my lips. 'Our business depends on you doing your repair work, not running around all day checking I'm all right, which Aidan is supposed to do, for a few more days at least. And I rather think Aidan needs a bit of a project after his sister's death. Which means I may have to go away with him. Fortunately, I'm UK-bound for a bit, so no long haul flights, thank goodness. We're talking about a boutique hotel somewhere. Now, what I want you to do for me is check the schedule of fairs we're booked to exhibit at – no, I'm not suggesting I help out, you silly child – and find accommodation that you can come back to at the end of your working day. I know you like lurking in our caravan, but imagine ending a tedious day with a hot bath, a luxurious bed and gourmet food!' He did the tiniest of little dances, which made me feel like doing handsprings, even though he did have to steady himself against the worktop.

'You're on! Yes, I'll miss the caravan, which makes me feel like Mrs Tiggy-Winkle, but a spot of pampering would be lovely. Oh, yes please. Can I email the list of fairs to Aidan? He won't mind? I'll just send it without comment,' I added.

'Excellent. Now, have a lovely evening with that young man. I know you're not smitten yet, but you never know.'

# Ten

'Thank God for Internet, say I.' Brian stirred his coffee. 'We do so much trade that way these days – you've no idea how keen the China market is these days.'

'China with a big C? Not a little C? Because I wouldn't describe the market in mid-range china, the sort of stuff we specialize in, as keen. Not even buoyant.' I used Griff's word of choice.

'So your skills come in useful?' His voice had an edge to it.

I wasn't sure which skills he was referring to, so I nodded as I took a sip of the coffee. When he didn't follow up, I grasped the nettle. 'Do you mean restoring? In which case, yes, that side of the business is ticking over nicely.'

'Of course it is; I've heard very good things of you. I meant the twitching nose skills.'

'It doesn't work to order, as I was telling Tristam. I couldn't rely on it to win the Lottery. Heavens, it didn't even tell me how ill Griff was.'

'But you've got a good eye, anyway. Picking out the only decent miniature from the lot Tris was checking over,' he reminded me. 'He's off with flu today. Or so he says. And worrying about those horses,' he added, when I didn't bite.

I felt as if I might be on surer ground. 'Have any others turned up?'

'Not round here. And nothing suspicious about

108

the quality. It's just the quantity. We auctioneers have reputations to maintain, same as you have. We thought of an informal little conference. Can we count you in?'

When I got back home, I was glad I'd said yes. Paul was looking distinctly sober.

'You know that little white horse? I had someone round at my house this morning asking for it back.'

'How did they get your address?' I flashed.

'A bit of logical deduction, I suppose. We'd talked about how far I'd come and where I lived and so on. So I must have given too much away. Mary's furious with me. She's made me up the security to match that on her cottage.'

Which had been installed by the clever people who'd fixed ours. 'Good. Anyway, what did you say about your horse?'

'I didn't. I just said I'd given it away, and that was that. I don't think they believed me, somehow.'

I bet they wouldn't. 'Do they know anything about your connection with Mary? Or me and Griff?'

'Mary, probably – because someone in the village would have told them if they asked about me. In any case, they'd only have to sit and watch the house and see her coming and going. And they'd easily follow us.' He added, with a faint grin, 'You've no idea what a circuitous route I took to get here.'

I nodded. He was a sensible man. How on earth had he come to be so confiding, a man whose profession demanded a padlock on the mouth? Because someone wanted the information, that's why. Maybe not for any particular purpose, just to keep handy should it ever be needed. And obviously they needed it to retrieve this horse. Because of the fingerprint? As good a reason as any.

'If I go to the police, what's left of them, that is,' Paul said, 'what can I say? They didn't threaten me, not exactly, just asked me to try to get it back because it shouldn't have been sold in the first place. At which point, I repeated that I didn't think I could.'

I managed a rueful grin. 'I'm sorry I've embroiled you in something I don't want to be involved in myself. And – I never thought I'd say this – I wish Morris and I were still together. He'd know what to do. Not because he's a man, but because he's a policeman,' I added quickly as Mary joined us.

She grinned, but asked, 'What about that police-*woman* you were friends with? The one with the funny name? The one the parson married?'

'Ah. Long story.' It was, very long. Freya and I more rubbed along together than loved each other as friends. And one day, when she'd been angry with me, she'd let rip in front of a fellow officer who'd turned out to be corrupt, with potentially disastrous consequences. But I'd lived to tell the tale, though I admit I would have been happy never to see her again. As a priest, rather than simply as her husband, Robin had suggested I forgive her. To his amusement – possibly – I'd agreed, so long as God made sure Griff came through his operation. Although Robin insisted that God didn't do bargains, I rather felt I'd got to keep my half. I'd conveniently forgotten the

110

whole deal till now, of course – though no doubt God would forgive me since I'd had a lot on my plate. But would this be pure forgiveness or – since I wanted her advice, if not her help – applied forgiveness? Maybe Robin wasn't the person to ask that particular question, not least because he was worried sick about her and their unborn baby, who'd wanted to pop out early. Freya had been stuck in hospital trying to keep the baby in place for at least two weeks. She was bored out of her skull, according to Robin, who'd assured me she'd welcome a visit. I wasn't so sure myself, and I'd have preferred the forgiveness to be more in the abstract.

But now it was clear it'd have to be face to face, which meant another hospital visit, this time to Pembury.

I might still have flunked it if Freya's other visitor, an older woman, hadn't caught sight of me as she got up to leave.

'She's very low,' she mouthed, as if Freya was blind as well as pregnant. 'Mind you cheer her up.' She tiptoed out and gave an exaggerated wave. If I'd been Freya, I wouldn't have been low so much as furious.

'I didn't know if you were allowed flowers,' I said, now properly in the bright but institutional little room, 'so I brought these.' I produced a pretty basket the local deli had filled with nuts, olives and other small and exotic nibbles. I had a moment of panic: what if there were things in here pregnant women shouldn't eat?

She stared at me and then the basket, dull-eyed.

111

So this was what low meant. I don't think I'd ever been low. I'd been angry and I'd been in despair, but a general state of lowness, where my face and shoulders drooped like Freya's, was foreign territory. I plonked the basket on top of a pile of fresh new magazines, mostly to do with babies, as far as I could see, and searched every last recess of my brain for something to say. Anything.

'Look, I didn't have time for any lunch,' I said, producing a sandwich from my bag. One of the deli's best – so full that the sides of the baguette had given up trying to meet. 'Would you mind?' Since all she did was turn her head away, I unwrapped it and took a bite. Garlic and herbs and gherkins and home-made mayo and Italian sausage and sun-dried tomatoes – they couldn't have crammed in any more. The inescapable hospital smell was overpowered, though not without a struggle.

She only started to cry, didn't she? So, abandoning the sarnie but still chewing, I found myself gathering into my arms a woman whose anger had nearly got me killed. Oddly enough I soon found myself crying too, good and hard, though I wasn't sure what for. Griff? Aidan? Morris? Nor to be honest was I sure what she was howling about: she'd got everything she wanted, hadn't she? A lovely husband and a baby and maternity leave with a good job to go back to and . . . But that was what being low was about, maybe. And maybe it was another name for depression, which I had read about. And maybe they couldn't give her any drugs to perk her up because of the baby.

'What the hell did they put in that sarnie?' she

demanded suddenly. Not as if she was blaming it for her tears. More as if she was about to snaffle it herself. Which was so like the Freya of old that I handed it over, just breaking off the part I'd bitten.

'I need to pick your brain,' I said as she tore into it. 'Fraud. Low level. I've got a fingerprint I need photographing before I return the thing it's on to its owner.' Since, cramming the baguette into her mouth as if she'd been starved, she wasn't in a position to ask any questions, I told her the whole story.

'And what does Morris say?' How she managed to sound sarcastic when she'd got a mouth full of salami meant for me I didn't know.

'Morris says nothing because I haven't told him. I haven't told him anything except goodbye.'

'About bloody time too. What made you see the light?'

'Leda sicking all over my bed.' I'd keep Tim out of it. 'After she'd weed in Griff's.'

She threw back her head and laughed, eventually adding sourly, 'Well, if you will play child-minder to someone else's brat – it's not even his, I gather.'

'He couldn't love her more if she was his,' I countered. Praise where praise was due.

'And more than he'll ever love any other female,' she agreed. 'Lucky you, then – on the loose. Anything promising on the horizon?'

'Only a row of pots and other things waiting to be restored. Which brings me back to the fingerprint.' I dug in my bag and produced Paul's purchase. 'Look at this.'

Frowning, she ran a finger over it, finally producing a grim smile. 'Oh ho!' She rolled herself and her bump off the bed. 'You couldn't pass me my phone, could you? Ta.' She tapped in digits as if the thing had offended her. 'DCI Webb here,' she barked. I'll swear her spine straightened and her shoulders went back. 'Yes, I know I'm on maternity leave. But I'm still ma'am to you.'

The upshot was that I was to take the small white horse to one of her colleagues, a forensic photographer, whatever one of them was. She also detailed a detective constable to what wasn't quite a case yet, as she told him, but might be. 'There. So tomorrow little white gee gee can go back to the shop it came from, complete with its print, and with luck that Paul of yours will be left alone. Any ideas who's behind this? Not that old villain Oates?'

'Would I be telling you about it if for a minute I thought so? By the way, do you and your mates know anything about gold picture frames? He wanted me to warn you about someone faking them.' I crossed my fingers behind my back. But Titus needed a few brownie points, didn't he?

'I doubt it. And do I want to? Just run one hare at a time, Lina, that's my advice.'

'Actually, there's another hare, too. A high-fired Ruskin one.'

'OK. Tell. Hey, are those stuffed olives I see there?'

Mary was more relieved than Paul to see the much-photographed white horse. She pushed him out into the corner of the garden where reception was best to phone the original owner. 'Now, tell me,' she asked, 'did you meet any nice handsome policemen?'

I nodded, just to wind her up. Actually, DC Carwyn Morgan had been drop-dead gorgeous, but more, I suspected, the sort of guy Griff's eyes would follow around a room. On the other hand, he'd got the makings of an ally, and just at the moment I rated a mate above a lover.

'Tell me,' she said.

'Only about five nine. But a lovely body – obviously uses the gym. Thirties – early. Blond hair already thinning on top. Nice hands. Really nice hands.' I mimed the way he'd handled the horse, as if it was a body he loved.

As if against her better judgement, and certainly doubting mine, she asked, 'And will you be seeing him again?'

I couldn't hold back a bark of laughter. 'Oh, if this white horse business takes off, I should think so.' He'd promised to update me immediately if the print showed up on their system, but I wouldn't hold my breath. 'But not otherwise. And just as a police officer. No more.'

The mixture of relief and disappointment on her face made me laugh again.

'I can't inspect every guy as if he's boyfriend material, can I? Not as if I was one of Lizzie Bennet's sisters, always on the catch for an officer.'

'There's something about a uniform, though.'

I shook my head. 'He's plain clothes.'

Her face dropped. 'Like Morris?'

'Heavens, I hope not!' How on earth had she startled that out of me? It was time to change the subject. 'You know, I suspect Griff's getting a bit bored in Tenterden, and I know he'd love to see you. If I take over the shop tomorrow, would you and Paul have time to nip over?' I'd pay her as if she'd worked every last minute, but there was no need to say that now. 'You wouldn't have to stay for very long: I should imagine Aidan will have the stopwatch on you. He insists on treating Griff as an invalid,' I added, wondering if I was being disloyal. 'And the trouble is, it's so nice for Griff to be pampered, I'm afraid he won't want to be independent again.' Maybe that sounded better.

'Aidan always terrifies me,' Mary said. 'There are some gays who love women, aren't there, like your Griff, and some men, like Aidan, who despise them. At least, *I* always feel thoroughly despised.'

It was something she did very well. My therapist would have said she had the same self-esteem issues as mine, even if she showed them in different ways. I wanted to give sound advice about not taking his attitude personally, but instead I found myself giving her a quick hug. 'Talk about the wedding plans,' I said. 'Aidan'll hate it, but Griff needs something to look forward to. Oh, Mary, I do wish he was safe here at home.'

She returned the hug. 'We all do. And I'm sure he does too. But he'd be afraid of giving you even more work.'

'That's what he said.'

'And he's right. You're working all hours to

116

keep the business afloat. Well?' She turned wide-eyed to Paul as he closed his phone and returned to the shop.

'Fine. I lied my socks off and told him I'd driven all the way to Cambridge to see my niece and would drop the horse off tomorrow morning. If that's OK by you, Lina?'

'More than OK.'

'We could go on the way to Tenterden, couldn't we, Paul?'

I could see him working out the dubious geography, but he smiled as if he'd always wanted to go to Tenterden.

'To see Griff,' she explained. 'And talk about the wedding.'

Another huge smile. What a nice man he was. Wouldn't it be nice to find such a kind and decent partner for myself, though I did rather hope I didn't have to wait till I was a widow in my sixties.

I left them wrapping the newly repaired Worcester vase ready for the courier who was due any moment. Where did my time go?


Mary and Paul were just leaving for the day, white horse, double bubble-wrapped, safe in the rear footwell, when Mary opened the passenger window.

'I don't think I reminded you. In the diary there's a note about a fair on Sunday. Great Hogben.'

I slapped my forehead; I'd completely forgotten. Griff would probably have said it was because though Great Hogben village hall antiques and collectibles fair was one of our regulars, I wanted to scrub it from our calendar. We never did more than cover our expenditure. But he insisted that even tiny events helped bring money into villages that needed it, and that we were, in his opinion, honour bound to keep going. It was only a couple of hours or so on a Sunday morning, he reminded me. 'Or so', indeed. By the time he'd chatted to all his old friends, all equally keen to stop going, but equally reluctant to ditch yet another fair, we never got back before four. Day gone.

This time, however, there'd be no Griff, of course.

I looked at my watch: should I pack for the fair tonight, or wait till tomorrow when I'd be in the shop anyway?

My phone decided the matter. DC Morgan? Carwyn Morgan!

'Hi, Lina. Bad news, I'm afraid. We don't have a match. But we do have some people on our radar whom you may recognize. Would you mind if I brought some mugshots round for you to look at on my way home?'

Mind? I'd be delighted. If I thought about it I had to admit I found the cottage horribly quiet without Griff – crazy, since often he was simply sitting reading downstairs, as quiet as a mouse. I fished out the nicer china in case he had time for a coffee. Was it too late to offer him one of Griff's lovely little cakes? There were still some in the freezer.

'We'd have liked to get prints off the exterior of the horse,' Carwyn said, 'but they were thoroughly corrupted.'

118

'By Freya Webb's and mine, not to mention our shop manager's and her fiancé's.'

'Shame: I love playing with a nice bit of kit which we take round with us – we just ask the suspect to shove his finger in and we can see if he's on the database. Just like that.' He clicked his thumb and finger.

I looked him in the eye. 'You may well have my prints on your database, though they should really have been destroyed by now. I was a feral kid at one time – it was only when Griff, the Tripp half of our business, took me on that I joined the human race.'

He looked around, wide-eyed, taking in the exquisite furniture and delicate china. 'He was taking a hell of a risk, wasn't he?' Then he frowned. 'Mind you, so were you. He could have been a raging paedophile.'

'I don't think Griff could rage if he tried. And he's got a lifelong partner. He's staying with him now while he gets over his operation.'

'And you?' he asked casually.

If I knew Freya and her mates, everyone would know about Morris and me, but I pretended not to know which question to answer first. 'Oh, I can rage. Pity it's not an Olympic sport – I could have got Gold for England. Funnily enough, I never damaged anything he cared for.' Except myself, of course. 'I didn't throw so much as a plate when my bloke and I split the other day,' I said tersely. Why we were talking as personally as this, I'd no idea. It was time to change direction. 'So you've got nothing on the print under the glaze?'

'Nope. And we have to remember that it may well

be that of a completely innocent employee. Though how it would get through quality control . . .'

At last he produced his laptop. It was easier to put it on the office desk, so we could both see without cosying up on the sofa.

We were doing fine, cracking loads of highly un-PC jokes about the owners of the faces he brought up, until I spotted Titus. Though I said nothing, he must have picked up my reaction. 'Him?' He pointed with a well-manicured finger.

At this point I remembered why I'd decided never to get close to a police officer: a relationship depended on honesty, and I couldn't ever be honest about Titus, or, of course, my father. Now wasn't the moment to reflect on why I'd made an exception for Morris.

'Of course I know Titus. He's a highly respected dealer,' I said indignantly, or as near as I could get. I could scarcely add that it wasn't china he faked. 'In fact, he asked me to pass on to Freya the information that, for some reason, someone had started to make a lot of little gold picture frames. I suspect she thought she'd left enough for her replacement to worry about without those.'

'Replacement!' he snorted. 'In the current economic situation?' But he must have gathered he was getting nothing about Titus from me, so he moved over to women's faces.

'Nothing. I'm sorry. She came to the shop at the very moment Griff was in the operating theatre,' I said apologetically. 'And I truly can't tell you much about her.'

'I quite understand. But anything you can think of would be good, too.'

I'd have loved to respond to his smile with one of my own. Instead, I sat on my hands, to stop myself hitting my face in frustration. 'I can't recall her name or anything. She'd given the horse she was trying to sell some stupid name, too. The trouble is,' I said, again shocking myself by my frankness, 'when you have a crap childhood like mine, you survive by shutting it out. At least that was what my therapist said. Griff's tried all sorts of things to improve my memory, but whenever something nasty happens, it all seems to go off in a grey mist. Until the flashbacks start,' I added bitterly. 'I could do without them. But our Mrs Walker, who'll be back in the shop on Monday, is a genius: she'll tell you all about her. And so,' I added with a grin, 'will our CCTV.' Why on earth hadn't I thought of it before? And as one thing popped into my mind, so did another. 'Ah! Of course! Mrs Fielding and Puck!'

Once he'd got the footage, including the entire recorded conversation, there was really no reason for him to hang around. He'd got all the evidence he needed. But – Limoges plate apart – there was really no reason for me to get rid of him. How I came to show him the plate, and explain what I had to do, I don't know.

Then he started asking intelligent questions. Not just about the repair processes. 'So if I wanted to buy a piece from your shop, how would I know it was kosher?' he asked, narrow-eyed.

'We always provide documentation with each piece. Where possible, we give its provenance. If necessary we detail any damage or repairs,

121

mine or anyone else's. If I do insurance work, both the client and the insurers get a list of what I've done. Tripp and Townend have a national reputation for probity. International, these days.'

He laughed. 'So how do you make a profit?'

'Apart from buying cheap and selling dear, which is what all dealers do? For some reason these hands of mine take on a life of their own when I'm repairing. People are pleased by the results.' Did I sound too defensive? With a bit of a challenge in my chin, I showed him the invoice for the museum work. 'So this is what keeps us in profit.'

Whistling softly, he nodded. 'What if I had something I wanted to sell on?'

I looked him straight in the eye. 'You're asking if we fence things? Never knowingly. Never. As for doing it accidentally, I'm sure Brian Baker – and you can't be much more respected as an auctioneer than he is – would say the same as me: you get a feeling for things, and for people. If in doubt, don't buy. If in doubt, certainly don't offer for sale. Hence we turned down the offer of Puck.'

'But you do sell, on commission?'

'You haven't half been doing your homework! Occasionally. I regularly sell on commission for my father, Lord Elham, who's got a wing of a stately home stuffed with artefacts, mostly tat, but some worth flogging. The odd dealer's tried to con him. I don't. Ever. And just in case you wish to know, I give him a receipt for any items I remove, and he gives me one for any money I bring him.'

He nodded doubtfully.

'There's one bit of homework you've missed,' I said. 'Come down to the office for a moment.' It didn't take me long to bring up the names of my French clients. 'These are people I've been working for recently – before I was the victim of a pretty nasty assault here in Kent – or, to stretch a point, it might have been Sussex – a couple of weeks back.' I sketched a few details, which made him raise his eyebrows in an altogether satisfactory way. 'You see, I help the good guys, Carwyn. Not the baddies.'

'So why are you friends with Titus Oates?'

He'd been doing what Paul's white horse people did. Lots of nice questions, all on a nice friendly level. And all he wanted was to nail Titus. What I wanted to say was that Titus was a good friend of Pa's. I had a nasty feeling that this was precisely what he wanted me to say. With faint praise I'd have damned them both.

'There are some people I'm happy to bad-mouth, Carwyn, but Titus isn't one of them. He's always been someone I can turn to. Now, I'm afraid I've got a date this evening.' It was with the Limoges plate, but he didn't need to know that. I felt angry and sad. I'd have loved to have a guy like Carwyn as a friend. But you couldn't run with the fox and hunt with the hounds, not in terms of personal relations. Perhaps, deep down, that was one reason why Morris had never committed to me – because he knew I had dodgy friends.

# Eleven

It was the most gorgeous late summer's day – just the weather to be outdoors, preferably on an empty beach with the wind in my hair, or even, if I had to, in the garden, which I'd neglected recently. Instead I spent Saturday closeted in the faint mustiness of the shop – no matter how clean Mary kept it, which was off the immaculate scale, the old items came with their own smells.

Occasionally, I had a customer, but I also packed up the stock to take with me the next day. Fortunately for my sanity, I had the book on miniatures to keep me company. Mary and Paul phoned to say they'd found Griff so cheerful and bright that they'd insisted on taking him for a tiny trip in the car, padding the space between his seat belt and his still tender chest with a little cushion. He'd loved it: though she had a feeling that Aidan had disapproved.

'But he's OK?'

'Tired, but in a good way. He's worried about you, you know, not getting out enough. I may have told him there was plenty of time for you to go on the razzle when he was back running the business, but I agreed with him. Lina, you do need some joy in your life. And some fun. And some silliness.'

With someone like Carwyn? Why hadn't I just stayed off my high horse and suggested a drink?

Mates, that's all? 'When Griff's better I shall go for all three,' I promised her. But once again my fingers were crossed behind my back. Tonight I'd have loved even one of those diversions, but the best I could manage was another wicked takeaway and a glass of wine. Tim looked thoroughly disapproving at the thought of my drinking alone, and sent me off to have a scented bath with candles and nice music. Pity I filled the bath too full and ran out of hot water.

Sunday dawned suddenly autumnal, wind slapping dollops of rain into your face and leaves wet and slippery beneath your feet, delightful – or not, when you're carrying plastic boxes full of china, even if none of it was particularly valuable: I'd selected the grown-up equivalent of pocket-money toys. Even if I didn't sell much, I might get a sighting of another dodgy horse or even some questionable Ruskin ware.

Neither. To be honest, I was quite glad: after all, many of the dealers were friends of Griff's. Most of them had sent him cards or flowers, and it was good to pass thanks and good news back to them. I didn't want them to have been conned into selling fakes – or, worse still, actually to have known they were diddling the public.

The very few customers came in with streaming macs and lethal umbrellas; those who came to our stall picked up one object after another, only to put each down with a disparaging snort. One or two dealers had people approach them asking them to look at an item they'd brought with them – getting a free valuation, in other words.

Round about one o'clock, when we were supposed to pack up, there was a little surge of punters who actually began opening wallets. One customer pounced on a pretty Coalport trio, reduced because I'd had to repair the plate, and another didn't even bother to haggle over a vase I'd have paid her to take away. At least, I reflected, as I stowed the last plastic box in the van, the driving rain slapping my hair across my eyes and making it hard to grip the handles, there was something to make Griff smile. There'd be precious little else if the rest of the day at Aidan's was as chilly as I expected.

Would Aidan manage to crack his face when I told him about the next few minutes? A woman fell in the car park – maybe she slipped on some leaves. There were two sounds: her scream and the sound of china being smashed. Other people were quicker to pick her up than I was, but naturally as soon as I'd made sure the box was safe and locked the van, I joined the knot of onlookers.

By now she was on her feet. Someone offered her a cup of tea, even though the fair was officially over and the hall was being locked up. But she insisted she was all right, and, picking up her plastic carrier and its bubble-wrapped contents, which had tipped sideways on to the tarmac, said she'd be off. Didn't I know that voice from somewhere? But perhaps I'd just heard it this afternoon.

Something fell out of the loosely swathed bubble-wrap. A little white thing. Surely, surely, a tiny horse's leg. I was too far away to be sure, though I'd have loved to pounce on it – helpfully, of course, in order to return it to her. Now I was

126

almost sure it was our Mrs Fielding, but with an elegant dark bob this time. As she scuttled away, presumably to a car parked in the village street, something got into me, and I leapt back into the van. I would give chase!

Actually, that was not a good idea – not with our names blazoned all over the sides of our lovely petunia vehicle. If only I'd come in the nice anonymous Fiesta. I brought the chase to an abrupt halt some hundred yards behind her – I stopped as if I had to take a call on my mobile. So when I saw her scramble into the passenger side of a Y reg Volvo outside the Three Tuns, at least I could try to get a few shots of her, and of the number plate. No, too far away to get a really good photo. Then I made a point of not following them, talking endlessly and with endless hand gestures as the Volvo did a U-turn and drove past me. In other words, I couldn't have been less interested. Just in case they'd clocked me and were waiting to see what I did next, I nipped diagonally across the road to the filling-station cum shop and bought a paper I didn't want and some milk I needed. There. Lina just being an ordinary girl.

Maybe.

Call me paranoid, but I wasn't about to lead them back to Aidan's, or anywhere else. Assuming they wanted to follow me at all. Assuming there was anything significant about the little white fragment I'd seen on the ground.

Just to waste more time, I bought a pretty vile sarnie too and retired to the van to eat it. And then, and only then, did I drift back to the village hall car park, looking hard on the ground as if I'd dropped something myself (I'd tucked a key in my hand ready to use as a prop just in case anyone noticed me and asked what I was doing). It was clear where she'd fallen – quite a skid. She must have hurt her own leg too. But not as much, I hoped, as she'd hurt the little white one. Because leg it was. In her haste to scarper, she'd left behind perhaps two centimetres of china hoof. I picked it up with the sandwich wrapper, which I bunched into my pocket. A little present for Carwyn Morgan. If he had a tame forensic photographer, perhaps he had a tame forensic ceramics expert too.

But though I went to the trouble of driving into Maidstone, I did no more than drop it off at the reception desk, with a short message telling him how I'd acquired it. I didn't expect him to be working on a Sunday, after all, and even if he was, there didn't seem to be any point in having a conversation, not the way Friday's had ended. In any case, I had a load of china to stow and a van to park before I set off to Tenterden. Should I take Tim and stay the night, which would mean Griff didn't have to worry about my driving through increasingly nasty weather? Or should I make the weather an excuse to leave early?

Since Griff was well enough to play chess with Aidan, I was glad I'd settled for the second option. The drive home was really tricky, but he didn't need to know that, and when I phoned to say I'd got in safely, he crowed that he'd just beaten Aidan.

So I did the routine security check with a light heart. Until the screen told me that someone had been sniffing round. A predictable hoodie, with the face ninety per cent hidden. Perhaps it was just a would-be opportunist thief, deterred by the obviously hi-tech system. Of course, there was a lot more that was even higher tech not on show. I saved the footage and double checked the shop and the cottage. All was well.

The following day, the usual deluge of emails matched the still torrential rain. Two struck me immediately. One was from Tristam, asking if I fancied lunch today. He didn't get it, did he, that I didn't do lunch? But before I could point this out, I had one from his boss, Brian, telling me he'd had another batch of pictures in and he'd welcome my opinion over lunch. Problem. Griff always insisted on good manners, and if I turned down Tristam's offer, how could I accept Brian's? Or vice versa? Tim suggested the best thing was to say no to both; I could offer to see Brian towards the end of the working day, when I'd finished the next stage of the Limoges plate, with a quick drink with Tristam afterwards.

'We did well with the fine arts sale,' Brian greeted me, 'and especially well with the lot including the miniature you fancied. Of course, as Tris points out, if it had been a real Isaac Oliver, it wouldn't have been offered here but in a higher end auction house. Anyway, the lot brought in nearly twelve hundred, so the vendor was pleased.'

'Have you any more lovely miniatures?' I asked.

His phone rang. Checking it, he pointed apologetically at the stack of pictures in the far corner. There was no sign of Tristam, so I was free to browse.

As before there was a strange mixture. There was something claiming to be a Turner, and a David Cox or two. Even I knew that the market was awash with David Coxes you wouldn't want to touch, not just by his son or the school of, but just plain fakes. As for the lowering cloudscape that claimed, by way of a signature, to be a Constable . . . Heavens, would anyone fall for that? But as I worked my way through, I came across another batch of miniatures. Some were even worse than those on Adrian's spare room wall. But as before there was one cracker. This time it was of a lovely young woman, in the sort of costume you associate with overblown Lely ladies, with the most beautifully depicted eyes and no hint of the Lely pout.

'Tell me about them,' Helen Baker said, appearing from nowhere. 'Brian's always on about this gift of yours. Tris too: he'd like to lay his hands on it even more than he'd like to lay his hands on you.' She pulled out the Coxes. 'Loadsa money in Tris's family. Oh, he says they're hard up but it's the sort of hard up that means they can't have a new Audi till next year – not that they'll need one then, because they last forever. And they can't go skiing twice this year – just the once. He'd be a good catch, Lina. Assuming you wanted to catch anything, of course. Even Tris's so-called flu. Back this morning with not so much as a pink nose or an apology. The young, God bless them. Now why don't I class you as young?' she asked. Her smile suggested it was a compliment; I wasn't so sure. 'Now, these 'ere Coxes.'

'In a minute,' I said. If I was called on to do party tricks I'd do them in my own time. 'This miniature.'

She checked in her apron pocket for a notepad. 'School of Gibson, according to Tris.'

Had I got as far as Gibson in that book? I must have done, but I couldn't remember anything about him. 'Only school of?' I queried, hoping I sounded as if I knew what I was talking about. 'Some pupil!'

'My sentiments exactly. The others?'

Crap. I couldn't use that word, of course, so I groped for the sort of word that Griff sometimes used. 'Dross. Unless they have some extrinsic value. Are they all from the same collection? Because if so I can't understand why anyone who liked her should like the others. Can you?'

She shrugged. '*De gustibus . . .*'

Thank God for Griff and his insistence that I must never look blank, even if I didn't have a clue what people were talking about. And then the thought of Griff reminded me I did know the phrase, but in a longer version: *de gustibus non disputandum est*. There's no disputing matters of taste. True. But that was such a difference of taste. Somewhere, deep in the bit of my head I can't explain, a little bell started to ring.

'The Coxes?' she prompted.

131

I shook my head. 'Ask me about china and I'll tell you things worth hearing. Possibly, though I don't know as much about them as Tris, even about little white horses,' I added with a grin.

She tapped the Cox. 'Like those in this picture?' She wasn't about to let this go, was she?

There were some genuine, absolutely authenticated Coxes in the library of Bossingham Hall. Lovely things. Everything seemed to be in the right place, in the correct proportion – the sort of effect the best landscape architects like Capability Brown were after. Everything about the picture she flourished was right. But not quite. The horses were great little nags. A shepherd the other side of the meadow looked good. But . . .

'I can tell by your face, you know,' she said. 'OK, one for the dodgy pile.'

'But you can't go on my instincts,' I protested. 'Not on something I've not a clue about.'

'Of course not. It's nice to have a second opinion, though, even if it is highly unorthodox. Tris has got plenty to research – and he'll have to dig deep, I can tell you. We don't want to get into trouble. Did you see that case in the paper, some Russian who'd paid millions for a painting and then sued the auction house because he'd got evidence that suggested it was a fake? We don't want to go there, believe me.' She looked across to Brian, who was making frantic gestures and pointing at the phone.

After a last look at the School of Gibson miniature, I followed her. Brian handed over the phone and again beckoned me into his new office. I ran a finger across his desk: the dust was already

132

settling nicely. There was a patina growing on his sparkly new keyboard, too.

'White Beswick horses,' he said.

'Fingerprints,' I responded. 'At least one.' I explained.

'But the print isn't on the police files?'

'Not yet. But it's the most definite ID we've got. And it's nice to know that we're not on our own.'

He snorted. 'Come off it, Lina – with the police decimated, and I mean that literally, not in the general woolly sense of being reduced by a lot, can you imagine them devoting much time and effort to chasing up bits of minor crime? Actually, I'm wrong. They say there are twenty per cent cuts, don't they? Hell, though antiques are my living, I'd rate small-scale fraud lower on a scale of importance than bashing old ladies.'

I had to agree. 'On the other hand, sometimes little crimes lead to big crimes. And big crimes tend to involve organized criminals sooner or later. Think international people-smuggling, child prostitution and drugs.'

'So in the interests of world peace, PC Plod should look at little gee gees. Come off it, Lina. Anyway, it's certainly appropriate that we should keep an eye open. After all, if they can't sell fakes, there's not much point in producing them.'

I couldn't argue with that.

'It's proving tough getting people together to discuss the issue; maybe we'll resort to video-conferencing. You're still up for it? You must be working your socks off, with Griff *hors de combat.*'

Whatever that was. I got the general sense and agreed. 'That's why I can't take proper lunch breaks,' I said, trying not to sound too apologetic. 'The end of the day's better, because my hand's getting tired by then.'

'Helen says the rest of you's looking pretty tired, too.' He laughed, and I had a shrewd idea what was coming next. 'I just think you're looking pretty, of course.'

'Thank you kindly, both of you.'

'Come and have a bite of supper with us one night. We'll even invite young Tris, if you want.'

'Helen's already tried a spot of matchmaking,' I said, 'thanks very much. Actually, I've agreed to take him for a drink tonight.'

'Interestingly put.'

'Nothing but the truth. You'll have to start paying him if you want him to take me out on a date!'

# Twelve

Whoever paid, I didn't see many future dates with Tris. We just didn't have enough in common, which sounds amazing when you consider our work. I tried to get him talking about all the research that goes into authenticating a picture – or damning it to the 'School of' category, of course. He just wanted me to pull identification rabbits out of a hat he didn't even have with him. Was this how professional comedians felt, honour-bound to make people laugh all the time?

At least I had a good excuse not to snog him: I didn't dare catch his flu, I said, when he tried it on, because of passing bugs on to Griff. Since he knew I was mates with Helen and Brian, he could hardly admit he'd just pulled a sickie because he wanted a nice long weekend. He did offer to drive me home but since he'd drunk enough for me to worry he might be over the limit I insisted on walking.

Last time I'd done that, of course, I'd had to take refuge in the takeaway and then had the nasty shock of seeing our cottage lit up like Blackpool illuminations; this time, my walk was quiet and uneventful, and our security nicely undisturbed. The phone rang just as I shut the front door, but years of Griff's training made me fasten every last lock before answering it. 'If they want us enough,' he always said, 'they'll hang on or ring

135

back. And if we want them enough, we can always dial 1471 and call them, can't we?'

Of course, there were some people who withheld their numbers, weren't there? And it was one of those who'd called tonight. But then a text came from a real human being – Carwyn Morgan. The horse leg was interesting, he said – and he suggested I pop round to Maidstone police station next time I had a moment to spare to talk about it.

People who work for other people just don't get it, do they? If you're self-employed, you don't just have moments to spare. In any case, assuming I did, what would be the chances of finding him in his office? Detectives aren't tied to their desks, are they? He might be out and about protecting the old ladies Brian was worried about.

On the other hand, I was interested in that horse, so I texted back suggesting he give me a specific time when he could guarantee to be around – or that he could pop into the shop if he were in the Bredeham area during the working week. That way he'd know I was tied up, and if he did take up the suggestion, it'd give Mary a frisson of pleasure, though it would take her three days to stop talking about it.

And so to bed. But before I headed upstairs, I gave the CCTV cameras one last check – it was nice, when I only had Tim for company, to know that anyone who approached the shop or cottage was still being photographed. Everything was fine. But on impulse, I checked what they'd recorded while I'd been out. I didn't like what I saw. When someone parks a car out of range

– and there's plenty of parking in front of the cottage, much to Griff's irritation – and sidles up to the shop and then the cottage as if to avoid being seen, I get alarmed. All the man who approached did was look. Maybe he was appraising the alarm system, which wasn't the most reassuring thought. But if he cracked that one, tough enough in itself, there was always the hidden one. I didn't worry about writing down a description: I just copied the footage, enhanced it as much as I could and sent it off to Carwyn. Let him and his magic gizmos work out who it was.

That was what I said, anyway. Aloud. Just to make myself believe it. But I was scared enough to grab Tim. Should I call the security firm and ask for one of their nice solid guards to come and babysit the place? Given the hourly rate for a heavy, no higher than it ought to be for a man lurking in a cold van all night, this was not the obvious option. A character in one of the books Griff had read to me had said something about even an unsuitable man having a certain abstract value, and tonight – only for a nanosecond – I hankered after Morris. Not Tristam, with or without the flu. At this point I did the obvious thing: I retired to bed with Tim in one hand and the panic alarm in the other.

The guy who presented himself in the shop on Tuesday morning looked highly official, with the security company's logo on the pocket of his bomber jacket. He even had his company ID to hand, flashing it at Mary Walker, who'd summoned me to deal with him.

'Good morning, Miss Townsend,' he said, with

a polite smile. 'We've detected some attacks on your system: would you mind if I checked it?'

My smile was equally polite. 'Just hang on a minute. I've got a new dog and I'm not sure how he is with strangers.'

He cocked a hand to his ear. 'Very quiet, isn't he?'

'I wouldn't be so worried if he was barking,' I said, with a smile at Mary. 'Give me a couple of minutes and come round to the front door. Mrs Walker's getting ready for a visit from our accountant and we don't want to waste her time. No sign of Mr Banner yet?' I asked her casually, not expecting her to say yes because Tuesdays were Paul's golf days.

'Not yet.' She checked her watch against the grandfather clock in the corner. 'I'll give him a call and see what's keeping him. Meanwhile,' she added with her kindest smile, 'why don't you go and sort out Saul? You may have to shut him in the office. Would you like one of my rock cakes, Mr – er—?'

'Clements. Home-made, are they?'

'Is there any other sort?' she asked. 'I use my mother's recipe, which involves plain flour and . . .'

Leaving her in blessedly full-flow, I sneaked out.

Don't think I didn't feel bad leaving Mary on her own with him: I did. But so long as our friend thought there was a man in the offing, I thought she'd be OK. The moment I was in, I speed-dialled our security contact, Geoff. 'There's a guy claiming to have come from you in the shop,' I said. 'Wants access to our security system. Wearing a uniform, carrying ID.'

138

'Is he now . . . Yes, I can see him on our system. He's putting something in his mouth and approaching the door now as if to leave. No, he's still talking to your shop lady.' Taking a breath, Geoff added, with a mixture of pride and reproach, 'You know we wouldn't send anyone out without contacting you first.'

'Of course I do. Which is why he's still in the shop waiting for me to chain up the Rottweiler. Which, unfortunately, I don't have.'

'You do, actually,' Geoff chuckled. 'Mr Tripp being on the elderly side I added a little extra last time we serviced the system. Didn't he tell you? Ah, well. Bottom left of the master panel – press Start now.'

What the hell? What hadn't he told me? But I pressed anyway, to be rewarded by what sounded like that dog in the Sherlock Holmes story. Baying, that was what it was doing.

'Bloody hell! How on earth do I stop it?'

Presumably his end Geoff was holding the handset miles from his ear. 'Excellent,' he yelled. 'Ed's on patrol your way – he'll be with you in four. Less. Ask him for the second, fourth and seventh letters in his password and text them to me before you let him in.'

'But I know Ed.'

'All the same. Cheers!'

'No! Don't ring off. How do I turn off the bloody noise?'

'Shout at it. Just like it was a real dog. There. All nice and quiet again, eh? If you'd pressed the button twice, it'd start again, just like a real dog. And then it'd shut up and whine a bit. When it's safe, you can press the Clear button. Hang on – ah, Chummie's leaving the shop via the front door. Press that doggie noise now. Twice, remember. Don't open the front door yet. If you feel you must, keep it – like Fido – on the chain! And Lina, my eyes won't leave this screen till I see you're safe.'

Fido – Saul! – still barking his digital head off, I called Mary on the shop phone. 'You're OK? Thank God. Now, lock the door and don't let anyone in – anyone, any age, either sex. Except Paul,' I added with a giggle. 'With his golf clubs, of course.'

It was hard not to respond to the doorbell, which was now ringing loudly. A bit more baying dog. It even came with the sound of large feet scrabbling on a wooden floor. I was so impressed I actually yelled at it to shut up.

And it did!

Then it started again, and this time I let it continue. Checking the chain was still in place, I opened the front door a crack. 'You'll have to wait till Griff gets in,' I said. 'He's the only one who can really calm him down. Give me your card and I'll call you the minute I can.'

The fake dog let out a terrific burst. Holding a card by the very end of his fingertips, the guy passed it quickly through the crack and left.

Talk about exit pursued by a bear.

Ed, like our previous visitor a man in his fifties, looked more like an old-style GP than a security geek, which was as good a disguise as any, I suppose. There was no sign of a company logo on his well-cut but not snappy suit. He didn't

140

flash an ID uninvited. And there was no problem with his password letters.

As much to calm myself down as anything, I made tea, and summoned Mary from the shop, with a request to bring those cakes with her.

'What was all that about?' she asked, sharply for her, setting the tin down on the kitchen table.

'Someone's tried to get unauthorized access to the property – both properties, in fact, Mrs Walker,' Ed explained, cutting across me. He pressed a tiny receiver further into his ear, smiling as he absorbed what someone, Geoff, presumably, was saying. Then he added, 'We think he was specifically aiming to tamper with the security system.'

'You mean leave us without a burglar alarm? And all those clever photos?'

She sat down hard. 'And was that woman who tried to get into the shop – no, I kept her out, don't worry . . . But, of course, you'd know that, wouldn't you, from your cameras.'

I didn't, of course. 'It wasn't the same woman as before? With Puck?'

'Mrs Fielding? No, I don't think so.'

'Could it have been her with a wig? I think I might have clocked her the other day at a fair.' I explained to her and Ed, now halfway outside one of the rock cakes. I helped myself to one. 'I'm still waiting for the police to get back to me about the bit of leg she left behind when she fell down. China horse's leg,' I added hurriedly.

'One way to find out,' Ed said. 'We check the photos. Geoff's got some really nice kit that compares faces. Excuse me just a second.'

While he stepped into the living room to make

his call, I turned to Mary. 'I was really sorry to leave you in harm's way like that.'

'I'll give Paul what for, insisting on playing golf on Tuesdays!' she said, with a slightly watery smile.

'No! He's entitled to enjoy himself. He's not even on the payroll! You are – and that means you're entitled to feel safe where you work.' Sighing, I put my head in my hands. 'If things go on like this, I'm tempted to say we close the shop and concentrate on our Internet trade.'

She pulled herself straight. 'As Griff would say, I Do Not Give In. Where would we be if we did? No, I shall carry on just as normal.'

Normal? There was no point in telling her to vary her route to the post office when she dispatched our mail order parcels – in a village this size there was only one route.

'It's true I shall be looking over my shoulder more till this business is sorted out. And perhaps Ed would install another panic button so we have one at either end of the counter.'

Ed, returning, caught her second sentence. 'I can run a sensitive strip the whole length. Geoff's got a bit of an emergency over in Essex, so he can't do the face comparison yet. I'll just get my stuff from the car.'

Catching his arm, she said, 'You're always reading in the papers about people being deliberately run down.' She listed several examples, one of which had actually made the national TV news. 'I wouldn't want you to be the victim of a hit and run attack. Do be careful.'

He gave a slow smile. 'That's what I'm paid to be.'

# Thirteen

Although Ed was far too professional to say so, I suspected that Geoff and his staff wouldn't rest till they'd nailed the man claiming to be their colleague. That was their business, not mine. But I did suggest quietly to Ed, as Mary set off across the yard to open the shop, that he talk very firmly to Mary about her and Paul's personal safety.

'When I can get a word in,' he said with a rueful smile as he opened the front door. 'It's the adrenalin – some people can't stop talking after a scare.'

I didn't disagree. No need to point out she could always talk for England. The phone rang. I reached for it.

He put out a warning hand. 'Let it ring. Could be a diversionary tactic. Lock me out, then answer it.'

He was taking things horribly seriously, wasn't he? *Diversionary tactic* sounded a bit too military to me. But he'd probably say it was his job to be serious. 'OK.' I withdrew my hand. Then I got serious too. 'And I need to talk to you about Griff's safety before you go. He's staying with a friend.'

'Best place he can be.'

When I got round to checking, I found our caller had withheld his or her number. Had we won yet another holiday to Florida? Or not. Before I could turn off my cynical smile, it rang again.

'Carwyn Morgan here, Ms Townend. I have to be over your way round about midday. Would you be in? Or, of course, we could meet over lunch somewhere?'

Oh, yes please! But then I remembered what Griff – and even Pa – would call My Duty. 'We've had a bit of a security scare, Carwyn, so you'll understand I don't want to leave my shop manager alone on the premises.' Mouth turning down, I mentally reviewed the fridge contents, and then had a brainwave – before Ed left I could nip to the deli. 'Why don't you eat here? So long as you don't mind salad and something?'

But even as he agreed, I remembered that whatever else we had to talk about, apart from the china horse, he'd almost certainly want to pick my brains about Titus. It would be a very careful lunch indeed.

'Tell me about this security scare,' Carwyn said, by way of a greeting. 'Mmm, something smells good.'

'The deli's speciality flan. Usually Griff cooks.'

'That's your business partner – and honorary grandfather. Right?'

'Right. He's still in Tenterden with his other sort of partner. Aidan and I don't always see eye to eye, so I'm trying to keep out of their way.' Here I was, gabbing on again, just as if I was Mary Walker.

'How is he?'

'Making excellent progress. But I wouldn't want him exposed – to any possible danger?' I prompted him. And then I slapped my head in fury. 'Hey, the guy who claimed he was from the security people gave me his card. It's over here somewhere. I promised to call him back when I'd tied up the dog.'

'Dog? What dog? I didn't hear one last time I was here.'

'You wouldn't. I didn't even know I had one myself until I called the security firm. It's a nice fierce one, but beautifully house-trained. Very convincing.'

'What about a real one?'

I spread my hands in despair. 'When would I walk it? Look after it generally?'

He smiled. It was nice to see the man behind the cop again. 'My gran got one after she was diagnosed as starting diabetes. She read that exercise might postpone the diabetes, so she started walking. Lost two stone. Even plays tennis again. And no diabetes – yet. So it might help Griff's heart. Have it as his dog, not yours. After all, you've got enough trouble with white horses,' he added with a smile.

'Would you mind if Mrs Walker was here while you updated me? She's been involved from the start. And then her husband joined in,' I explained. 'Plus I don't see why she shouldn't have a share of that flan.' Did I detect a tiny frown? Annoyance at being asked to share sensitive information? Hell, it couldn't have been disappointment, could it?

*No, Lina, you do not do policemen. Remember?*

Of course I remembered – and hadn't I thought he might be gay when I first met him?

'So I think you're right about someone repainting and refiring these horses,' Carwyn declared, rejecting a further helping of salad. 'That's what our forensics people with their clever gizmos have been able to prove – it's no longer just a matter of your keen eye and professional expertise, Lina. And thanks to your fiancé's nosiness, Mary, we're two steps closer to finding out who's doing it. They certainly put your fiancé to a lot of trouble to get back what we think is the prototype forgery.'

'What would they have done if he hadn't returned it?' Mary asked, her voice muted.

I squeezed her hand. She might never Give In, any more than I would, but if someone threatened Griff directly, I'd hand over anything, even the contents of our hidden safe. And she loved Paul enough to be marrying him in a very few weeks' time.

'He did return it. It's all over. No worries.' But she clearly didn't believe him, so he continued, 'All the same, I'd be grateful if you told him simply to report any other white horses to us, not to try to buy them. These people aren't fools, Mary: they were able to track him down once. They may be inclined to believe he really did have a niece at uni who is now minus a nice gift. But if he made a habit of scouting for white gee gees, you can bet your life the word would get round, and there's nothing to stop them getting on to him again. Tell him to leave it to us. Please.

146

And that applies to you too, Lina. You can repair china wonderfully – but you might not be so hot on repairing your own bones.'

I couldn't hold back a shudder. A criminal had threatened my hands once before. I held them out in front of me, meeting his eye with a silent question. He gave a tiny nod.

'There's talk,' I said, 'of a mini conference of auctioneers in this area. They want me to be involved. Would you be, too?'

He pulled a face. But then he seemed to make a decision. 'It's not exactly the Met's Fine Arts people's bag, is it? So I'll make it mine, so long as my boss gives me permission.'

'Tell your boss it looks as if they're moving up a notch. *Sang de boeuf* Ruskin.' I told him about the identical high-fired ginger jars I'd seen in Folkestone. 'They're after hundreds with the horses, but thousands if they nail Ruskin ware.'

'I'm not familiar with it,' he admitted.

'Let's have our coffee in the living room,' I said, suddenly thrust into hostess mode. It was always Griff who managed such things, but now it was up to me. 'Then I can show you what they're copying. It's the most beautiful stuff.'

In response to a buzz on the shop doorbell, Mary left us to it, rubbing her hands at the prospect of a sale.

'The strange thing is,' I told Carwyn, 'that Mary prefers to sell ugly dross. I think she sees it as a bigger challenge than selling beautiful things.'

'Which she'd rather keep for herself. I don't have a problem with that. Neither do you or your grandfather,' he added, gesturing at the rest of the room. His eyes lit up, and he headed towards the display cabinet. 'Is that the Ruskin ware you were talking about?'

Unlocking the cabinet, I placed the vase gently into those lovely hands of his. He inspected it with something like reverence and returned it to me to put back in its place. He smiled as I adjusted the spotlight slightly to bring out its deep rich purples and reds.

'Actually, that Ruskin's one of the very few perfect artefacts in the room. Most of the others are lovely one side, but too damaged elsewhere to think of selling. Which is how I got into restoration. But tell me, how did you get into policing—?'

'Long story.' He was just settling back into his chair when his phone rang. I gestured – he could take it here while I busied myself in the kitchen. As it happened, our office phone rang too. Pa! Of all the people I'd rather not have in my life in the next ten minutes.

'Crisis, Lina. Major crisis.'

My God, they'd arrested him! Or Titus!

'Dropped my last two bottles of shampoo. Oh, not the good stuff in the cellar. Can't touch that on my own. Your inheritance, Lina, that's what that is. No, the ordinary muck.'

The stuff that usually came in at twenty-five pounds a bottle, even with discount for quantity.

'Any chance you could get me some, old girl? Oh, and one or two other odds and sods. Got a pencil handy?'

When he'd dictated an A4 sheet-long list, he paused. 'How's that old bugger of yours?'

'Griff's doing fine, thanks, Pa. Still at Aidan's, over in Tenterden.'

'About time he was home. Or do you sleep over there?' His voice sounded both suspicious and jealous.

'Occasionally. But you know how Aidan and I are together.'

'Two dogs, same bone. All the same, time Griff was heading to his own home – you need someone to keep an eye on you.'

'Me? Who's broken two bottles of bubbly? Anyway, all I can say is I'll do a supermarket run when I can. Perhaps a late-night shop tonight. Then I could drop the stuff in first thing tomorrow. I can't talk any more. I've got the police here.'

He cut the call immediately.

Carwyn wandered in clutching his phone. 'My boss,' he said.

I pointed to ours. 'My dad.' As Carwyn's face clouded, I added, 'He's just broken his last bottle of champagne, which is pretty serious. Alcoholic,' I added, bending my arms and wrist vigorously. 'Starts the day with a nice healthy Buck's Fizz – to get his vitamin C, you understand. And then he thinks he might just as well empty the bottle. And the next.' This time I demonstrated the shakes – an arrant lie, because I'd never seen Pa's hand less steady than mine. Well, with his line of work . . . 'Mind you, he gets a lot of time to watch TV. When Griff was having surgery he was a mine of really useful information, having seen every medical programme going.'

He opened his mouth to say something and then shut it, with something of a snap. 'I've got to move on to another investigation, I'm afraid. Ten minutes ago.'

Damn it if my face didn't fall.

He added quickly, 'But I'm still running this one. So copy me in on any invitation you get to this conference on horses, will you?'

'Of course I will. As I was saying to Brian Baker, it'd be good to have official involvement. You might want his number.' I held up the phone so he could copy it. There, that was better. Altogether more professional. I added, with a touch of malice, 'Mind you, he thought Kent Police'd be too busy protecting old ladies from armed robbers to worry about minor fraud.'

He put his head on one side, eyes slightly narrowed. 'And what did you say?'

'That little crimes led to bigger ones. And I spouted a lot of crap about money-laundering, drug-running and people-trafficking. Proper little head girl, I was.'

He nodded appraisingly and laughed. Then his face was serious again. 'Are you over that assault yet? Nasty, from what I gather.'

'Heavens, I've got to be. I shan't enjoy going to court and reliving it all, but at least both Griff and I are alive to tell the tale. Unlike your under-cover colleague,' I added soberly. After a moment I continued, 'Would you mind leaving via the shop, by the way? And reminding Mary to keep Paul's sleuthing under control?' Which was the best way I could think of to tell him to push off and let me get on with my life.

At least until the white horse conference.

150

# Fourteen

I'd just picked up my paintbrush when Aidan phoned. He'd forgotten he had an engagement at a charitable function he really ought not to miss, and wondered if it wouldn't inconvenience me too much if he asked me to cook Griff's supper and stay overnight.

'No problem,' I said. 'What time do you have to leave?'

But if Pa needed rations, my being in Tenterden by six forty-five did cause problems. Big ones. Putting down the brush still unused, I toddled down to the shop. Mary was busy rearranging the main shelf. A quick glance told me she'd managed to offload five hundred pounds' worth of early nineteenth century Derby plates.

'We're running out of stock! It's no good, you'll have to go to a sale or two soon,' she greeted me.

'I know.' I was ready to tear my hair. 'But I've made no progress on my pile of restoration and there's more coming in. Griff needs babysitting tonight, and on top of that Pa's run out of supplies. Where do I start, Mary?'

'With your brain, Lina. Order the supermarket stuff online: have them deliver it.'

'I tried that once. Pa's lane broke a spring on their van. He's blacklisted.'

'Well, have them deliver it here, and then you can take it tomorrow. Or Paul and I can drop it off – we're at my place this week.' She paused. 'But he only runs out of supplies when he wants to see you, doesn't he? And when he wants you to sell more of his goodies?'

I nodded. 'So it'll have to be me. But the Internet order's a brilliant idea. I'll go and do it now.' But not until I did what I should have done two or three times this week. 'Before I dash off, tell me how the plans are going. Have you sorted your fascinator yet? That nice shop in Hythe?'

The arrival of Paul cut her mercifully short, but I stayed long enough to ensure she passed on Carwyn's message about safety. And Geoff's, for good measure. Then I left them to it; they had parcels to wrap and get to the post.

*They* . . . What about putting Paul, who was working his socks off for free, on the payroll too? He wouldn't want me to, but offering was the best way I could think of to say thank you. I'd discuss it with Griff tonight.

It then occurred to me I could do even better than have to wait in for a delivery the following day. I could collect everything from Tenterden Waitrose and even add a few fun things for my feast with Griff tonight.

'Thai salmon! My darling, you don't know how I've longed for this. And how foresighted of you to bring all the spices. Fresh coriander too. When I was afraid of dying – though we both pretended to each other that there was no chance of that, didn't we – I told myself if I reached heaven I'd know because of the scent of coriander that St Peter would organize specially for me. And here

152

it is – safe on earth.' He threw his arms round me and gave me the best hug we'd had since his operation. With not even a wince.

And then another miracle: he grabbed Aidan's pristine pinny and started pottering around, clearly ready to cook. I didn't argue.

We talked about how far he'd walked each day – and how very, very much he'd relished the little car trip with Paul and Mary. Why he hadn't been for a spin in Aidan's Merc I didn't feel I should ask, any more than he ever asked me about any relationship problems I might be having. That was part of our unspoken deal. I wouldn't even ask about the night nurse, though I was intrigued that she was never, ever mentioned.

Then talk drifted to the wedding.

'There's absolutely no doubt at all I shall be well enough to fulfil my promise,' he declared, eyeing with interest the champagne I'd also bought. 'But of course, dear one, there is the problem of the shop in Mary's absence. Their honeymoon, dear one. For all they're not in the first flush of youth, not to mention the fact that they've lived together for months, they're entitled to some private time together. I tried to make it one of our gifts to them, but dear Paul said that a man was entitled to pay for such an intimate gift to his new bride. Such a romantic.'

'And too romantic to divulge the location, of course. But did he say how long they'd be away? You've no idea how wonderfully they've looked after me. So maybe they wouldn't tell me if they were going to take two or three weeks off, in case I panicked.'

'Panic not. I shall be back on the scene by then, and though we may have to reduce our opening hours—'

'But—'

'My dear one, don't look so horrified! I had this operation to make me better. The scar may tug from time to time, but I walked right to the high street and back without stopping today. Three times. And I was venturing to dead-head some of Aidan's flowers, but then his gardener arrived. Now, they gave me a leaflet about returning to work – it's in my bedroom somewhere. I'll get it while you test the rice.' He paused in the doorway. 'Even doing a proper job I'd be back at work after six weeks. And you can't say that selling *objects d'art* is as taxing as teaching, say.'

'Not if your pupils are like I was,' I admitted. Fancy him doing all that walking! And going to fetch the leaflet himself. I did a little pirouette of joy. Then I remembered he'd still not told me how long Paul and Mary would be away. How on earth would I cope without them? With that huge backlog of repairs and precious little in stock? At least over supper we could talk about finding some means of paying Paul for all his work.

'There,' he said, thrusting a leaflet into my hand. 'Read that and be reassured.'

Funnily enough I was. Enough to open that champagne.

Since a chunk of my day would be occupied ferrying Pa's provisions across to Bossingham

Hall, I left Tenterden before six. Not to go to Bossingham – Pa didn't do early hours. But I could make a start on some repairs: normally, I preferred to give each item my undivided attention, but it was clear that if I was to make any progress I'd have to organize batches of things with similar problems – a sort of triage system, which might just work if I was meticulous in recording which item belonged to which owner. But we were out of labels, both adhesive and tie on: dead serious, because we'd need both for the next fair. Before I could hit myself with frustration, I told myself that I didn't even want to work that way, and all I had to do was add them to our office supplies Wanted list, which Mary would deal with. Soon my hands were steady enough to make huge progress on a vase for Harvey Sanditon. There'd be no need to worry about taking that to the post – he used a courier I knew well enough to have seen pictures of his grandchildren. I was so absorbed that I worked on without a break, till it dawned on me that I'd not yet heard Mary's cheerful voice asking if I'd had breakfast. Nearly ten, and no Mary? And no Paul, of course.

And no response from any of their phones, landline or mobile. I swear I had the phone in my hand to dial nine-nine-nine and report a double kidnap – or worse. It was only when I hurtled into the kitchen, out of my mind with worry, that I saw the diary propped up against the kettle. She'd put it there to remind me of something, hadn't she? Now what the hell was I to recall?

There it was. P and M: meeting vicar.

So they were. I'd better get my own breakfast and deal with all the email enquiries in the shop using my laptop. In whichever order – and someone was already ringing the shop bell.

'Looking pale and wan, my girl,' Pa declared. 'Told Titus I was worried about you. It's the old bugger who's supposed to be ill, not you.'

'Tell you what, Pa, why don't you dig out some tea bags and make us a nice mug of green tea. No shampoo for me, thanks – not on an empty stomach.' Very empty. Nothing since a mid-morning brunch of scrambled egg on toast. And now it must be – heavens – well after seven. 'I'll have a mooch round for some things to sell, shall I?'

He produced a strange grin – enigmatic, I think you'd call it – and waved an airy hand. Off I went to prospect for suitable goodies. The trouble was, although I'd occasionally tried to make order out of Pa's total chaos, as often as not I'd find he'd undone all my good work while he was hunting for something he thought would bring in a load of cash but which I knew was so out of fashion that it was worth peanuts.

Now why should this pile of plates, Worcester mixed in with Woolworth's, be in this room? And why was there a load of furniture huddled in the old housekeeper's room as if afraid to venture beyond the door? He knew I couldn't help with furniture. Maybe Titus had started a new sideline – though surely not with such unfashionable curli-cued Victorian stuff as this?

156

I assembled a stash of some decent Art Deco china, and then plunged off down the hall – servants' territory, remember, with dark green painted dados and not a dazzling chandelier in sight – to see if there was anything else I could pick up without disturbing a pick-a-stix tower of books and papers. Oh dear – some worrying Elizabethan map books there: horrible evidence of Titus' activities. Then my nostrils picked up a strange smell – familiar enough, but strange in this context. Paint. Emulsion paint. Gloss paint.

The next room should hold items from about eight different dinner services, which had been scattered piecemeal all over the wing, including the stables and other outhouses, some of which weren't strictly Pa's territory, of course. Another reason not to get involved with another police officer. Some tureens and soup bowls had managed to survive from a late eighteenth century Sevres set: I was after those to complete this evening's haul. Instead I found an almost empty room. Someone had cleaned and even polished the original floor boards and installed a single bedstead (so far without mattress and bedclothes), a chair, and a Victorian dressing table. There was a rag rug on the floor and under the bed . . . a chamber pot. My first thought was that some media company must be wanting to film a period drama here. The second, equally disbelieving, was that Pa had organized a bedroom for me. A real one, not one of the giant historical rooms in the part of the house that the trust owned.

Pa appeared in the doorway, clutching not tea, of course, but what smelt like really expensive champagne in two of his priceless flutes. 'Thought you ought to have a bolt-hole whenever old Tripp goes gallivanting,' he said gruffly, opening his arms awkwardly as I hugged him. 'Titus is organizing a mattress. Hey, hang on, old thing.'

'Nothing to beat a bit of salmon,' Pa said, pushing back from the table. This was from a man whom I'd rescued from an exclusive diet of Pot Noodles and champagne. He still sank more bottles in a month than the average man in a lifetime, but at least now, despite what I'd told Carwyn, he augmented the alcohol with occasional mugs of green tea and his supermarket list had included fresh fruit. I'd discovered I could persuade him to eat some fish if I disguised it: tonight's was cooked in Bart's Cajun spices and came with broccoli and carrots. He'd consume vitamins and minerals if it killed him. Or me.

I promised to buy some bedding and curtains for my new room out of the proceeds of my latest hunting expedition and left him happily preparing for an evening in front of his huge flat screen TV. Mysteriously, he'd acquired satellite channels, quite an achievement since dishes were absolutely forbidden on a grade one listed building.

'Don't forget to lock up and set the alarms,' I said as I hugged him goodbye. 'I'd hate anyone to come and crack your skull for you.'

'Know what? They wouldn't find much in the way of brains. They've all come down to you, Evelina.'

# Fifteen

Brains? It was more hands and feet that I needed.

Much as I'd have liked to spend the rest of the week in my workroom, our need for stock sent me scuttling off to Brian's Thursday morning auction. I'd missed the public viewing and there was no time for a proper look round, so I'd have to trust to my judgement when it came to bidding. Hardly to my surprise, they got Tris to stand up and show off each item as it came under the hammer – glamour sells, doesn't it? And Joe Public – or in this case Jo Public – wouldn't know that he was actually as dull as ditchwater. Perhaps they didn't need to – no one asked the IQ of pretty women draped over posh cars at motor shows, did they?

For some reason the sale was poorly attended, with very few dealers I knew. This suited me: more and more these days, if people saw me bidding they assumed I must know the lot was worth having, so the price shot up. So we did a lot more commission bidding, leaving offers in advance with the auctioneer. But you needed to see things before-hand to do that. Time. If only I had some!

But at least now I had some more stock, most of it remarkably cheap, and nothing relying on my divvy's instincts. Helen drifted over as I was settling up and with a flick of an eyebrow invited me into her office. Without asking, she pressed buttons on the coffee machine, and then dug in a cupboard for biscuits.

'Notice anything about today's catalogue?' she asked.

'A couple of items withdrawn,' I said.

'Quite. White horses, both of them. Thanks to a phone call late yesterday afternoon from Kent police in the form of a young man with a quite delightful voice. Ah, I see you know him.'

'Carwyn Morgan. It's his hands I like,' I admitted. 'Not that they've been closer to me than handling the odd vase. But I'm glad he's officially on to the white horse business, because I think the owners might have been getting cross with me.' I told her about our security men, fake and genuine.

She nodded. 'Like those guys who phone and say there's a problem with your perfectly healthy computer only to make sure there is when you follow their advice. Yes, they tried it with us the other day. Bastards. But at least they were only on the phone, not on the premises. How did you cope?' she asked.

'With a fake dog,' I explained.

'As opposed to a fake horse. Well, fair's fair. Now, these here horses. Young Carwyn wants the conference brought forward to next week. What's your best day? And would you like to travel up to London with us? Can't be Tuesday, of course – our fine arts day.'

Not to mention Paul's golf day. We agreed on Wednesday, wherever it was fixed.

'Do you want Tris to sit on the back seat with you? Hold hands?'

What made the words fly out, I don't know. 'I don't even want Tris to know about this gig.' In horror I covered my mouth with my hand.

She stared.

I back-pedalled. 'I just don't want Carwyn to get the wrong idea about me and Tris seeing each other.' Perhaps I didn't. But whatever the reason I couldn't bat images of miniatures out of my head. Anyway, I popped on a smile and added, 'He's as lovely as his voice, Helen – just wait and see.'

Forget checking and washing the day's haul. The minute I'd unloaded it I was on the phone to Titus.

'Have you and Pa been messing with miniatures?'

'He's good but not that good. Why?'

'Twice I've seen at auction one really good miniature amongst a batch of also-rans—'

'One good one amongst a load of crap. Why not?'

'Twice? Just wondered if it ties in with the gold frames you mentioned.'

'Eh? Ears open, anyway. How's the old bugger?'

'Better every day. Home soon. But his posh friend wants to take him on a holiday.'

'Stay at your pa's?'

'Maybe. Curtains and mattress, first.'

End of call. But that was Titus' way. What I could never work out was how and why I ended up speaking in the same staccato way.

'Portugal. A cruise up that big river to Spain. Just a week.'

Heavens, even Mary was talking like Titus now. But only because she was concentrating on washing the china I'd bought – a mixture of Regency and Art Deco. If punters didn't want Victorian, let them buy something else. I dried some and left the rest upside down to drain – I didn't want to stick a great hand up inside elegant vases, did I?

'We're going to buy one of those iPod things and fill it with our favourite music so we can dance each night on deck under the stars. How romantic is that?' Putting a saucer back in the bowl but not drying her hands, she waltzed round the kitchen table. 'All those classes we've been to, it'd be nice to put what we've learned into practice.' She returned to the sink. 'These'll be just the thing for that fair in the Cotswolds.'

I put down the plate I was drying very carefully. 'Fair?'

'Oh, Lina, you're not very good at checking the diary, are you?' This time she did rinse and dry her hands. She picked up the weekly diary, still by the kettle where I'd abandoned it the other day. 'Look: not this weekend but the next one. Warebank Court. Near Cirencester. It's a three-dayer. And Griff's pencilled in: *Prepare caravan. Enough stock???* Oh, and there are the labels I got for you – Londis, of all places. I took the money out of petty cash.'

Thanking her for being such a wonderful secretary, on top of everything else, I gave my mind to the problem of Warebank Court and its wretched fair.

Even as the word *cancel* floated into it, I

162

remembered what Griff had said about the three of us staying at a nice niche hotel, which would at least knock out the need to clean out and stock up the caravan. But would he be up to a journey like that? On the plus side, Warebank Court, a stately home hiring out its great hall for a twice-yearly event, always made us a lot of money, the top of the range items we'd not dream of taking to any other fair flying off the stall. Usually. But during a recession like this? I still thought cancellation was the best plan.

'Let's just finish these plates and I'll talk to him,' I said aloud, wondering how I could fit in a London trip too. And knowing I couldn't. Or do everything else crowding in on me.

'Warebank! I'd forgotten all about that. My darling, the Cotswolds heave with good hotels. I'll put the notion to Aidan and get back to you. Oh, what a treat!'

So I really couldn't say I was about to phone to sacrifice our deposit in order to gain a weekend.

Returning to my workroom, I was so panicky that I almost dropped five thousand pounds' worth of Chelsea figure. Deep breath time. I put it carefully back on the shelf and surveyed the rest. One of our regular customers bombarded me with requests to repair what were pretty well the only things I really loathed – Toby jugs. There was a mini rogues' gallery of them, all glaring balefully down at me. I glared back. I'd wipe the smiles from their faces – or, in the case of the least valuable, put it back. Reaching for my paints and adjusting the light, I sighed and began the task.

It was far from the most important, and certainly not urgent, but at least it would be finished by the end of the afternoon. And there'd be one thing I could cross off my list before I started the next. I challenged myself: could I finish the whole squad and get rid of their ugly faces?

I was just wondering how long I dared try to work without a break when Griff phoned.

'You were still in your workroom,' he said accusingly. 'I counted the number of rings it would take for you to put down your brush, wipe your hands on your apron and run downstairs. Angel heart, it's gone ten o'clock. And have you had supper? No, I thought not.'

'Guilty as charged. Toby jugs,' I said. 'Tomorrow I can get rid of them all and make room on my shelves for the next batch. Business is booming, Griff.'

'And there's only one of you to do it all. To do everything,' he said, sighing.

'Not with Mary and Paul here. By the way, they're only taking a week for their honeymoon. And guess what they aim to do!'

He sighed again when I mentioned the romantic evenings they planned – not, I suspected, because he yearned for them for himself but because he worried that my evenings were far less pleasurable. Then – and I could almost hear him squaring his shoulders – he said, 'But we have an extraordinary piece of good fortune, my child. It turns out that Sir Richard Walker, the owner of Warebank Court, is an old friend of Aidan's. We're going as his personal guests. All of us.'

'You mean—?' I prompted stupidly.

'My love, whereas last time we enjoyed an al fresco delight in the sylvan setting of his grounds, never penetrating, as mere tradespersons, beyond the scarlet rope separating the haves from the have-nots, this time we will be sleeping under his roof. I've no doubt we shall be waited on and butlered – or is it butled? – to pleasurable death. Though not literally, I hasten to add.'

'Does this guy know a mere tradesperson will be leaping across his have-not rope a couple of times a day?'

'Indeed. It seems he remembers you clearly from our last sale – you pointed out an imperfection in a *famille rose* plate he was about to buy. He was most impressed.'

But, as I recall, backed out of the purchase. 'Why didn't he know about you and Aidan before?' I asked bluntly.

'Apparently, he did – but he only knew my first name, and, I gather, had no idea that his old public school chum should be associating so – er – intimately with someone so low in the food chain.'

'*Associating* – how many years have you two been together?'

'Since before it became acceptable for people like dear Aidan to come out, sweet one. Theatrical types like my friends have always been tolerant of homosexuality – indeed, accepting, welcoming. But other people made laws against it, and enforced them, remember.'

All before my time, of course – but I was fuming at what I could only see as cowardice on

Aidan's part; cowardice that kept such vital information about him from even his own family.

'Now, we must make sure we have appropriate togs, dear one.'

'Black tie?'

'I was thinking more of the heated indoor swimming pool.'

And I was thinking that we didn't have anything to sell.

Since I was downstairs I raided the freezer for supper (the healthy M and S option I'd spurned a couple of weeks back), going round the house drawing curtains and setting room alarms while I waited for the microwave to ping. No wine. Not if I was going to get another couple of hours' work out of my hands. I couldn't manage anything requiring fine detail, of course, good though the lighting was, but at least I could unglue some of the badly repaired items people had passed on to me to restore properly. I told myself I simply had to complete at least five repairs by the end of the weekend.

There were times, I told Tim (when, at past midnight, I persuaded my aching back – it felt like a question-mark – into bed), that it was a good job I no longer had a boyfriend to worry about. Or one in the offing, of course, I added.

His smile was extremely smug.

# Sixteen

I hadn't intended to stop working all day Saturday, but a phone call from Robin changed my mind. He claimed my visit to Freya had lifted her spirits and hoped I might manage to pop in again. If I knew her it had been the good food, not me, that had done the job, so once again I popped into the deli for supplies. Since I hadn't had any lunch myself I bought two baguettes this time, one – because I was hungry – filled with the sort of unpasteurized cheese I knew pregnant women were forbidden.

'What are you doing in Kent? Hasn't Morris won you back yet?' she greeted me, her eyes full of unshed tears.

'He must have found a new babysitter,' I said lightly. 'How are you?'

'Still here, still pregnant,' she said. 'Did you know that that basket makes you look like Little Red Riding Hood?'

'I think maybe it's my waterproof,' I said mildly, slipping it off and letting it drip unhygienically all over the floor.

She looked blankly at the window. 'I didn't even know it was raining. Is that Coronation chicken in there?' She tucked in, retrieving odd bits of chicken as they fell on the sheet. 'Now, how did you get on with my team?'

I braced myself for all sorts of awkward

questions about Carwyn, but to my relief Robin, as wet as I'd been, put a streaming head round the door, rewarding me with his angelic smile. To divert Freya further, I told them about Griff's plans for the Cotswold weekend. Robin looked really interested, but it was hard to tell with Freya. Thinking I was what Griff – and Morris, come to think of it – called *de trop*, I shrugged on my coat again and prepared to leave.

'Sir Richard Walker?' Freya put in – just when I thought she'd not been paying attention. 'Name rings a bell. Is he kosher?'

'Far as I know,' I said, taken aback.

'Freya, darling – he's a friend of Aidan Thingy, Griff's partner!' Robin looked genuinely – but, of course, naively – shocked. 'An aristocrat.'

'There are some dodgy aristos around,' she said, adding, looking straight at me, 'and some have extremely dodgy mates.'

Despite the weather, Griff had been for another walk and had even ventured into some shops. As he sliced late beans for the supper I found myself cooking, he declared that his next target was to walk to St Mildred's for Communion the following morning. He'd got a lot to thank God for, he insisted, when Aidan growled anxieties about other people's germs on the Communion cup, and he agreed to compromise by dipping his wafer into the cup as if it were he who had an infection.

Admittedly, the next morning, he sat for the prayers, instead of managing his usual courtly kneel, and he was clearly glad to get back to

168

Aidan's after battling with a quite vicious wind. Aidan tepidly suggested I might want to stay for lunch; I said with absolute truth that I had so much work on that I simply had to get back. When I told Griff which clients were waiting he practically pushed me out of the house, but not before he'd pressed a foil pack into my hand, bulging with enough of last night's chicken to keep me fed till Monday night.

A warning call to Titus that Freya clearly had him and Pa in her sights wasn't as easy as it sounds. For one thing, it isn't exactly legal to warn someone you suspect of committing a crime that the police are on to them. So Titus had told me never, ever to implicate myself in such a thing. I had to introduce a completely innocent-sounding word into the conversation – easy enough when people natter for hours, but, of course, that wasn't our style. Most of our conversations lasted less than a minute. So I worked out in advance what I had to say, said it, and then destroyed even the piece of paper I'd written on, burying the charred remains in the compost bin. It wasn't just Titus' skin I was worried about, remember, it was Pa's – and mine and thus Griff's, too.

For the rest of the day, I developed a manageable routine, alternating between emails and Internet enquiries and restoration.

By pacing myself I found I could spend much longer in my workroom, though Griff would have been furious with me for toiling till Sunday midnight. Even angrier when I started before six on Monday morning.

When the rest of the world woke up, I contacted Geoff, our security contact.

'I'm worried about tomorrow,' I said baldly. 'Most of the time – as I'm sure you've seen from the footage – we have Mrs Walker's fiancé keeping an eye on things in the shop. Our own private muscle. Tuesdays are his golf days, and I wouldn't want him to think he should give them up. So what can we do extra, for those times Mary's alone in the shop?'

'Ed fitted an alarm strip, didn't he? So all she's got to do is touch that and we check our screens here and alert whoever's on patrol. Right? Or are you thinking something extra? One of our staff on duty? Inside or outside the premises, of course. Maybe something more sophisticated like a utility company digging up the street?'

'That's all a bit heavy, Geoff,' I said. And the bill would be astronomical. 'I'll have to consult Mary and see what she thinks. Meanwhile, any news of the guy who pretended to work for you?'

'We know who he is – an ex-employee, as you've probably already worked out.'

'The logo and the ID might just have sucked me in. But a uniform? When your people always look like chance visitors? Why should he think I'd buy that?'

'Because people do, sweetheart. People always fall for a uniform and an ID shoved under their noses. Think of all those dear old ladies letting fake gas men into their cottages – all smiles and cups of tea, and meanwhile Chummie there is stealing their poor little engagement rings worth tiddly-push and all the cash they'd hidden in a safe place. Safe! Ha! Robbing bastards,' he concluded viciously.

'So you know who he is but not where he is?'

'Couldn't put it better myself.'

'Do you think he'll be back?'

'That's the question you've been wanting to ask all along, isn't it? Well, nothing's shown up on my monitors, and I've been keeping my beadies open, as you can imagine. But the trouble with villains is that they never really change their spots, if you get my meaning. Or do I mean they're like dogs returning to their vomit? So all I can say is that I certainly wouldn't rule it out.' He must have heard the snatch of my breath because he continued, 'But there's nothing for you to worry about, sweetheart – not with us watching over you.'

Not while I was in fortress Tripp and Townend. But sometimes I'd have to leave it – as would Mary and Paul, doing their daily commute and generally going about their business.

'And don't worry about extra personnel tomorrow,' he said. 'I'm on duty myself so I'll keep my very own eye on you – how's that?'

'Couldn't ask for more,' I lied.

I was just checking our emails when a text came through from Carwyn. He was working flat out, he said – no time for a trip to London. So how about that video conference?

Excellent, I said. At least a text wouldn't betray my huge sigh of relief. As for Helen and Brian, when I emailed them, they thought the same. Good result all round. But I still urged them in one last email not to tell anyone else. At all.

171

Mary seemed perfectly happy to hear that Geoff would be keeping a special eye on her – 'Like having a guardian angel,' she told Paul happily. 'And no more talk of giving up your game tomorrow – they say it'll be mild and dry for a change. Now, Lina, Mondays are always quiet – can I contact some of your owners for you and get them to collect their pots? Safer than the post, after all. Any that can't, Paul and I can start wrapping.'

'Which reminds me,' I said, blushing, now it came to it, at having to mention money to people who were friends, 'Griff's been worried about the amount of your time you've been devoting to us, Paul. It's one thing you sitting in the corner writing poetry: it's quite another us absolutely depending on you to help Mary.' My blush deepened. 'Would you be prepared to come on our payroll – at least until Griff returns and can start pulling his weight again?'

His blush matched mine. 'There honestly isn't any need, Lina. What would the tax man say?'

'If anyone could predict that, you could,' I retorted, with a grin.

'Thanks but no thanks,' he said. 'I appreciate the thought, but I'm happy to be wherever Mary is, and doing whatever she has to do.' He turned to her and kissed her.

Yucky or touching, depending on your point of view. Touching, in my book. Inspired, I headed back to another pair of devoted lovers, this time a Dresden shepherd and his shepherdess, both with damage to their headgear.

\*     \*     \*

172

Tapping on the office door, Paul brought me a cup of tea, setting it down beside the computer. I was hoping that the Internet would help me track down some local sales, which might well supply what we needed for our weekend away.

He peered over my shoulder. 'Lyminge Auctions?'

'Yes: it's still trying to establish itself, and it always attracts a really mixed bag – both stock and punters, come to think of it.' I pointed to their virtual catalogue. 'This is what's coming up on Friday. And I'd better be there.'

'Why? You can do it online. Or over the phone.'

I shook my head in shame. 'I can never get a true sense of what's on offer just from pictures and descriptions.'

'But I've seen people on TV paying thousands for what they can't see – at least in the flesh, or whatever you'd call it. And you certainly don't want to stop people doing just that for items we offer.'

*We*: he really thought of himself as part of the firm, didn't he? 'Quite. And where would we be without them? But I couldn't do it myself.'

'But it would save you hours. And think of the petrol you waste. This calls for a rethink, Lina.'

I was afraid he'd stay and argue. Instead, nodding home his point, he picked up the cup and saucer and headed off.

There was another auction on at the same time the far side of Hastings. Why did everyone want to sell things on the same day? Crazy. Surely the local auctioneers could have got their heads together and avoided clashes. The Hastings one looked more promising, with some highly desirable china and some fine art. Though the guide prices were low, I suspected that the actual prices would be much higher. As I couldn't be in two places at once, perhaps what Paul said made sense.

He repeated his arguments over lunch.

Mary answered for me: 'You forget that sometimes Lina relies on a sense the Chinese long-distance bidders don't have.' She touched her nose. 'Don't you? Your divviness.'

Paul shook his head, as he always did when my weird gift was mentioned. But then, he was an accountant.

'As for your father,' he said, out of the blue, 'I think Mary's already suggested we could take food parcels when he needs them. We live practically next door, half the time at least.'

I swallowed hard. Even assuming Pa would let him in, what would he find?

He might be an old crook, but he was my father. What if anyone else happened upon those Elizabethan books he'd left casually lying around, all with lovely unused pages at the front and back, ready for him to remove and print his lovely fake words on? I might tell myself that no one else would understand their significance, but that wasn't the point. Pa and I had never actually spoken about his 'work', though he was quite happy to discuss what he did with Griff. It was time we had an adult conversation. But not yet. Maybe I wasn't quite grown up enough. More likely he wasn't. Meanwhile, Paul was awaiting a response.

'I'd be really grateful – you know that, Mary – but he's pretty weird, you know, and might not even open the door. Which would be a shame after you'd buggered your suspension going up the track to his wing. And he is my pa, after all,' I finished lamely.

'Quite. And ought to be thinking of securing your future, as I've said before.'

I had a weird vision of Paul trying to give Pa financial advice as he handed over a jumbo pack of loo rolls. 'As for my future, Paul,' I said quietly but firmly, 'it doesn't lie with him. It lies with me. In these.' I held out my hands.

'But if your father and Griff aren't careful, those hands won't be living in this cottage or working for this firm.'

I wanted to shout that it was none of his business. But, of course, since he was an accountant that was exactly what it was.

Mary stepped in, pressing more salad on me. Who'd have thought a lettuce leaf could prevent a quarrel? But it did, or rather the little slug sharing it with me did. I don't know which of us shrieked loudest. By the time we'd all calmed down, the moment was passed, and I dug out some of the *noblesse* that was supposed to *oblige*. 'Tell me, have you decided where you're going to live? You won't be commuting between the two cottages for ever?'

Apart from regularly popping into the shop to make sure Mary was OK, my working life continued to involve little more than watching paint dry. At least on Wednesday morning I was

175

due to be part of the video conference. I'd never done anything like it and was half excited, half anxious. But I needn't have been either. At the last minute – I was literally just getting dressed in what I thought might be a videoconferencing outfit – Carwyn phoned to say it had been postponed. His boss wanted him to drop everything to tackle something else. Brian and Helen had wanted it to go ahead without him, but he insisted he wanted to be part of it. How about Friday?'

'Brian's auction day.' As I listened to his muttered swearing, I added, 'You know what Brian will say?' I told him without waiting for a reply: '*I told you so.* That's what they'll say. And they'd be right.'

'Please don't take it personally.' He sounded quite upset.

'Carwyn, as far as I'm concerned fraud is personal. Particularly when I'm dragged into it by Mrs Fielding and her darling little Puck.'

# Seventeen

More drying paint, then – not to mention, of course, drying glue. But suddenly I wanted air – maybe it was the glue fumes getting to my brain – and bolted, without telling Paul exactly where I was going, because I was off to check the two auction houses' offerings.

There was nothing top-end worth bidding for at the Lyminge one, but I left low bids for some items that should do well in the shop or in everyday fairs. The Hastings one was more interesting, with one or two gems tucked away in quite unexciting lots. Real gems: an eighteenth century Lowestoft bowl shoved under a twentieth century Winfield basin – Winfield being Woolworth's range, of course. Perhaps that one would have sentimental value, as opposed to the very real value of the Lowestoft. And there were other things in the room too. I didn't know exactly where. But there was something I had to respond to.

At last I found a pile of china, as haphazard as any of Pa's heaps still awaiting my attention. There were some decent Victorian plates, part of a dinner service, some twentieth century Wedgwood, and other odds and ends. And sandwiched between two very handsome late sixties Royal Worcester dessert plates was a piece of Delft. Eighteenth century. Adam and Eve. With the least bit of TLC it'd fetch upwards of three thousand pounds. I checked. The estimate for the entire lot was one to two hundred. OK, that was my Friday booked. But since other people were milling round, I simply put on my uninterested face and drifted on. Miniatures. No, I was absolutely not interested in miniatures.

Why wasn't I surprised to find a crop of very ordinary ones and one quite spectacular one? All one in one lot? The good one was of a guy in Restoration clothes, long cleft chin, gorgeous hair, his heavy-lidded eyes languorously regarding the world. Was that the right word? Or was it *sensuously*?

At least I wasn't ignorant enough to think I'd happened on a picture of Charles II. But I knew I'd found something. Not that the paperwork agreed with me. Unknown man, unknown artist. From the collection of some guy in Worcestershire, just like the other, ordinary ones. Estimate six hundred to eight hundred for the lot. I nearly squawked in disbelief. If only I'd had time to finish studying that magic book, I might have known something about the good one. And, come to think of it, I'd left the book at Aidan's. Not that I could have sat down and studied it here. Apart from anything else, that would have given the game away something shocking.

Yes, that miniature had to be mine. Not even Tripp and Townend's. Mine. Along with the dross that came with it if necessary.

So much for Paul's theory that you only needed the Internet to trade. If I hadn't been there in the flesh, I'd never have seen any of the precious items I wanted to bid for. Wouldn't have sensed them.

Even as I stuck a mental tongue out at him, however, I realized that he might have been right about something else. Phone bidding. No point in arousing interest by bidding for something people didn't associate with me. Why not do it anonymously, either via the net or by phone? Since, on the whole, I thought I'd rather hear a voice putting in my bids for me, I toddled off to the office and gave them my details.

Yes! The game was afoot.

So why was I feeling guilty?

In the past I'd have self-harmed till I could shut out a nagging doubt. Griff had suggested an alternative: hard work. But even as I geared myself up for yet another evening with nothing more cheery for company than a paintbrush, I puzzled over what felt like a tarnished conscience. My father regarded finding as keeping, no more and no less. Griff's dictum was *buy cheap; sell dear.* That was what trade was about. I hadn't stolen anything. I hadn't hidden the plate I wanted. I wasn't the person who'd given what I was sure was a poor provenance for the miniature. So I had done nothing wrong. Could I have done more that was right? Should I have alerted the auctioneer – not a man I knew, even by reputation – to the fact that my antennae were twitching? 'Hello, my diviner's instinct tells me your learning and experience are astray?'

I'd done it professionally in France. I'd told aristocrats their inheritances were dodgy and informed the Prime Minister that he'd wasted money from the public purse. But I hadn't done it this afternoon.

As I picked up the figurine I'd marked out for the evening's work, I let her slip. A hundred pounds' worth of Chamberlain's Worcester milk-maid, entrusted to me to have a churn restored to her right arm, lost the other. Just like that. So now – because that was how I did business – I had to do the whole repair for free, explaining that I'd been a careless idiot. The waste of a complete evening and a tiny chip on my reputation.

It was only as I finished all I could do on the milkmaid for now that I realized what I'd done wrong. Or failed to do right. It was nothing to do with the miniatures. It was that I should have had my eyes open for shady white horses and suspicious Ruskin ginger jars. And I hadn't, in my lust for goodies, even thought about them. I headed down to the computer and checked. Yes, there they were. Both of them. Tomorrow's job – and not for me. For Carwyn.

For some reason I couldn't concentrate any more. There was no point in risking another breakage, so I did some ungluing and cleaning, before heading downstairs to do some of the boring office tasks that would probably have had Paul rubbing his hands in glee. If only I hadn't rushed my fence with my offer of payment. I should have sidled up to the idea, saying I couldn't cope with paperwork, real or virtual, and asking if he would become our office clerk. It was true about the paperwork. Griff had made

180

huge efforts to educate me, but I'd missed years of schooling, sometimes through wagging off, but more often because of Social Services' inadequacies, moving me from one home to another without any thought of continuity. These days I could write a decent sentence, but then, halfway through a paragraph, I'd forget how I'd begun. And words would float away, just out of my reach. I could see the general shape, but it was only the dear, precious computer spell-check that stopped me making some absolute howlers – malapropisms, Griff called them. He'd taken me to see *The Rivals*, but I hadn't been able to laugh at Mrs Malaprop's mistakes because they could so easily have been mine.

After no more than twenty minutes, I fancied a drink. One of Griff's best hot chocolates. No Griff to make it, of course, and I had to agree with him that drinking-chocolate needs full-fat milk, not the red-top I'd made him use when his heart problems started. For some reason I still bought it even though he wasn't here to worry about.

Forget the hot chocolate, then. I prowled round, checking and double-checking every lock and camera. At last I stopped myself. What was I up to? Sometimes I behaved like this when thunder was brewing, but it was just a miserable murky autumnal night, with rain in the air swiftly becoming thick swirling mist.

At least that made one decision for me. It wasn't a night to drive to Tenterden. I'd have been soaked through by the time I'd got the car through all our security, and though the trusty Fiesta had fog lights, the roads just didn't encourage a random visit. And a phone call would have scared Griff half to death and made him insist on coming home to keep an eye on me. Actually, that was just what I wanted. Even an overnighter at Pa's would have seemed halfway attractive if only I'd remembered to get bedlinen and curtains.

Eventually, I did what I should probably have done an hour ago. I headed to bed and to Tim the Bear.

And awoke with a huge jump in the middle of the night. A pulse racing, heart pounding sort of jump. The sort that has you frozen in bed, listening for intruders.

Tucking Tim firmly between the pillows, I reached for the old swagger stick Pa had given me in the belief it was now legal to whack intruders round the head. I couldn't see it. And then, ever so slowly, considering how poised for fight or flight I was, I realized I needed to switch on the bedside light to see. Normal: we don't have street lights in Bredeham, of course, so when it's dark, it's dark. Not normal: the bedside light didn't work. Nor did the main light.

At last I had the swagger stick in hand and could feel my way downstairs. The sensors picked up even this stealthy movement and the security system emitted a set of increasingly hysterical beeps, until I prodded in the area code number. Once in the kitchen, I wasn't greeted by friendly greenish glows from the microwave or the oven clocks. So the power was out, as well as the lights.

We had one clever burglar if he'd managed to throw the mains switch.

Even though I knew the alarm system was still working, I was ready to scream. I clamped my hands across my mouth. Better me than someone else. Breathe, Lina, breathe from your diaphragm.

Once the panicky whooshing in my ears subsided, I made myself listen. Griff's favourite clock. That was all. No, it wasn't. There were lots of other noises, but from outside. Car alarms? No, house alarms.

Damn me if I didn't head into the living room to check. The sensor got very ratty. I withdrew smartly and re-set it.

By now I'd just about recalled that though our alarm system had a huge battery back-up in the attic for when the power failed, other houses became either noise machines or burglars' paradises. To save power, the cameras shot fewer frames. The sensor beep was quieter and less frequent. The exterior alarm remained silent – unlike those of several of our neighbours, intermittently lighting up the street. So it was a general power failure.

So why did I still feel twitchy?

On impulse I called the night-time equivalent of Geoff, the screen-watcher. This was what we paid our massive bills for – someone to tell us our property was intact. Answering first ring, the man grunted his name: Phil. I'd not come across him before, never having bothered the night shift in the past.

Phil didn't sound reassuring. 'No street lights in your location,' he said.

'Never are,' I said, explaining.

'But there's no one making your floodlights come on. So everything should be fine. Let's just have one look-see. House, OK. Inside and out. Shop – fine too. Hang on, there's a car parked just opposite. Let's see what I can see . . . Yep. There's someone in it, pretending to be asleep.'

'Pretending?'

'Why should someone sleep in a car in a village street?'

My heart did a funny little dance. I knew only one person likely to park up to catch me first thing in the morning – someone who was fairly sure of his welcome, but not sure enough to wake me up at midnight or thereabouts. For all I knew it wouldn't ever work, for all I knew I'd made the right decision, just at that moment I'd have given anything to let Morris into the house.

Phil clearly thought he'd asked a question I didn't need to answer. Rhetorical. 'Looks like obbo to me. Anywhere you can check from? Upstairs window? Don't let anyone see you.'

'Phil, it's pitch black out there – no street lights, remember, and it's getting really foggy.'

I could almost hear him grinding his teeth at my stupidity. 'There's a burglar alarm on the house he's nearest to. Every time it flashes on and off you can see him. Come on, Mrs Tripp, if there's enough light for your camera to pick it up . . .'

He'd obviously passed his customer relations course with highest honours – or not.

The only window looking at that particular angle was in the bathroom, and it involved putting

184

a stool on the loo seat, holding on to the blind for dear life and, since the window only opened about three inches, peering through a very narrow gap. It wasn't a regular manoeuvre of mine. Yes, there was a car. A very old Subaru: he must be talking about that. Unfortunately, the eerie blue light didn't reach as far as the sleeper's head or face.

At this point my heart stopped dancing. That wasn't Morris's sort of vehicle, not at all. But it was vaguely, very distantly familiar. I could picture it somewhere.

Inching down, I sat on the edge of the bath to consider.

Griff had made me play endless memory games – objects on trays I'd have a minute to scan, before he whipped them away and told me to list them. And of course my job had helped – repairing a badly smashed vase was like doing a three-D jigsaw. So I told myself I could do it. I could. But the more I insisted, the less I could conjure the image. I was just picking up the phone to call Phil and report failure when it came to me: I'd seen a car just like it in Baker's Auction House's car park. It wouldn't be Brian and Helen's. They sported his and hers Beamers, come to think of it, which said something about the state of the auction trade. Could it possibly be Tristam's?

And if so, what on earth was he doing outside our shop?

# Eighteen

One thing was certain: I was not going to find out tonight, as I told Phil when I reported back.

'Lovelorn swain, is he?' He cackled at his take on village life.

'Could be. He'll be a cold lovelorn swain by the morning, won't he?'

'You're a hard woman, Mrs Tripp. I'll cast a beadie over him from time to time, so you can go and get your beauty sleep.'

Tristam's car had gone by the time I woke up to a chilly house in the morning. So there was still no power. When I phoned the emergency helpline I got a recorded message assuring me that they knew about the problem and were working hard to solve it. Well, they'd hardly say that one man and his dog would have a look when they'd finished their breakfast. Local radio was more informative. Someone had nicked a whole lot of cable from our local substation and replacing it would take till noon at the earliest.

Great. Last night's mist had become fully-fledged fog, so with no lights the chances of finishing any delicate repair work were zero. Nothing I could do using the computer, either.

I called Paul and Mary to suggest they didn't come over till there was some reason to open the shop: like lights, a till and a working credit card terminal. I left a large handwritten notice to that effect on the door. I phoned Carwyn, but he wasn't in the office and wasn't expected back till noon the following day. Great.

So leaving the cottage and shop under Geoff's eagle if far distant eyes, I set off on foot to Brian's premises.

They were, of course, in darkness too. Brian, phone clamped to his ear, was too busy trying to locate an emergency generator to do more than flap a hand; Helen stared longingly at the coffee machine; the office staff huddled together as if their mobiles would provide heat. But where was Tristam? There was no sign of his car.

'Oh, he looked like death so I sent him home,' Helen said, offhand. Then her eyes gleamed. 'Of course, if I'd known you were hoping for a *tryst* with him . . .'

'I hope you breathalysed him first,' I said unkindly, cutting across her little joke. Or whatever.

One of the office staff abandoned her phone, turning to me with huge eyes. 'Tris? Was he ill?'

'Not as far as I know,' I responded coolly. 'He just spent last night slumped behind the wheel of that car of his outside our shop. The security people didn't spot him till midnight and I wasn't about to toddle down in my nightie to offer sympathy and a hottie bottle. Not with the security cameras following my every move,' I added.

'But what if he'd died?'

There didn't seem to be an answer to that. Eventually, I settled for something neutral. 'All I want to know is why he should choose my

187

cottage to park by. Which is why I came down,'
I told Helen. 'To ask him.'

Tris's fan pushed forward again. 'I could call
him? Text him?'

I nearly snarled, 'So could I.' But I'd been
young and in love once. I produced the most
grown-up smile I could, horribly patronizing. 'I'd
prefer to speak to him face to face, thanks.'

Since there were still a couple of hours to go
before the power was likely to come on again, I
headed out to Smeeden. It wasn't a particularly
pretty Kentish village, but it did have a small
antiques and collectibles fair every Thursday – so
small, and so focused on collectibles rather than
genuinely old items, that Griff and I no longer
took a pitch. The question was, would it have
electricity? It did. So I handed over my one pound
entrance fee and strolled round casually, just like
any other punter.

Battered teddies; Dinky cars with no paint; lots
of Fifties' china; a huge area of second-hand
books. There were a few more interesting stalls,
at one of which I found for fifteen pounds a
mauve Fieldings' Devon lustre planter, just right
for one of the plants Griff had acquired while he
was in hospital. A willow-pattern meat dish –
genuine Chinese, would you believe it? Not
hugely valuable, but worth much more than the
fiver I had to fork out. Another root around
unearthed a Shelley bonbon plate, which I bought
just because I liked it – and, come to think of it,
it matched a couple of other items in store so I'd
have a set to offer, which was always more
profitable.

Next, a stall groaning under model animals. Normally, I wouldn't even have paused, but Puck and his friends had given me an irritating interest. Yes, Puck's cousin, in brown, was there, badly chipped and on offer at fifteen pounds. I didn't have the least inclination to buy him and embark on the spot of restoration Rob Sampson might have encouraged me to do to improve the price. What I liked much better was a little model of a cat. It was only about six inches high, a purply-grey colour, with far bigger eyes than it should have had and its paw on a cartoon-like mouse. But Tom and Jerry it was not. I didn't know anything about it, but my divvy's instinct was working overtime, so I would have coughed up the sixty quid the stallholder was asking without turning a hair. I might have asked for – and probably got – trade discount, but I preferred not to. As it was, with hardly a haggle, I got it for fifty. Just to show there was no ill-feeling, I pottered around a bit longer, buying some home-made cakes (at the WI stall) as a bonus.

The power came on just as I opened our front door. The return of civilized life. Computers. Lights. And – in response to my phone call – Paul and Mary.

I wanted to nip down to Tenterden to show Griff the cat and pick his brains about its identity, so at about four I phoned to invite myself to supper. Griff sounded delighted but cautious – the fog was already getting thick, and he didn't want me to take any risks. How about tomorrow evening, weather permitting?

It was no more than murky in Bredeham, but,

189

since they'd not seen a customer all afternoon, I sent Mary and Paul home early, as usual locking up the big yard gates behind them. This was one time when our fortress was vulnerable – the gates were, of course, heavy, and even at my briskest I couldn't move them quickly. In the past I'd have been carrying keys – now, in the most recent upgrade, we'd changed to touch pads. Griff hated them because he was always afraid he'd forget at a crucial moment.

The first was closed, and the second halfway there when a figure appeared. In an instant what was really no more than mist seemed to become the sort of swirling fog you imagine at the start of *Great Expectations*, but at least it wasn't Magwitch that materialized on the pavement outside. It was Tristam.

I couldn't read his expression at all. If I'd been him, I wouldn't be best pleased. In fact, I might owe him an apology: I'd given away information about him he'd no doubt have preferred to keep to himself. Whatever sort of conversation was about to take place, it was going to take place in front of our cameras. Leaving the gate ajar, I stepped into the street.

'I know it looked bad last night,' he said. 'I know it did. But I just wanted to see you. And you know that song – about the street where you live.'

Him! Love me! Nah, didn't buy that, not for one minute. I didn't even think he had a crush on me, not the way he'd behaved when we'd had those drinks together.

I mimed a phone. 'Call? Text?'

'But not at that time of night. I just wanted . . . and then I fell asleep,' he admitted.

I must not laugh. Absolutely must not. 'Anyway, here I am.' But I found myself folding my arms. Defensive? Or combative? If I wasn't sure how it would look, it was because I wasn't sure how I felt. I added an encouraging smile. Was this how Morris felt when he was dealing with me, an adult indulging a kid?

Fog or no fog, I could see his blush from where I stood.

'I was wondering – would you fancy a drink?' he blurted. 'The Crown?'

A quick check of the watch. I ought to get at least two more hours' work in, preferably more. 'About half seven? But then I have to do some more work – I've got a contract to finish.' In other words, *Tris, you're not coming back with me.*

His mouth opened a few times which I took to mean yes.

'Great,' I said. 'See you then.' I tried to make my retreat behind the gate look leisurely, but all the same I was happiest with it locked.

Drat the boy. I really didn't want to go out, especially with him, because there were a lot of things I didn't want to let slip, especially to someone else in the trade. I'd have to stay on the wagon and make sure he did the talking, which he usually did anyway. But not about me and my doings.

That was what was different about this evening's drinks, which, as I'd expected, I bought. I drew the line at buying us both food, though – I was telling him the straight truth that I really did want to get back home to work. Even as I made the point I felt mean – after all, I had a sound income, and occasionally busted a gut to earn it. And I'd have to eat something anyway.

He started picking my brain about other auction houses in the area.

I countered with another question. 'Are you fed up with Brian? He's got a wonderful wide range – you must be learning a lot there.'

'I was just thinking of a paying job,' he said, tugging at my heart strings.

'Brian and Helen are the only people I'm friends – as opposed to friendly – with. I couldn't give you half a dozen names and tell you to phone them and say, "Lina Townend says you should give me a trial." I'm just another dealer to most auctioneers.'

He wouldn't take no for an answer, listing all sorts of firms in Kent and Sussex, and asking for my opinion. But I hadn't had years of training – both dodging trouble on the streets, and then, for professional reasons, with Griff – to know when to keep shtum. Mention the Lyminge Sale Room and the one near Hastings I would not, just in case I mentioned my plans for tomorrow. Double tact; double silence.

'What about people in your line? Dealers. There must be someone you know who'd give me a job. I mean – while your partner's ill, couldn't you do with a hand? National minimum wage – that's all I'd ask. As a friend. Come on, think about it – someone to do all the heavy work. And didn't I hear that old bat of yours, the one that yacks all the time, is going on holiday soon? How'll you manage without someone in the shop?' He grabbed my hand.

Now how did he know that? Of course, Mary wasn't the most silent and discreet of people. But I didn't like to hear her described like that, not one bit – even if, especially if, that was how I'd once thought of her.

'Mary's a highly experienced shop manager,' I said curtly, removing my hand. 'But at least I'll talk the idea over with Griff. Another half? Because it's time I got back to work.'

'I *told* you that you needed help!'

'I'm just about to make from scratch an entire hand for a Staffordshire figure, and paint and glaze it so well that no one but me will be able to tell what I've done without looking at the documentation I give them and their insurance people. When you can do that you can help.' I shouldn't have said that, not in that tone: it was too brutal. I added with a smile, 'I'm really sorry, Tris, but you've got a wonderful brain and plenty of brawn, but not these.' Safely out of range, I waved my fingers at him.

'It's not fair. I've studied for years. I've got all the qualifications anyone could dream of, and a few more. And no job. But you – you don't have so much as a GCSE, do you? Sorry. Shouldn't have said that.'

Damned right he shouldn't. But how did he know?

He had the grace to blush, and he changed the subject quickly. 'Are you going to bid for anything at the sale on Friday?'

193

Should I go for his jugular? On the whole I couldn't be bothered. Besides which, getting angry made my hands shake. So I answered coolly: 'Not this time. In fact I—' I'd nearly dropped it out, hadn't I? 'In fact, I'm expecting a vase from Harvey Sanditon. He'll expect absolute priority – and pay for it,' I added fairly, even though I was lying through my teeth about the vase.

'That's the upmarket guy you were shagging, isn't it?'

Who'd told him that? I suppose the world of antiques was small enough. 'How dare you! He's married, and I don't do married men. Or, to be frank, men who sit outside my house at midnight. Sorry, Tris. But at least you know where we stand. Mates.' At best. At very best.

'But Lina—'

Hell, he was only trying to snog me, here in the bar!

'You emptied the ice bucket over him!'

'Only a couple of cubes.'

'Even so, he won't like that!' Afzal looked more serious than amused. He tipped extra salad between the thick cheeks of the naan bread. 'Some guys don't cope with humiliation. Look, I'm just making up a takeaway order. Rafiq'll take it and give you a lift. Just in case.'

Rafiq was another cousin – how many did he have, for goodness' sake? I'd never met him before, but he seemed to know his way around the village.

'You're that antiques lady, innit?'

'Right.'

'Cottage and shop, innit?'

'Right.'

Pausing only to make sure the delivery order was anchored, he set out. Talk about bats out of hell! Still, maybe that was how they drove in Birmingham. So he didn't see me gripping the seat as if my life depended on it – maybe it did! – I mentioned that Griff had once taken me to Edgbaston for a day at a Test Match. Well, I didn't reckon he'd want to hear about my adventures at NEC antiques fairs.

Bingo. We nattered about cricket during the short journey home in his van. But to my amazement he shot straight past the cottage.

'Someone there,' he said. 'In the shadows opposite. Saw the light of his mobile. I'm going to deliver this order and then bring you back. OK?'

The speed he was going it had to be OK, didn't it?

At last he screeched to a halt, grabbed the insulated bags and hurtled off on foot. I called the security firm, to flag up – in his own words – to Phil that we might have someone to worry about.

'No sodding street lights, are there, Mrs Tripp? Want my advice? Just let yourself into the house smartish and lock up quick as you can. Press your panic button if nec. Only, I've got to keep my eye on some posh place in Tenterden.' He cut the call.

I froze. What if it was Aidan's place? I almost called him back, but stopped myself in time. He wouldn't have told me if it was, would he? Couldn't, for heaven's sake.

Rafiq bounced back into the van. 'Right, time to sort out that guy, innit?' He rubbed his hands, raring for a fight.

'Let's just hope he's gone,' I said under my breath. But I tried to enter into the spirit of things. 'Tell you what, let's just drive very quietly, very gently, and surprise whoever it is.'

Poor Rafiq was really mortified to find all his unnatural driving had been in vain. The street was deserted. A perfect gentleman now, he strode round to the passenger side to help me out, and he shone his torch at the door lock to help me let myself in.

'Won't stir till you call and tell me everything's OK, innit?' He folded his arms and turned round to face the street. I was being guarded with his life. It wasn't until I'd turned both thumbs up that he accepted I was safe and sound. With a wave, he got back in and drove away.

Before I could think of eating, I had to check it wasn't Aidan's house under special surveillance. Hang Aidan, and his *objects d'art* – it was Griff I was worried about. The landline was engaged, and both their mobiles switched to voicemail. I left a perky message on Griff's, asking him to call me to talk about my purchases from the fair. Texted him, too. Nothing to panic him – after all, if Phil and the team were doing their job properly, he and Aidan might not even know there was a problem.

OK. Time to eat. Fine except for one thing. I'd left my tikka and naan in Rafiq's van.

\* \* \*

196

Having had no response at all from Griff, and with Aidan's landline engaged whenever I tried it, I was reduced to talking to the cat. 'I wish I could keep you. But you know I only bought you as an investment. And what do I find? That you're a really pricey pussy. Faience, that's what you are, according to the Internet. And you're as old as I thought you were. Late eighteenth century, probably all the way from Brussels. How about that? And when I put you up for sale you'll have a really nice price-tag on your paw. Two and a half thousand pounds, that's what it'll say, Cat. How about that?'

For five minutes I toyed with the idea of a real cat, the sort that would sit on my lap and purr. But there were three arguments against. Griff hated cats; cats and china did not mix; and Tim the Bear would be speechless with jealousy.

The phone rang at last.

'Phil here. Van heading your way. Cottage, not shop. Suspicious-looking guy. Front door now.'

Just like a visitor, then. But I couldn't think of anyone likely to visit me, suspicious or otherwise.

Not until I checked the security camera.

It was Rafiq, with my supper.

# Nineteen

Friday morning brought good news: Tripp and Townend were awash with euro-loot. Some of the invoices I'd submitted to our French clients had been paid, and the others, according to the bank, were in the pipeline. Paul tapped busily at his calculator, sorting out today's conversion rates to pounds sterling and coming up smiling.

It meant, though I didn't tell even Paul or Mary, that I could go higher with my bids for the items at today's auction – I could take a risk on that miniature. Even so, when it came to it, though part of my everyday job was making bids at auctions, my hands were greasy with sweat and my voice kept cracking. And that was just for the plates! But I got them for peanuts, far less than I'd mentally set aside. Which left all the more for the lot of miniatures.

Which dropped into my hand like a ripe plum. As easy as that. I couldn't believe my luck. Or was it a horrible misjudgement? I wouldn't know whether I'd made the right call till I had it in my hand, so, abandoning the vase I should have been working on, I headed straight out, taking a couple of plastic boxes stuffed with bubble-wrap for the china.

Willpower time. Lyminge first. It was like making myself eat the vile grey porridge I knew was really good for me before toast and Griff's home-made marmalade.

'You bought this for less than a thousand pounds?' I'd never heard Aidan squeak but he came pretty close to it now. A squeak, in his elegant drawing room – the one too posh for the family miniatures!

'This and half a dozen little friends.'

His eyebrows disappeared as he passed it carefully to Griff. In awed tones he continued, 'A Samuel Cooper?'

I didn't like to admit the name meant nothing to me. I managed a dry smile. 'Unknown artist, according to the catalogue. Unknown man, too – but I'd guess from your expression you know who it is.'

'Not precisely. But it has to be a relative or by-blow of one of the Charleses, doesn't it?' *By-blow*: that was Aidan's euphemism for *bastard*. Perhaps he used it to spare feelings I didn't really have about my illegitimacy. 'Such quality . . . Lina, when you come to sell this, may I have first refusal?'

I could feel Griff's eyes on me. 'Of course,' I said. 'But the thing is, Aidan, I don't want to sell it. At all. I know that's what dealers are supposed to do. But I want to buy it from Tripp and Townend and hang it on my own wall. If you don't mind, Griff.'

'My darling, the only thing that stops me telling you to have it for free is the fact you paid for it using our funds. Our accountant would die if I did. So we will do it officially, with every scrap of paperwork being entirely official and above board. What it does call for is champagne . . .' His voice tailed off. This wasn't his house, after all, to be hospitable in.

'What a good job I stopped off at Waitrose,' I said. 'I even got it out of the chiller cabinet, so it should be ready to drink.'

Far from being delighted with Aidan's reaction to my unknown man, I was actually quite worried. The more I looked at it, from the delicate gold frame to the wonderful living quality that the artist had achieved, the more anxious I became. From being good, the vibes I was getting were bad. There was something altogether wrong about my purchase.

Should I ask Tris? He was an expert, after all. On the whole I thought not. The unknown man and his unknown artist could both stay that way until I'd made more enquiries myself. Until I had, I wouldn't – perhaps couldn't – hang him on my wall. As for his mates, perhaps they'd better stay with him. Just in case.

I wouldn't explain to Griff till I got him on my own. Meanwhile, we had other things to celebrate: the Adam and Eve delftware plate had him literally jigging with pleasure, which was more than enough excuse for champagne in my book at least.

When I'd told Tris I had a rush job on for Harvey Sanditon I'd been lying, but by some coincidence, as I laid the table for supper, still festive and cooked by Griff himself, a text came through from Harvey himself. A valued client had had a disaster: could I help?

Leaving the napkin-folding to Aidan, who did such things so much better than I, I retreated to call Harvey. My eyebrows were still probably sky-high when I returned to the dining room.

'A week's work, I'd say,' I told Griff quietly as Aidan brought in soup. 'So urgent, the owner will pay me a bonus on top of my fee if I can deliver by next weekend.'

'Can you manage it? As their Big Day draws ever closer, Mary and Paul must have things to do that will take them away from the shop.'

'I shall just have to focus . . . Thanks to today's auctions I think we've got enough stock for the shop. And I picked up a few things at Smeeden – including a really cute faience cat.'

Griff looked at me; even though I meant to sound casual, he knew it was another item I didn't want to part with.

'He – *it!* – should do well at Sir Richard's gig. As for more top of the range stuff, we'll have to bring one or two things out of store – and the Adam and Eve plate should help.'

Aidan was quiet to the point of looking suspicious. It was clear he didn't like our shop talk. So we turned our attention to the food, and said nothing more.

I could only hear parts of their after-dinner conversation, which took place in the drawing room while I ferried the dirty dishes from the dining room to the kitchen. The rest I could imagine. I wasn't trying to eavesdrop, but as soon as I heard my name my ears wouldn't switch off.

'Lina lonely!' Aidan said in loud disbelief.

'What gives you that impression? She might be on her own more these days but she's always struck me as an extremely self-contained young woman.'

'She wants a cat and she's bought a picture of a handsome young man. Exactly what I'd do in her situation. She's been on her own long enough. And Aidan, much as I'd love to flit around London for a couple of days with you, I think it would be too much for me.'

'And the connection is?'

'I don't want to stop you going up to town and enjoying yourself. I would like to spend some time with Lina before the weekend in the Cotswolds. The connection is that you can go to London and I shall return to Bredeham.'

'And you'll exhaust yourself trying to look after her.'

'If I know her, she'll exhaust herself trying to look after me. But we can be like two playing cards propped up to make the foundation of a card tower. We shall support each other and thus achieve a lot more. If I do no more than answer the phone and check the Internet purchases, it will get me back into the business, nice and slowly, and it will get some of the pressure off her. You must have noticed how pale she is.'

Pale? Was I? I'd certainly got a couple of random spots which I could well have done without. More than a couple. And goodness knows when I'd last had my hair cut. That was something I must get done before the Warebank Court weekend. And I must think about clothes, too. But where would I find the time for buying them? I'd really messed up by not buying anything for autumn going into winter while Griff was in hospital, though Ashford would have provided a good basic wardrobe. But why not look beyond basic? Griff had blown more euros than I could imagine on chic French garments for me, and some of them would go with me to Warebank. There, decision taken.

Now what were they saying?

No, it was time to concentrate on loading the dishwasher, preferably with a bit of a clatter, and to close the ears to their private conversation. Probably Aidan thought much the same – I heard a door close firmly and the voices disappeared.

I didn't dare hope that Griff would come home. Or did I almost hope he wouldn't? What if he was too poorly to do all he wanted? What if he was taken ill? What about all his medication?

There was a terrible crash. I stared at my hands. How could they have dropped something precious? Something of Aidan's!

I stared at them in horror. They'd let fall – ah, just an old crock basin, one Griff whisked eggs in. It had landed on a le Creuset casserole. More noise than mess. All the same, I found myself crying, and, as usual, once I'd started I found it hard to stop. In no time, I felt Griff's arms round me, loving me better. Why should that only make it worse?

But a hissed question stopped me in mid-sob.

'Dear God, the girl can't be pregnant, can she? Like father, like daughter, you know.'

Griff spoke before I could. 'I can think of no

one less like her father than Lina. As for pregnancy, that's her business.'

'And not possible,' I declared. 'I shan't embarrass you with details of my contraception, but believe me, Aidan, it's foolproof. Which means, in case you're concerned, that even I can't mess up.' Deep-breath time. A big row would be really bad for Griff's heart, wouldn't it? 'Look, I'll clear up here and then head for home. No doubt I'll see you at your mate Sir Richard's place,' I added, my accent as ugly as I could make it.' A big hug and kiss for Griff. 'See you soon. I love you. Don't worry – I'll drive as safely as if you were there beside me.'

'My love, I will be there beside you. I'll get my things while you repack all your precious items.'

It wasn't all quite as neat as that. Aidan was full of the most grovelling apologies and kept finding other reasons to keep Griff with him. Most of the time I simply kept out of his way, loading the car with all my purchases, including the book on miniatures I'd left behind last time. I'd also ferried Griff's luggage, which was pretty minimal but more than he'd come with, since he didn't care to leave any dirty clothes at Aidan's. At last, as Aidan almost leapt up and down with anxiety, I said, 'Come on, Aidan, all lovers have tiffs. But sometimes a little space is good for both partners. I'll look after him, I promise.' Maybe my being calm irritated him even more than if I'd lost my temper, as I wanted to. If I had, I knew I'd have well and truly lost it – used words that were general currency when I'd been a street kid and which he probably wouldn't have understood. But if I had, it wouldn't have done Griff any good.

'And you'll be seeing him next weekend,' I continued, all nice and cheerful and grown-up. Could I be adult enough to say what I ought? I'd try, at least. With a deep breath and in a bit of a rush I said, 'He's always told me not to let the sun go down on a quarrel.' I drifted away to let him take the hint.

But if he did, Griff didn't say anything to me as I picked my way home to Bredeham through the misty lanes.

Once we were safe, his belongings either hung up or in the wash, and he had a glass of his favourite Rioja in his hand, I tried again. Handing him the phone, I said, 'You know what you told me about quarrels. Go on. You know you ought.'

Saintly or what? All the same, as I discovered when I logged in to check the day's emails, I was still shaking with rage. Or terror. All that passing out. This crying business. I couldn't – could I – be carrying Morris's child?

# Twenty

Tim the Bear was his usual reliable self. Looking at his calm face, I told myself I knew I wasn't pregnant, didn't I? If anyone was meticulous in the matter of contraception it was me. Belt and braces. Hardly surprising given my father's random dispersal of his seed. Meanwhile, I'd better go and see that Griff wasn't suffering any ill effects from the row and the car journey.

He didn't seem to be. He was sitting up in bed looking remarkably perky, in fact, reading glasses perched on his nose and a copy of *The Grand Sophy* in his hand. A real book, not an electronic one.

'You've no idea how wonderful it is to be home,' he said with a smile that stretched beyond his ears. 'Home with you. Where I belong. In my own bed – even though it has a new mattress, which you'll no doubt explain when you're ready. Aidan and I will always love each other dearly, but life isn't restful with him. It never has been. Ever. Between ourselves, he's a teeny bit of a snob. Intellectual as well as social.' It seemed as though he meant to add something else, but instead he simply stretched out a hand, patting the duvet with the other. 'You were wonderfully restrained earlier, my love. I'm surprised you didn't deck him – is that the term? Or let loose some of that wonderful vituperative language you used to employ.'

I sat beside him. 'Does *vituperative* mean very rude? Because I wanted to. But I didn't want to let you down, and most of all I didn't want to give you a heart attack.'

He pointed to a bubble pack of pills, propped up against a glass of water. 'I think they're designed to prevent that. Those or the ones I take first thing in the morning. We must devise a system to remind me to take them – I feel so well I've nearly forgotten them a couple of times already.'

'Well? How well, on a scale of one to ten?'

He knew me better than to lie. 'Probably seven, because I do still get unconscionably tired and there's still pain from where they sawed my breast bone. But overall I feel better than I've felt for months. And the medics assured me that if I do as you tell me – loved one, all that walking! More than I've done in years! – then I shall soon feel better still. I can't imagine wanting to try cycling or swimming, but I was thinking about taking up dancing again. We'd need proper classes, of course – you to learn and me to remember.'

'But you're still convalescent.'

'In a few more weeks. And there is absolutely no doubt that I can lead dear Mary down the aisle. Has she driven you mad yet, my child?'

I shook my head. 'She's kept me sane! She and Paul. I forgot to tell you she made me find a darling little fur tippet to wear over my brides-maid's dress – yes, she assumed that lovely evening dress you bought me in Paris was meant for the wedding.'

'And you said?' He looked anxious.

'Nothing. She's been too kind to risk upsetting.'
I caught him yawning.

'But I'll tell you all our other doings in the morning. Now, where are your painkillers?'

His shrug told me he neither knew nor cared. 'I don't take them any more. If things get desperate I might consider a paracetamol, but I've not had one of those for a week or more.'

Arms akimbo, I demanded, 'What did your night nurse say about that?'

'I think I'll save that tale too . . .'

Although he still got tired easily, Griff only had difficulty with one thing – pulling on his heavy support socks (like flight socks, only white) after his morning shower. Mary Walker proved a genius with them too, having had to do the same for her late husband, she said.

'Make sure you let him do what he can,' she whispered to me later. 'The more independent he can be, the more independent he will be. Of course, doing some things will hurt or tire him, but he'll know when to stop. Just let him be – and you get on earning our living! Now, I'm off to Ashford on my way home – is there anything you need doing there?'

I smacked my head: the library book on miniatures. 'Goodness knows how big a fine I'll get.'

'Petty cash!' she said gaily, seizing it.

Over the next few days, I spent more hours in my workroom working on the bonus-earning vase than I'd have thought possible. Griff assured me it was part of his treatment to carry cups of tea and coffee upstairs, and to prepare lovely light meals for us. The very fact he was in the house with me calmed me down and helped me concentrate. Between times, he selected the items for the weekend sale, walked round Bredeham a very great deal and sometimes dozed.

When he thought I'd worked long enough, he'd summon me downstairs and I'd find him dressed for whatever the weather was doing, looking for all the world like a dog ready for walkies. Off we'd go together, talking all the time because he was supposed to (something to do with walking at the right pace, which I didn't really understand), and extending what he called our constitutional by a couple of hundred yards each day. Griff was clearly a man who meant to get fit. And I was a woman who lost her spots, thank goodness.

I was half expecting Tris to try for another date – or whatever he liked to call it – but all I saw of him was a broken tail-light as he drove too fast out of the village two evenings in a row. I was happy enough to hope he had a date with another more amenable girl – with deep enough pockets to treat him.

Had Griff and Aidan not patched up their quarrel, I suppose we could have taken the caravan to the Cotswolds, but he obviously thought that staying under a baronet's roof was a much better option. I'd even have been happy for Griff to travel down in the luxury of Aidan's Mercedes, but Aidan was calling in somewhere en route, and Griff assured me that a few hours in our van wouldn't harm him.

Since it had taken me till just after nine on Thursday evening to finish the profitable vase, we couldn't set out till very early on Friday morning. The M20 was clear enough, but as usual the M25 was full of unexplained hold-ups and speed restrictions. Thank goodness for the open road of the M4. Even so, we turned into the grounds of Warebank Court only an hour before the event was open.

'Someone knew his landscape gardening,' Griff said as I gasped at the vista. Each turn of the long drive gave another stunning view, before eventually the house itself came into view, a mixture of Tudor and Elizabethan, with a quick burst of Georgian somehow pulling everything together. All in lovely Cotswold stone. At this point, as if on cue, the sun broke through. We could have been looking at the set of an upmarket movie.

Following the signs, I parked in the stable yard, behind the house itself. I made Griff wait in the van while I ferried the boxes of stock, via a dark corridor that reminded me of my father's wing at Bossingham Hall, to the hall itself. But I had to leave them there. Aidan had made it clear that, as house guests, we had certain obligations to our host, so I dashed back to the van and helped Griff out. Even as I did so, someone arrived to spirit away our cases.

Sir Richard, in his sixties with a surprisingly gentle face considering he'd spent most of his life in the army presumably killing people, was waiting in the Court's double-cube entrance hall with a crew of his Reynolds and Gainsborough-painted ancestors. He held out his hand to Griff with what looked a genuine smile of pleasure. My turn next.

I was afraid that Sir Richard and I should find a mutual loathing inspired by our mutual acquaintance, Aidan, who was standing beside him. I was rattled in any case, given how little time I had for a polite exchange of courtesies, but I did my best to smile and let Griff take centre stage, something he always did very well. In fact my main concern was that Griff'd be so busy hogging the limelight at the fair itself that he'd get over-tired. Another was that he'd feel obliged to help me on the stand.

Aidan introduced me as if I was his protégée, not Griff's, and had a tendency to bask in what he implied was my glory. I didn't mind him being nice to me in public; I just wished he'd try a little harder in private.

Sir Richard was charm itself. Even as he was inviting us all for coffee, he must have seen me glance anxiously at a spectacular long case clock. 'Ms Townend, would you prefer to take yours in the hall? I'll get someone to help you, shall I?' Somehow it wasn't the sort of question you could say no to. Suddenly, a young man he introduced as Charles, his secretary, materialized. Griff, who might as well have had *matchmaker* printed on his forehead, beamed happily as we went off together. And why not? Charles must have been a few years older than me, perhaps thirty. He was about five foot eleven, and neatly built. He had a public school accent, but I decided, since he had a lovely voice, not to hold that against him. He had the sort of face you could miss in a crowd, and a very nice smile.

I'd never met anyone who needed a secretary before, not a private person, anyway. Some time I'd ask what this involved, but not now.

I followed Charles through a gloomy and under-lit ante-room, where other dealers I didn't even have time to wave at were clearly ready for action, to the hall where we'd booked our space. He quietly and deftly unpacked our plastic boxes, leaving me to lay the contents out and to adjust the lights. I kept some items back, of course, in the hopes I'd need them to fill the gaps left by nice profitable sales. Not quite to my surprise, Charles seemed to think that returning the empty boxes to the van was part of his job description too, not to mention finding me biscuits to go with the now cold coffee. No wonder people liked to have a secretary.

Usually, I had time to whizz round all the other stalls, often picking up trade bargains. This time I'd just managed to apply a bit of lippie and greet with a wave my sort-of friend Harvey Sanditon, looking older than I remembered him but as chic as always, when the doors opened. In surged – quietly and politely, but no less ruthlessly for all that – the first wave of exceedingly well-dressed and well-spoken punters.

'And what do you think you're doing in here?' I greeted Griff, at what felt very much like lunch-time to someone who'd had breakfast at five and hadn't had time to eat Charles's bikkies. 'Don't even dream of taking over,' I added as he started tinkering with my layout. He was right to, of course. I'd not had time between sales to refill the shelves.

'My angel, when you look as fierce as this, I wouldn't even contemplate the possibility of dreaming. No, I came to press a little flesh – there are so many people here who sent me good wishes, not to mention flowers, aren't there? It would be churlish not to thank them. Heavens,' he whispered with a mock shudder, 'pray tell me that that isn't Titus Oates lurking over there.'

'He must have a stall in the ante room,' I said. The dingy space was much more the sort of location that he'd prefer, even if every last item on his stall was as genuine as I hoped and prayed it was. As I looked in his direction, he raised an eyebrow by perhaps half a centimetre. I was being summoned. In response, I opened my eyes a fraction – he'd have to wait.

None of this went unnoticed by Griff, of course. 'If you need to powder your nose, dear one, then I believe the ladies' cloakroom lies that way. Don't worry – it won't kill me to keep shop for five minutes.'

And looking at him I didn't think it would. Indeed, he'd only sat down for half a minute when his cronies came paying court. So no one would even be looking in my direction as I drifted past Titus.

'Done a spot of spring-cleaning,' he said. 'And at your dad's too. Clean as a whistle.'

'That pile of Elizabethan books,' I said accusingly.

'Like good Queen Bess herself, each one *virgo intacta*. Every page in place. Horses?'

I shook my head. 'The police don't seem very interested. Or in the fake high-fired Ruskin.'

'Just in me? Never mind, doll – the filth'll soon be privatized and run by Americans who wouldn't know their Adams from their Hepplewhite.'

'Don't you believe it: half our trade is with Americans these days, and very knowledgeable they are too.'

'Mmm. What's this about buying miniatures? Not your line.'

I didn't ask how he knew. 'Just liked one in a small lot.'

'But?' My offhand reply hadn't deceived him for a nanosecond. His eyes narrowed. 'Dodgy? Watch it, doll.' And there he was, gone.

I used the loo anyway and ran a comb through my hair – no, I'd not had time to have it cut – before heading back to Griff, who was now mysteriously armed with a glass of champagne. Charles, appearing behind him, flashed a most gorgeous smile – I had a nasty idea he thought the huge beam I'd sent Griff was meant for him. But here he was, asking about my lunch preferences – it seemed Sir Richard was worried I'd not taken a break. A sandwich? Salmon or crayfish? And a glass of champagne too? And would I mind, he asked, when a few minutes later he brought a tray loaded with goodies, if he joined me? Since there was no longer any sign of Griff, and I'd seen Harvey leave with a very glamorous Eastern rug expert, I didn't mind at all.

\* \* \*

'Well?' Griff demanded, appearing from nowhere – had he been taking lessons from Titus? – a minute after Charles had left with the empty tray. Apart from a few stallholders, most of whom were keeping an eye on their neighbours' stands for them, the hall was pretty well deserted. Either there were long queues for lunch, or the food, like the so-called snack that Charles had shared with me, was so delicious that they were all lingering over it.

'Well what?' I parried straight-faced.

'Tell!' he demanded, sitting down, ready for a long chat.

'About Charles, I suppose,' I said, with a sigh. 'Can't a girl have a secret romance these days?' I added melodramatically.

'So long as it's secret between the two of us. Does he make your heart beat faster, loved one?'

'He might do,' I conceded. 'Once I get to know him. Him as opposed to facts about him. And I don't know many of those. He went to some school he seemed to think I should know about but was too polite to seem to mind when I didn't. Millfield? Does that mean anything to you?'

'A public school renowned for sport. Heavens, Lina, several of the England cricket team went there, so you should know that.'

'So I should. But we didn't mention cricket. He just told me about uni – Durham, I think. History. The trouble is,' I confessed, 'I like his voice so much, it's hard to concentrate on what he's actually saying.'

'Did he say how he came to work for Richard?'

'Ooooh, we've dropped the Sir, have we?' I

crowed mockingly. 'Isn't he his godson or something? There's some family connection. Actually, he kept asking questions about me, which was polite of him.'

'But it's something you don't like, isn't it?'

'Talking about my past, somewhere like this?' I gestured. 'It's a good way to get sent back below stairs, where I belong, isn't it?'

'Your father wouldn't agree you belong there,' Griff said sternly. 'It's possibly the only opinion we share, of course.'

I grinned. Now wasn't the time to tell him about Pa's plans for a pad for me at his place. 'Hey, have you seen your bedroom yet?'

'I have, and very grand it is too. Whether I'll ever find it again without assistance I doubt. I meant to leave a trail of breadcrumbs, but someone would have hoovered them up straight away. What have I said?'

I pulled a face. 'A building like this must cost an arm and a leg to maintain. Yet it's not rented out for weddings or conferences or any other money-spinner except these fairs. What I've seen of the grounds suggests they're immaculate. You mentioned a swimming pool. There are staff wherever you look – not to mention Charles the secretary. Tell me, how does Sir Richard pay for it all?'

# Twenty-One

Before Griff could answer, he had another crony to greet and I another client. It was like that for the rest of the day. I was worried that he was overdoing it, but amazed when he stood up and announced it was time for his walk.

'Every day, without fail, was what I resolved, and while I'm having the time of my life I mustn't stop,' he declared. 'Besides which, I wish to explore the grounds.'

This from a man who only ever walked from A to B because he had to! Since I was cradling three thousand pounds' worth of porcelain at the time, all I could do was smile and tell him to take care of himself.

By the end of the afternoon, we'd made a decent profit. I was wondering what to do about stowing the stock back into boxes, when a posse of men in uniforms turned up. It seemed we could leave everything as it was: it was to be under the eyes of security staff all night. Someone – Sir Richard or Charles – clearly had an eye for detail. I was even more impressed when Charles appeared from nowhere to bid goodbye to the other stall-holders and invite me to afternoon tea.

And then dinner. Did posh folk never stop eating? At least I had time to shower and change before Griff and I presented ourselves for sherry before dinner. Sherry? I felt as if I'd been sucked back into the era of *Downton Abbey*. And as terrified as a tweeny would have been in those days. But I had to be part of the conversation, not an underpaid onlooker.

Fortunately, I'd been partnered (partnered! It was as formal as that!) with Charles for dinner itself. Might Pa be a conversational asset? No, I couldn't make mock of him, not to a stranger. If not him, what or who? I couldn't leave everything to Charles, who seemed to have developed a talent for small-talk at the same time as he cut his milk-teeth.

At last I recalled what Griff had said about Millfield and cricket. And won the jackpot. Suddenly, he was a young man with passions, instead of politeness, and I heard all about how he'd wanted to be a professional batsman until he'd injured his eye when a ball had somehow squeezed between his helmet and the protective visor. It was only after a few uncomplimentary comments about several well-known players that he remembered where he was and came to a sudden halt. 'But you can't be interested in all this,' he said apologetically.

But I could be and I was, and soon we were talking about matches I'd watched with Griff on TV: he'd actually been to some of them.

It was only when Griff caught my eye that I realized I should have been giving some attention to the man the other side of me, allowing Charles to speak to the woman beside him. I grimaced back. At least, thanks to him, I hadn't got the cutlery wrong as well as the etiquette.

\* \* \*

At some point on Saturday Charles popped into a heaving hall to ask me if I fancied going to the village hop after dinner. In a lowered voice, he told me he'd cleared it with Sir Richard, who thought it was an excellent idea. As did Griff, of course. There was only one problem. I had work clothes and smart clothes. Nothing remotely village hoppy. Cinderella had nothing on me. But at least I had a fairy godfather.

'If you think I can't take over from you for an hour while you nip into Cirencester or even Cheltenham you are sadly mistaken,' Griff declared. 'Two hours! Whatever you need. I'm sure that Titus will always take over if I can't cope.'

And I had a terrific time at the dance. OK, everything about it was amateurish. The hall was badly lit and the floor wasn't sprung and the sound was like a bad radio in a bathroom. But Charles and I danced pretty well non-stop till time was called at the rural witching hour of eleven. I couldn't think of anyone I knew who would have thought it was fun to rock and jive all night in the slightly fussy ballroom version of the dances that Griff had taught me – and that someone had clearly taught Charles. We had no breath to talk – and wouldn't have been able to hear each other anyway. Which, considering how much I liked his voice, was probably a good thing.

'It seems, dear one, that you may have to sing for your supper tonight,' Griff murmured over breakfast on Sunday morning. We were the first ones down and had been invited by a maid, no less, to help ourselves while she went in search of the green tea Griff had asked for. 'It's regrettable, but as host I suppose he does have some claims.'

'Like having me suss out a few items to sell on commission so he can pay his bills, like I do for Pa?' I asked ironically.

'Quite,' he said with a twinkle. 'You weren't very late last night,' he added, sounding disappointed.

'Chucking out time is eleven in the country,' I said. 'Actually, it's half-past ten in Bredeham, isn't it? So we were gay to dissipation.' I wished I could remember which book I was quoting but my brain was too furry this morning. 'What's Sir Richard want me to look at, anyway?'

'Who knows? Miniatures?' He threw me an impish glance as he helped himself to smoked salmon and capers from the sideboard. Wholemeal bread and no butter. He was taking this health business seriously, thank goodness.

'But I don't know anything about miniatures! Anything at all. I even let Mary take that book back to the library,' I wailed.

'I dare say you'll find he's got several learned tomes on the subject. But I digress. I was hoping you and Charles . . . might have established a little rapport, shall we say?'

'And how do you suppose Aidan would have reacted if that rapport had extended to a quick shag under his mate's roof? It would have confirmed all his worst opinions about me.' But I mustn't let the merest hint of wistfulness creep into my voice. 'Roll on those dance classes you were talking about.'

After all, it had been the dancing that was fun – hadn't it? Not that Charles wasn't a great person to be with. We had such good fun, though, and nice friendly sex would have been a lovely but horribly complicating way to round off the evening. If we lived closer I might even have been smitten, but I'd had more than enough of long-distance love affairs.

Business was very slow till almost lunchtime, so at last I had a chance to gossip in a very Griff-like way with some of my fellow dealers. None of them would have been in the market for Beswick horses, of whatever colour, but some of them ought to be warned about the dodgy Ruskin ware. One of them was Harvey Sanditon. Since the rug woman was busy, I drifted over to him, to be greeted with a flamboyant double-air kiss.

'Never think that my eyes have left you for a second!' he declared for all the room to hear. 'But you've been perpetually surrounded by attractive young men, dancing attendance on you and plying you with lobster patties and champagne and goodness knows what else.'

'One, and he was paid to,' I said with a theatrical sigh. I added, more quietly, 'Harvey, I wanted to thank you for the wonderful flowers you sent Griff. And the work you've put my way.'

I could hardly hear his next words: 'I meant the flowers for you, Lina – you know that, don't you? I was so afraid – for you both, of course. As for the work – I'd no idea how you'd be placed financially if anything went wrong and . . .' He took my hand and kissed it.

221

'Thank you.' The moment lengthened. He'd loved me, I didn't doubt it, and I suspected he still did. No doubt his wife suspected he still did. I continued more briskly, 'Now, I know it's only a little thing, in return for what you've done for me – but something's going on you should know about . . .' I withdrew my hand.

He listened intently, as he always did when money and his reputation were involved. At last he stroked his chin. 'I do have a terrible suspicion . . . An art potter in Totnes who was very much down on his uppers has suddenly shown every sign of increased prosperity . . . But the South East – not his patch at all . . .'

Totnes: that might explain why the guy who sold a horse to the dealer at Folkestone had a West Country accent.

The rug lady finished her transaction and headed possessively towards us. He must have noticed – in fact, turning towards me, he raised an ironic eyebrow – but he kissed my hand again. 'If ever I can help, in whatever way, you only have to ask. You know that.' And he turned and embraced the rug lady as if all he'd ever wanted to do was inhale more of her quite vicious perfume. What would his wife say when she found lingering traces of it on his clothes?

My conversations with other china dealers were altogether less dramatic, but also, in one case at least, productive. A woman from Yorkshire I'd hardly met reported seeing more white horses than usual in her area. Since she was married to a Trading Standards officer, she promised some action.

\*     \*     \*

Was I disappointed not to see Charles, who'd not put in an appearance all day, at the informal cold supper Sir Richard had arranged for Sunday evening? Probably. Particularly as I'd have liked his take on Aidan, who was inclined to hold forth. Our host himself plied us with food and drink and let him get on with it, until Aidan asked him about some detail of his military career. It seemed he'd worked as part of a UN peacekeeping force, which had seen, in his words, serious action. Griff and Aidan started to bicker about the military hijacking of the word *theatre*, which Richard didn't seem particularly interested in. Since there were only four of us at the table, starting a supplementary conversation with him might have seemed rude, but I'd have liked to know more about him – even if I wouldn't have had the cheek to ask outright how he'd come by enough cash to maintain a place like this.

Funnily enough, it was cash that he collected. Roman cash. A numismatist? Is that right? He'd led us from the dining room to what he called his snug. Snug! In a room the size of our cottage, he had drawers and drawers of coins with neatly printed cards detailing each one as if it were part of an important museum collection. In my heart, I had no doubt that that was where they should be – available for all to see. But now he was talking about the access he allowed scholars.

'Students too,' he continued with a smile. 'After all, I fell in love with coins when I was young. It's good to encourage others when you get the chance. Though I've never had a protégée like yours, Griff. Lina, may I ask you to help me?

Aidan tells me you're a dowser and can sort wheat from chaff in an instant. Are these what they seem?'

'Aidan will also have told you I know absolutely nothing about coins,' I said with a shake of the head. I might have sounded grudging, because I was. Being an expert on things you know at least something about is one thing; fishing anonymous rabbits out of unknown hats is another. I managed an apologetic smile. 'Anything I'd say would be guesswork. Which is your favourite?'

He looked taken aback, but pointed to what looked like a battered bit of tin. 'That one. I found it in my very first dig. It suddenly dawned on me as I held it in my palm that I was the first person to touch it for eighteen hundred years. Instant connection with the past. It was like an electric shock. That was how this started,' he added almost apologetically, gesturing at his vast collection.

'And it means more to you than everything else in the house, doesn't it?' I blurted.

He produced a huge smile, unembarrassed about showing unwhitened teeth and receding gums. 'You see, you are a dowser!' Locking the cabinets and then the door behind us, he led the way down a wide corridor: we must be in the Georgian part of the house now. 'I am too, in my way. I could tell that you were shocked that one man should have so many things in a private collection. But at least I enjoy them, and encourage, as you've heard, others to enjoy them too. If they were in a national museum, they'd probably simply be locked away in a safe, and never, ever be seen or handled. Such a waste. A friend of mine has a similar collection of miniatures, which I understand are another of your interests.'

Drawing to a halt beside a cabinet full of presumably undamaged *famille rose*, I said firmly, 'I might like them – I do! – but I don't know anything. Whereas I could give you chapter and verse on these—'

'Including the vase I didn't buy,' he said.

'Quite! I happened to buy a miniature the other day because I just fell in love with it. But really, truly, I'm totally ignorant about them in general. There's an intern at our local auction house who puts me to shame. Knows every painter's dates and training and chosen medium and best work. Can set a value on it at a glance. Brilliant.'

'Would he buy one just because he loves it? I think it's you my friend would welcome. Shall I make a phone call? Toby's house is pretty well on your route home. Valleys, it's called.'

We waited while he fished out his mobile and dialled. The conversation was short. At one point Richard frowned as he turned to us. 'Can you be there at nine? Excellent. Nine tomorrow morning it is, then.'

I didn't care how many people he might have killed in his past, or how he'd made his loot; in my book Sir Richard was suddenly a friend. Particularly as it was clear he wasn't including Aidan in the proposed visit.

# Twenty-Two

Valleys, not surprisingly, was tucked away where two streams joined, deep in the eastern part of the Cotswolds. I suppose its chief security lay in the fact that no chance traveller would guess it was there, the drive like just another farm track, with no entryphone or obvious security cameras.

Likewise, the house looked ordinary – large, yes, if not on the scale of Warebank Court; late Jacobean; beautifully weathered. It wouldn't have been out of place in the National Trust portfolio, but it was far too ill-kempt to be taken for a publicly-visited stately – more like my father's territory, for instance, than the trustees' chunk of Bossingham Hall land.

A man about Pa's age and with a similar disregard for the niceties of fashion, not to mention shaving, opened the door. 'Toby Byrne,' he said, shoving out a hand. 'And you must be Mr Tripp and Ms Townend.'

'Griff and Lina,' Griff suggested politely.

He nodded. 'Toby. Welcome to my poor abode.'

I wasn't so sure about that description, because now I could see some serious security – only partly concealed by the door frame was another frame, with the sort of sensors you get in some shops that scream if you try to leave with tagged goods. All the windows were locked, too, with gratings in place where there weren't original

226

shutters. Deep within the house some very large dogs bayed – and though they sounded as if they came from the same sort of electronic source as our Fido, I didn't want to go and check.

'No trouble, no trouble at all!' he declared, overriding Griff's murmured apologies. 'There's a steady stream of students and scholars – not the same thing at all – coming to look at my collection. I'm sure Richard told me, but I forget: which are you? Student? Scholar?' He nodded at each of us in turn.

'Neither,' Griff replied. 'I'm a humble antiques dealer. My young partner is an international expert on fakes and forgeries – just back from an assignment for Interpol.' Talk about over-egging the pudding. But he wouldn't want me to glower at him in public.

Toby regarded me from under eyebrows that needed reaping, not a simple trim. 'Background?'

'Not academic,' Griff put in again. 'In fact, as Richard may have told you, she's an unqualified success.'

I managed a demure stare at my shoes. But I was squirrelling away the phrase for future use – on someone like Tris when he sneered at my background.

The two men laughed at his joke. They seemed to have taken to each other. How would Aidan feel about that?

'Coffee? Before or after you've looked your fill – not during, as some young people seem to assume. Would you believe I caught one eating chocolate with one hand, a priceless specimen in the other? This way then,' he continued, assuming we'd gone for the latter option. 'Oh, just leave your coats and bag there, please. The room's kept at a constant temperature; constant humidity too.' He pointed to a bin which he locked, pocketing the key. All very efficient, no matter how informal he might be.

Toby Byrne had chosen an inner room to house his collection, and, like Sir Richard, he stored it in long, shallow flat drawers. 'Look your fill. Please use that desk and those pencils if you want to take notes. Use the spotlight sparingly. And, of course, cotton gloves at all times. Even when you're jotting – don't want you forgetting to put them back on.' He barked a laugh and stepped outside. 'I'd prefer to lock you in, which is my usual practice, but Dick assures me you're kosher. All the same, I'd rather you pressed this button when you want to come down.'

Rather to my surprise, out on the landing Griff got into a technical discussion about security systems and their pros and cons; I let them get on with it. All I wanted to see was the contents of the drawers.

They were arranged chronologically, with sections for major artists. There were subsections marked 'Attributed To' and 'School of'. Unable to resist, I headed briskly for my favourites, Hilliard and Isaac Oliver – but stopped myself. 'Attributed To' and 'School of' first. Porridge first, and only then the marmalade.

'Oh, you can have more light than this, young lady!' Toby declared, making me jump out of my skin. As he twirled the dimmer switch, he added, 'Your grandfather's gone to the lavatory. So listen for the bell – I'll need to escort him back. Now, why are you wasting your time on the Championship players when you can have Premier League? Look!' He closed the drawer I was looking in and opened the one above it. And howled like an animal in pain.

In the centre, in pride of place, was a card marked Nicholas Hilliard: unknown gentleman. Above it was a delicate gold frame. But it was empty.

The bell rang – Griff needed to be let out. But it was clear Toby wasn't going to leave me alone this time. He slammed the door on me, and I heard the bolt shoot home. And no matter how long and how hard I rang the bell, nothing happened.

I could pretend that I gave calm thought to my situation and made a rational response to it. Or I could admit to spending a few minutes howling in terror and banging on the implacable door. Gradually, it dawned on me that he wouldn't keep me there for ever – just until the police or his security people arrived.

A few minutes of the breathing my therapist had taught me brought a few more ideas. Since I was locked in with things I wanted to look at, I might as well look at them. So, drying my eyes, I did. Drawer by beautiful drawer. Each drawer responded to being opened by supplying extra light. What a good system.

And what marvellous works – and what dodgy ones – were mine alone, for a few minutes at least. No wonder people became obsessive collectors – paintings, matchboxes, whatever. I was so absorbed with them at first that I didn't register the vibration in my jeans pocket. Bloody hell, I'd still got my mobile on me! And a signal in the middle of nowhere, while we struggled for coverage at home.

The caller was Rob Sampson, of all people, with news that he'd been offered a white Beswick horse. He was inclined to chat, but since I was getting low battery warnings, I cut him off short. First I called Griff: voicemail. Who next? I was just about to call the police and ask them to arrest me, when I thought of our security system. It was a long shot, but what if Toby was his client? He'd know if there was a hidden exit button, just in case Toby ever locked himself in by accident.

By some miracle it was Geoff who was on duty. I rattled off my password. 'Is Toby Byrne, who lives at a place called Valleys, one of your clients? Quick, Geoff – running out of battery.'

'Oxfordshire?'

'Yep. I'm stuck in his strong room. Help me!'

'I shouldn't tell you this.'

'I know. Battery's almost dead.'

'Bottom drawer – those long shallow ones. Right-hand side . . .' And the voice faded.

Finding the drawer and indeed the right-hand side – hardly rocket science. But what was I looking for? There were no hidden catches, no secret buttons.

There was only one thing to do. Sit still and listen. I'd done it before, with tricky furniture that didn't want to be examined. How about I do it now to save my skin?

No ideas at all.

So I'd do the obvious thing and look at the miniatures before me. I was comfortable enough, after all, and they had their bonus light. Why not make a virtue of necessity – again?

But by now I was really worried about Griff. Why wasn't he riding to the rescue, as I knew he'd want to? What if he was having a long row with Toby – no good at all for his health? Why had I brought him to this out of the way place, miles from ambulances and hospitals and defibrillators and all the other things on which his life depended?

Bottom drawer. Right-hand side. What if I tried to lift it out? It wasn't moving. There wasn't room for even my small hands to get between the side of the drawer and the wall of the cabinet.

I tried the panic button again. Nothing.

Bottom drawer. Right-hand side . . . What if I lifted out the not very exciting miniature? Would I get an electric shock or be squirted with permanent dye, both weapons in Geoff's armoury?

Shielding myself as much as possible, and braced for the worst, I reached for the miniature and lifted. And the door opened as sweetly as a nut.

What I didn't expect was to step into the arms of two policemen.

I think they were as surprised as I was. Which gave me the chance to ask, 'Have you arrested an elderly man? Because he's just had heart surgery. Serious.'

'And I'm the Pope's grandma,' said the younger one.

'He dies on your watch, you'll look good, won't you?' I might have sounded cool, but I could hardly stop the tears. 'Please, just check he's all right. Then I'll cooperate in every way I can.' *Which may not be in the way you expect*, I added under my breath.

While the younger one, seriously overreacting, handcuffed me, the older one spoke into his radio, edging away so I couldn't hear the response.

'Police informant? You don't seem to be registered.'

This wasn't going quite as I'd hoped. I'd not been allowed to speak to Griff, who'd been taken in for questioning, apparently, but at least a spotty young man who introduced himself as an FME, whatever that might be, popped his head round the door of the interview room in which I was trapped with two hostile officers. One was the officer who'd used his radio earlier; the other was an overweight young woman in plain clothes. All three of us stared.

'A doctor,' he explained, seeing my blank face. 'Is it you who's ill?'

'No. My business partner, Griff Tripp.' I explained how recently Griff had had surgery and rattled off the names of the pills he relied on. 'You can check for yourself – they're in his overnight bag. Except that's in our van, isn't it? He's also got one of those little puffer-sprays for if his angina returns. He might just have that on him. But look at his scars if you're not convinced.'

He nodded cautiously and withdrew.

'So what's this story about being an informant?

232

Not very helpful for a young woman caught in the act of removing someone's property. Come on.'

I wouldn't be rushed. 'I'm not going to be awkward and demand to have a solicitor before I answer any of your questions. First up, I didn't say I was an informant. I said I was working with the police on a fraud issue.' Griff would hate me for using such a grey word, but maybe they'd think it sounded professional. 'And,' I continued, 'I'm about to give evidence in a major trial. I'll be in the witness box, not the dock.' My smile was bleak. It wasn't something I was looking forward to.

The woman regarded me coldly. 'Does that prove anything? Didn't Blunt work for the Queen herself while all the time betraying his country?'

Who? No point in shouting my ignorance. 'I'm not an informant, but I repeat, I am working with Kent police. At DCI Freya Webb's suggestion, I'm liaising with one of her colleagues.' Whose name I'd forgotten. Bloody stress. Often if I kept talking the missing word – or name – would come of its own accord. 'Why don't you fish my mobile out of the evidence bag it's no doubt lurking in and charge it up? You'll find the name of Carwyn Morgan. He'll tell you what I've been up to.' Like he'd tried to get me to finger Titus, and I'd refused. I ground my teeth. No, better to keep talking. 'I told him some time ago that I believe someone is engaged in fraud. They take an ordinary cheap model horse and repaint and reglaze it so that it fetches at auction ten times its worth. And maybe the same person, maybe

233

someone else, is doing the same for some art pottery called Ruskin ware. I've kept DC Morgan informed and was due to join him in a video conference alerting auction houses to the scam. He's been too busy,' I added bitterly.

'And what's a slip of a kid doing playing with the big boys?'

It was out before I could stop it. 'That's remarkably sexist language!' That got them on my side, I don't think. Since I'd lost them, I continued in what I hoped was assertive, not aggressive mode: 'I really think you and Toby Byrne have got hold of the wrong end of the stick. He panicked when he discovered one of his miniatures was missing. He trapped me in his strong room and probably locked Griff in the loo. But the painting was missing when he – not I – opened the drawer. I don't know what's become of it. I wish I did. A Hilliard.'

'You had another one in your hand when you exited the room.'

'So I did. A really poor one. I was wondering why it was in there with others that were so much better. I picked it up and the door flew open.' I'd better keep Geoff out of this, hadn't I? 'As for the Hilliard, to speed things up you can search me. Strip search me if you insist.'

'I presume that's because you handed it to your accomplice,' said the stout young woman.

'Couldn't have done. He was in the loo. And Toby had locked my bag away when I went into the house. Officers, I'm as puzzled as you are. It's like an old-fashioned locked room mystery.'

There was a tap on the door. The stout female

DC left – or exited, of course, to use their jargon. She was replaced by someone else who slid silently into the corner just behind me. It wasn't reassuring to see the uniformed guy mouthing something – it looked like a question – and getting a response I couldn't see, which he acknowledged with a flick of the eyebrows.

It was no use getting rattled, however. Not if keeping calm would get me back to Griff more quickly. I concentrated on breathing: I'd always got stressed out of my mind when I was in a situation like this. It had been better when I'd had Morris as back-up, but I'd have to be on my way to the Old Bailey before I'd ask him to vouch for me.

The stout DC returned, looking scornful. 'Seems she's got friends in high places,' she said. It was either the cat's mother she was talking about or me. She opened the door and gestured with her head. I was to leave. Exit.

The guy reunited me with my phone and bag, sneering at my scribbled signature, and escorted me at breakneck speed through to the reception area – reception indeed! Griff was there, looking grim but healthy, and so were Sir Richard and Charles. Sitting down behind the others was Toby Byrne, grey-faced and looking far worse than Griff had ever done. I went and joined him, taking his icy hands between my warm ones.

'It wasn't me who stole your Hilliard. I promise. I also promise I'll do everything I can to help you get it back.' Less dramatically, I continued, 'But you'll have to trust me. And so will the police, I'm afraid.'

He said something I didn't hear. If anyone needed the spotty young FME – it now dawned on me that the initials stood for forensic medical examiner – surely it was him. Moving away as unobtrusively as I could, I said as much to Richard, who responded prosaically by suggesting we all get some fresh air. It seemed he and Charles had arrived in his Merc – the same model as Aidan's, only more recent – and I deduced from the bewildered way Toby was looking about him that the police might have brought him along, though I couldn't see why. Come to think of it, it was more likely that Richard had picked him up en route. Our van was still at Valleys, unless the police had impounded it. So it seemed logical for us all to pile into the Merc and head there. Richard drove, and Charles, sitting beside him, made a lot of phone calls. The rest of us sat like three shocked monkeys in the rear. I couldn't be sure whether either of the others was hearing or seeing evil; none of us was speaking it.

But I was sure as hell thinking it.

# Twenty-Three

At last Sir Richard turned the car on to the Valley's track with a convincing spurt of gravel. Boy racer, eh?

Although it was Toby's house, Sir Richard took charge at once. Because the place was still swarming with purposeful-looking people in white suits, he didn't need the alarm code, so he strode straight in, herding us into what was presumably Toby's sitting room, complete with sagging sofas and a TV Noah probably chucked out of his Ark. At least it had a digibox in attendance. Longing to take a duster and hoover to the place, I drifted to the window. The curtains, rotting where the sun had faded them, smelt of age-old dirt. At one time Toby must have smoked cigars.

'Charles: see if you can find some clean cups in the tip he calls his kitchen,' Richard ordered. 'Toby: do you have any medication you should be taking? For God's sake, sit down, man. And you, Tripp.' He pointed to the sofa.

They both sat. 'Bedside table,' Toby muttered.

'What are you waiting for, Charles? Be off, man, and find it.' Charles did as he was told. 'Tripp: that medic said you were OK, but do you need a second opinion?'

'And spend hours mouldering in A and E when all I want to do, to be blunt, is go home? No, thank you, Richard.'

237

Charles reappeared, clutching a packet of tablets and a glass of water. He selected one of a nest of tables, which he moved one-handed to Toby's side. Toby popped two pills and sipped, nodding his thanks.

'Good man,' Richard declared – to Charles, I think. 'Coffee all round? Tripp?'

'Coffee would be good. Unless Lina's secreted some green tea in that bag of hers, in which case, Charles, a mug of boiling water would be better. Thanks.'

I produced a tea bag. Silently. Charles nodded, and was off.

Meanwhile, I braced myself for Richard's next utterance – to me. Except he was very much Sir Richard, now, with no hint of informality about him. I hoped he wouldn't speak to me as I expect he wanted to, or my self-control might just disappear with an almighty bang.

'And Lina – ah, Lina . . . I absolutely believe that you are completely innocent. But that was an extraordinary comment you made back at the police station. Am I wrong to deduce that you know who did take the precious miniature? And if so, why, in heavens name, did you not warn Toby – and preferably the police?'

'Because I know nothing. Nothing at all. But I feel as if I ought. Griff always says that I have a pair of antennae to pick up the vibes that objects are sending my way. Like when I said that stuff about your coins.'

'Your antennae . . .?' Sir Richard prompted, as if angry to be reminded of his moment of vulnerability.

'Are working overtime. And it feels as if they've tripled in number. People say, "I can't hear myself think," and that's how it feels in my head. I've told many people before, Sir Richard, and I dare say I'll tell a lot more. I just can't be a divvy to order.'

'That's regrettable. Because I'm sure we could all do with the benefit of your insights, and sooner rather than later.'

Charles reappeared, carrying a tray. He flashed me a kind smile. 'I wasn't sure if you wanted green tea as well, Lina, so I've brought both water and coffee.'

I pushed forward another of the nest of tables – Edwardian, a nice rosy mahogany – and instinctively reached in my jeans for a tissue to use as a duster. He passed mugs to Sir Richard and to Toby, while I dunked the tea bag for Griff. Usually, we simply shared one, but I had a feeling that such meanness – or greenness, depending on your point of view – wouldn't go down well at the moment. So I settled for the surprisingly good coffee. None of us touched the plate of biscuits Charles'd dug up from somewhere, even though it was well after our usual lunchtime.

Toby, not looking much better, said, 'I thought the system was foolproof. The alarms everywhere . . . even a watch will set off that system by the front door. I lock up bags and cases and coats.'

'But you didn't confiscate my phone,' I murmured.

'I assumed it would be in your bag,' he countered. 'I must ask you to delete any photos you took.'

'Did you send photos to anyone?' Sir Richard piled in, for all his protestations that he believed I was innocent. 'They must be deleted too, if it's not too late.'

'I didn't take any and certainly didn't transmit any. Why should I?' I asked reasonably. 'I don't know anything about miniatures, let alone deal in them. And since as far as I can see there's no way of getting the things out even if I wanted to, I wouldn't be about to steal to order, would I? Unless,' I continued, slapping my face in frustration at my rotten memory, 'I did what your thief did. Unless I left the frame behind. And it'd be easy to stow a miniature in a pocket, even in your underwear. And no, I didn't.'

Toby was blinking in disbelief. 'I never noticed. You're sure?'

'Ask him,' I said, gesturing with a thumb at a white clad and hooded SOCO – or were they privatized these days? – in the hall. 'You're entitled – it's your picture, after all.'

The polar bear lookalike tapped on the door. 'Excuse me, sir, I was wondering if you wanted to make sure that the Hilliard was all they took. There was another picture out of place, by the way, but a slot left vacant that it might just fit.'

Toby heaved himself off the sofa and headed upstairs after him.

'Why in hell did you say nothing about the frame before?' Sir Richard demanded.

'Because I'd been frogmarched off to a police station, having been forcibly detained? Because I'd been worried sick about Toby, not to mention Griff?' I went to sit down beside Griff, tucking my hand into his. Maybe this would calm me down. 'And maybe, just maybe, because I'm an antiques dealer, not a detective?'

'I don't think our cottage has ever been more inviting,' Griff declared that evening as he filled the kettle, though he leaned with one arm on the work surface to do it, and I had to pass him the teapot and cups and saucers. Easing himself into his favourite room in the whole cottage, the living room, he said with a deep sigh, 'I want to hug everything in every last corner. But not necessarily that.' He pointed to Morris's last bear, which I'd still not got round to moving up to my bedroom.

I tucked it under my arm, head first, as if it was a battering ram. It growled, faintly but definitely. I stopped dead and stared in its poor ugly face before tipping it again. This time I'd swear the growl was plaintive.

'You know we were wondering how to ensure you never forgot your pills,' I said slowly. 'Well, this chap is the answer. Every day, when you've made your bed, you can pop your tablets in his lap, and you can't get into bed until you've taken them.'

'And where do I put it then?' he asked. 'It's not sharing a bed with me, not like your Tim.' He shuddered with revulsion.

'On that pretty nursing chair that's too low for you to sit on – or, rather, to get up from,' I added unkindly. 'Or you could sell the nursing chair and buy one for you both to share. Why don't you go and discuss it with him? Him, not it,

241

please note! Yes, have a rest – even a sleep. You look absolutely done in, and who can blame you? Not just the Toby business but that hold-up on the M25.'

He nodded. 'When you empty the van, sweet one, just stack the plastic crates. I'll stow the contents tomorrow. If I'm tired, you must be exhausted.'

No point in arguing. 'Would you like supper in bed?' I'd microwave the last of those frozen healthy meals.

'Absolutely not! We have some standards, this bear and I, and eating in bed falls far beneath them. Wake me at eight, prompt.'

There was much more to do than simply stack the crates, of course, though it was clear that Mary and Paul had kept on top of the emails and prioritized those that needed a response from me or Griff. There was also a little job I had to do that Griff didn't need to know about.

'Little gold frames,' I greeted Titus.

'That miniature of yours in one, is it?'

'I never thought! But there's a Hilliard on the loose somewhere that needs one.' I explained, but kept everything nice and anonymous.

He whistled. 'Good wheeze that. Something you'd do again and again. Like at the V and A, for instance. Or the Wallace Collection. Even the Tansey Collection, if the bastard risked the same MO in Germany.'

I might have whistled too: there were times when Titus could still surprise me. 'In fact,' I concluded for him, 'anywhere there were

242

unsupervised study areas for people who appeared to be *bona fide* students or scholars. 'I'd better go and look at mine,' I said – but I said it to a dead phone.

Getting out the ready meals triggered something in my brain. Something alarming. Nothing to do with the food itself, or with Marks and Spencer. A sort of non-memory, if you like, of a time when I associated a late meal with fear. But it swam away and allowed the microwave to do its usual mundane and invaluable job.

Happily fed and watered, Griff retired to the living room. There he sat very still, his post-supper glass of red wine untouched beside him, and the miniature I'd bought at auction – was it only ten days ago? – in his lap. He put down his eyepiece. 'It's a very serious crime, faking hall-marks. Heaven knows what the penalty would be. But that's what you fear may be the case here.' He touched the miniature, or rather its frame, which, despite my fears, looked authentic enough: just a little battered, just a little scuffed.

'Would it be a worse crime than stealing a masterpiece and passing it off as a very inferior product?'

'Why should anyone do that? I fear, my love, that since my operation my thought processes have become painfully slow.'

'Because if you wanted to sell a named item – let's say a Hilliard or an Isaac Oliver – at auction or to a respectable dealer or even a respectable private collector, you'd have to have proper provenance. Detailed provenance. And somehow I don't think *Nicked from the private collection of Tobias Byrne* would quite hack it, do you?'

He sipped slowly. 'So if you sell it as part of a poor lot, you get rid of it with very few questions asked. I begin to see. And you'd bring in a reasonable amount of money – not a huge sum, but if you paid nothing for it in the first place, at least something.'

'Exactly. Actually, I think the first miniature I saw at Brian Baker's probably was a Hilliard, maybe even Toby's Hilliard, rather than a school of Isaac Oliver, despite the intern's verdict on it. But because it was one of a batch from a collection somewhere in the Midlands no one bothered to raise an eyebrow.'

'Not even Brian? He's usually most meticulous.'

'*He* is – but he'd dumped a lot of work on to his unpaid intern, remember.'

'So you think this lad's been slipshod? But ultimately it's Brian's responsibility, my love. If what you suspect is true, of course.'

'Big if. Dangerous if, possibly – because people won't like being caught out, will they?' Or even suspected. I shivered, and not just because we'd left the central heating off while we were away and the cottage was taking its time to warm up again. I'd been on the receiving end of enough little scares recently to tell me that I'd annoyed someone, even if I'd not understood who. Had that woman who'd made me take refuge in the Indian takeaway – ah, that explained my frisson of fear earlier! – really been tailing me? Puck's Mrs Fielding, perhaps?

244

It had been bad enough when I'd been on my own – what would it be like if I had Griff to worry about?

Pushing the fear to the back of my mind, I said tentatively, 'Do you think, after all he's been through today, Toby would still send me a copy of the Hilliard he's lost? Because I'd recognize it. I know, I know: I should have thought of this when we were with him.'

'But at least you've thought of it now. Shall I phone Richard and ask for his help? It might be better if he suggested it to Toby.'

Passing him the phone and his wallet, I nodded gloomily. 'If I'm right, it'll mean no end of trouble for Brian and Helen. And for Tris. Police – no way out of it.'

'And you'd rather nothing was done? That you didn't keep your promise to Toby? Who looked to me, incidentally, as though he was in very poor health.'

'So I've got to restore Toby's picture to him before he dies? Oh, Griff. That's under the belt!'

He had the grace to blush, and applied himself to the phone. I worried a hangnail while he did so. If it was the picture I'd seen, then the trail leading to the new buyer, who'd no doubt bought it in good faith and would be dead miffed to lose it, should be easy enough to follow.

'Richard will phone Toby for you. And he sends his profound apologies for being what he calls abrupt with you earlier today. Oh!' He picked up second ring. 'Oh. Oh dear. Thank you very much. We'll hope to hear from you soon, Richard.' He looked at me. 'There's no reply

245

from either of Toby's phones. Richard's going round there now.'

For Richard, read Charles, no doubt.

Eventually, I made Griff go to bed, with his Kindle and Tablet Bear for company. I busied myself with the computer, supposedly sorting the business wheat from the advertising chaff.

It must have been nearly midnight when the phone actually rang. Charles. To say he thought he'd got to Toby in time. The paramedics had revived him, and he was now in intensive care. Charles would wait at the hospital until there was hard news. Then he said something odd: 'I wish it hadn't ended this way, Lina.'

That was all. He'd cut the call before I could ask him what *it* was.

# Twenty-Four

There was no point in hanging about, so I headed off to bed. Griff was dozing over another Georgette Heyer paperback, always his comfort food when he was stressed. The bear sat beside him, an empty bubble in the pack of tablets. One of them at least had had some medication.

Next morning, before I could change my mind or get diverted, I texted Carwyn Morgan. *Huge big SOS. Really need help.*

Understatement it was not, but surely that would do it?

Mary – no Paul, of course, since Tuesday was golf day – arrived before Griff was awake, let alone up. I was terrified and kept popping my head round the door. Was he going to die in his sleep? He'd been under so much stress. But now I was under some too. The phone rang with news from Richard – who'd no doubt slept in his own comfortable bed while Charles had hung around at the hospital – that Toby still hadn't regained consciousness, though the medics insisted he was stable. Perhaps this wasn't news to tell Griff.

By eight I was ready to shake Griff awake, but the front doorbell, rung loud and hard, might have saved me the trouble. It was Carwyn Morgan, waving at the security camera. He was flourishing a brown paper bag. Bless him, he'd only brought croissants, which were still warm.

Perhaps it was the smell of these, or perhaps the sound of an attractive young voice, that brought Griff, splendid in his most theatrical dressing-gown, downstairs. Despite what he'd said yesterday, he helped himself to coffee and swept back up to his room; soon we heard the shower running and his accurate but now reedy tenor treating us to gems from the opera.

'Before breakfast,' I said, which could have applied to Carwyn's arrival or Don Jose's aria from *Carmen*.

'SOS sounded serious,' Carwyn said with an encouraging smile. He sat opposite me at the kitchen table, dolloping Griff's best strawberry jam on the side of his plate but declining butter. He grinned to see me pour his coffee into an eighteenth century handless can, but didn't demand a mug.

'It was meant to. And this time it's not problematic horses but a stolen miniature.' I explained as succinctly as I could. 'The sad thing is I have a horrible feeling that a miniature I bought as one of a lot the other day might be stolen too.' I took a deep breath. 'At one point you tried to get me to grass up my friend Titus Oates. I insisted he was on the right side of the law. In fact it was he who warned me that someone was making gold frames and asked me to alert DCI Webb, but . . .' I gave an extravagant shrug. They'd not had the time or the inclination to pursue it, had they? 'I wouldn't mind betting that this miniature was removed from its frame at the museum or wherever it ought to be and rehoused, as it were.'

'Surely not a museum! Their security—'

'Is probably no better than Toby Byrne's, which is really excellent. After all, metal and tag detecting equipment isn't designed to pick up vellum.'

'But someone would notice a gap.'

'There's so much art work of all sorts in museums and galleries that never sees the light of day that it's possible that store number three, or whatever, is never opened except by request. And don't forget that guy who made quite a good living by filleting bits out of rare books and selling them at auction – it was a very long time before they caught up with him.'

'It was.' He nodded sadly. 'And all those beautiful books ruined . . .' Was he fishing for information about Pa and Titus? If so, all he got was another can of coffee. 'May I see this miniature of yours?'

'Maybe in my workroom?' I mimed sticky fingers. 'Another of your croissants first?'

'What about saving them for Griff?'

'Dear boy,' Griff declared from the doorway, making us both jump, 'since my life-saving surgery I find I have to treat life like one long Lent. So it will be wholemeal toast and Benecol spread for me.'

I pulled a face. 'Right out of bread.'

'So baking will be my first task this morning. In the meantime, perhaps just one. Thank you, Carwyn. But no jam and no butter, thank you. Any news of Toby Byrne?' he flashed at me.

'Unconscious but stable.' I turned to Carwyn. 'The trouble is, while Toby is ill, he can't supply you with a list of the scholars and students who had access to his collection. He can't supply us with a copy of the one that was stolen either.'

'A neat segue from *you* to *us*,' Carwyn said with a dry grin.

'If my miniature is stolen property it gets very personal.'

'I don't think I've ever been so close to anything so lovely,' Carwyn breathed, cupping the miniature – which he, too, had picked out instantly from the others – in those gorgeous hands and tilting it backwards and forwards under the strong lights. He reached to switch them off. 'These things should never be exposed to high light levels, should they?'

'Not for long, at least. Any idea who the subject might be?'

'He's got a very strong look of Charles the Second, hasn't he?' He looked me straight in the eye. 'Do you want me to take this into protective custody, as it were? Just in case?'

'Just in case it gets nicked or just in case it was nicked?'

Now my treasure, along with its companions, was out of the house, I actually felt happier. With Griff producing delectable smells, and popping into the shop to gossip with Mary, I could put my head down to my restoration work without having to worry. Possibly. At least when I came up for air it was to feel relieved that at last other

250

people were taking my worries seriously, with two police forces involved. Clearly, Toby had been robbed; clearly, they no longer suspected me. It would be their job, not mine, to hurtle round museums and auction houses checking records, and their unpleasant task, not mine, to break it to people who thought they'd got a bargain that they'd probably fallen in love with someone else's property. Huge plus.

Possibly.

Unless I put it about on Twitter and Facebook that I was no longer hunting thieves and fraudsters, then no one would know. In any case, since a lot of criminals were pretty bright, even Pa (on a good day), it wasn't impossible that one or two of them would think back on conversations with me and do the right sums. I sighed. In any case – thinking about the phone call that had indirectly got me out of Toby's strongroom – the police weren't necessarily going to be on the trail of the white horse forgers. I'd best phone Rob Sampson to apologize for not getting back to him earlier, hadn't I?

'You'd better come and see what you've done,' he said. And ended the call.

Carwyn was there before me, and so were several other officers. After all, Rob's emporium was within spitting distance of his local police station. So far all the discussion was outside, in the narrow street, while the SOCOs hunted round inside. They couldn't make out why a total stranger should turn up and demand to speak to the owner of what was now a completely trashed

251

shop. The only thing that didn't seem to have been broken was the white Beswick horse with the damaged hoof. Rob caught my eye imploringly: what he wanted me to do was all too clear. Could I fix it for him? And say nothing?

I could. Whether I would . . .

Rob must have taken my silence as a negative. He pointed at me. 'It's her fault. She said there were dodgy Beswick horses in circulation. So when I was offered one, knock-down price, I said no. And told them why. They seemed to take it on the chin, but I came back this morning and found this.' He gestured at the shards around him. He looked me in the eye. 'Why didn't you keep your fucking trap shut? I'd have offered them a couple of hundred, take it or leave it, and that would have been that.'

Carwyn said gently, 'It wouldn't, you know. Would it?'

'You think everything I'm offered—' He shut up abruptly. Sensibly, if he'd been going to add that he'd not just been offered suspect items, but had bought them and gone on to sell them.

'My colleagues here will do all they can to discover the people who did this,' said Carwyn. 'Ashford's got plenty of CCTV, and they'll know who to look for. The problem is, the people that came with the baseball bats or whatever may not be the ones who tried to sell you the horse. I'd like you to tell me all about them – unless you've got a security system yourself that might have taken some helpful shots?'

He shook his head despondently. 'Shop wasn't making enough to keep it up, was it? And then the insurance people upped the rates . . .' He spread his hands.

So he wasn't covered. I was almost in tears. And then I thought of what even dear, kind Griff had said about him – that he was ripping off old people when he knocked at their doors and offered to get rid of the rubbish in their attics. Rubbish! Personal treasures, not worth a mint but far more than the peanuts he offered. And I'd bet that decent white horse over there that the best stuff never ended in this tatty shop, but got sold on to other unscrupulous dealers. Or even, of course, to people like Griff and me. To think I'd once cleaned his windows!

'I've got some mugshots on my computer,' Carwyn continued. 'Would you like to come along to the police station and we'll have a look at them? I'm sure they'll find us a room and you a cup of tea. And they'll be able to give you the name of professionals who'll clear up this mess in no time.'

'At a price, no doubt,' Rob said bitterly. 'No, I'll have to sort this out myself.' He looked hard at me. Did he expect me to get busy with a brush and spade?

'Tell you what,' I heard myself saying, 'if you like, I could repair that white horse. My usual terms,' I added firmly, holding his eye. 'In other words,' I added to Carwyn, 'that all restoration is declared to the purchaser. In writing. May I have a word before you go?'

He raised his eyebrows but stepped away from the knot of other officers.

All the same I dropped my voice. 'I did mention

this horse business to a fellow dealer in Yorkshire, whose husband's a Trading Standards officer, so they might be worth contacting. And one of my colleagues says that there's an art potter in Totnes who's suddenly flush, after years on his uppers. As he said, Totnes is a long way from Kent . . .'

'If you were in his position, would you foul your own nest? Or stable?' he added with a smile to die for.

'No. But there's such a rash of them round here. And don't forget the guys from Hastings were dead keen to get their horse back.'

'I'll get straight on to that. Which shop?'

'Don't know. And Paul's playing golf today. This is his mobile number.'

Copying it, he continued, 'Did your Devon contact give you a name?'

'No. But there can't be all that many potters in Totnes, can there?'

'You've got to be joking! Tap and they'll come out of the woodwork.' He snorted. 'Still, that'll be Devon and Cornwall's problem, not ours. And their budget,' he added, with another wonderful grin. More seriously he added, 'How reliable is your colleague?'

'At least as reliable as Titus,' I said, turning on my heel and walking briskly away.

I'd got to the car park before he caught me up.

'Look, Lina, you must know we've had an eye on Titus for some time. But I have to tell you the word is he's gone straight.'

'Gone?'

'And the word also is that he's done this for you. Are you – are you seeing him?'

For a moment I couldn't speak – I just stared, goggle-eyed. 'Me? Titus?' I managed. 'He's – he's—' Hell, I nearly said he was a career criminal. 'He's old enough to be my father.'

Mistake. I got a very old-fashioned look at the word *father*. But I mustn't give him an inkling that I knew what he was on about. Change the subject!

I managed a rueful smile. 'As is the Devon colleague I mentioned. And actually I did have the hots for him at one time.'

'And?'

This didn't seem to be a conversation about cops and robbers any more. 'And then I found out he was married. Shame. Horrible wife. But he'd got kids and—' I shrugged. 'You don't need his name, Carwyn, you really don't. They're still together, and a policeman turning up on their doorstep with a hot tip from me . . .'

'Isn't going to improve their domestic harmony,' he concluded. 'But if Devon and Cornwall can't find this potter, you may have to tell me eventually. I liked the way you made that thieving bugger up there writhe,' he said as I unlocked the car. 'Written evidence isn't exactly his thing, is it? You know what, if he hadn't claimed he had no insurance I'd have put good money on him having wrecked that shop himself.'

'You know what? So would I. And if I were you I'd get your mates on to all the insurance companies you can think of. Just in case.'

The conversation ended with a smile that started as conspiratorial and ended simply friendly.

I drove home via Sainsbury's – where I found

bedlinen, but no curtains, plus food and champagne – and then via Bossingham. Pa was pretty subdued, which didn't surprise me. Bored to the back teeth, I suspected, now the work for Titus had dried up.

'It's for the best,' I said. 'You know exactly what I mean, so don't argue. And don't even dream of looking for another dealer, because the moment you do I'll strip these new sheets off the bed and make the biggest bonfire you've ever seen. With any fakery on top. OK?'

'OK.' He didn't sound particularly remorseful. 'Fancy a drop of this shampoo, old thing?'

# Twenty-Five

Griff claimed to be amused by Pa's response, but I knew he was saddened that I'd taken Pa's offer of overnight accommodation seriously enough to help prepare a bedroom, even though I insisted I'd only ever use it if Pa himself was ill. Oh, and when Titus had organized the mattress.

'It was either that or sneak into the main part of the house and have my sleeping habits exposed to the world,' I said lightly – and truthfully – as we ate a very late lunch. 'Any news of Toby? This bread is some of your best ever.'

Griff shook his head. 'Only if no change is news. Richard tells me that he doesn't know of any family who should be notified.'

'You mean that Charles hasn't been able to run them to earth yet. What a weird job for a young man,' I said. 'Or for a young woman, come to think of it. Why should he put up with being at someone's beck and call twenty-four seven? He's not even spoken to politely.'

'If the alternative is the dole-queue . . . I should imagine, of course, that he earns a decent amount.'

'I should hope he does – but I bet a lot of it comes in kind, not cash. "Charles, dear boy, finish the smoked salmon and champagne."' Where was his spine? Putting up with such treatment!

'Was I wrong to think you quite liked him? Charles, I mean?'

257

'I might have done. But I liked the outward things, if you see what I mean. Like the fact he's a good dancer – jives like the guy in *Dirty Dancing*.' We shared a giggle. 'Not that he looks much like him, of course – more like a cricket captain. Pity about his eyesight. Perhaps that's why he ended up where he did. Though I'd have thought that with his voice he ought to become a vicar.'

'I fancy you need more than a wonderful pulpit manner to be ordained.' He smiled: he was prepared to let the matter drop. 'Speaking of which, any news of poor Freya yet? No? You have been a little too busy to enquire, perhaps. Though you could have dropped in at the rectory while you were visiting your father.' For *while* read *instead*.

To oblige him, I texted Robin immediately, and for good measure texted Freya too; even if hospital regulations forbade the use of mobile technology, I wouldn't mind betting she'd ignore them.

As he cleared the plates, Griff asked, 'If you're not keen on Charles, which palpably you're not, what are your feelings about that delectable young Welshman?'

'Carwyn?' Who hadn't come back to me with news about the people who'd wrecked the emporium, despite what I'd thought was tacit agreement. Meanwhile Griff, who missed little, was waiting. 'But . . . I thought he was gay,' I admitted.

'Campish, sweet one. But I'd say he only dances at your end of the ballroom. Preferably with you, I'd have thought?'

258

'Really? You don't mean—' Occasionally, Griff still managed to make me blush. 'I just thought he was a really nice guy. But – and it's a big, huge, giant, enormous *but* – he's a policeman. And after Morris I really do not do policemen.' I took a deep breath. 'It's all about trust, isn't it? Pa and Titus: I hate lying about what they get – correction, *got* – up to. But I'd never grass them up deliberately, and I'm always on edge that I might do it accidentally.'

'And though you might ditch Titus – not that for a minute I'm suggesting you do, loathe him though I may – you can't ditch your father. I quite understand. Any more,' he added with a rueful grin, 'than I could ditch Aidan. Who hasn't been in touch since we got home. I hope he's all right.'

I thought of that beautiful house and its wonderful contents, including the miniatures, of course. 'So do I.' Flipping the phone across to him, I said, 'Your turn to text.'

By supper time there'd been no response to any of the texts, and there was no denying that Griff was quite agitated. He even tried the old-fashioned phone, leaving a message, but that made matters rather worse. I looked at the rain trickling down the windows and listened to the howl of the wind in the chimneys, but had to say it anyway: 'When we've eaten, do you want me to nip across to Tenterden to see if everything's OK? And no, you can't come with me.'

'Yes, I can, and yes, I shall. Even if I do no more than sit in the car with the mobile phone ready to summon the cavalry.'

'That's all you do – promise?' I slapped the side of my head. 'Griff, Aidan uses the same security firm as us! If Geoff's on duty he should be able to tell us if everything's OK. And if it isn't, he'd be the first to know.'

Griff smiled. 'He would indeed. Whether he'd tell you anything—'

'How do you think I got out of Toby's strong room?' I asked, touching the side of my nose.

But it was someone I didn't know who was on duty, and hearing his voice I decided not to push my luck. Even a hint of what Geoff had done could get him the sack, so I invented a trivial enquiry – actually, not so trivial, since I asked if the people his colleagues had regularly seen lurking near our premises were anywhere around. The answer was the sharp negative of a man who rightly suspected his valuable time was being wasted.

Thank God I'd insisted on fog-lights when we'd bought the car. Not that it was foggy, but it was raining so hard that it was difficult to tell where the road ended and the verges began. Half the time the wipers were on maximum speed. I didn't dare switch on the radio in case it distracted me, though I know Griff would have liked some music to think about. In fact, it wasn't long before he started *King Lear*, the bits about it being a naughty night to swim in and hurricanoes blowing.

Aidan's house looked occupied: lights were on in several rooms, and they went on and off as if someone was moving around. That might have been as a result of his security system, of course, but there were two cars parked on his drive, one his own, and the other, further from the security light, vaguely familiar. However, this weather didn't invite car inspections. No one responded when I pressed the buzzer to ask for the gates to be opened, even when I smiled and waved at the cameras so he'd know it wasn't an invading army waiting to rampage.

When I turned to Griff with a shrug of frustration, I found him already halfway out of the car. Without a blink he tapped in the code, and we were in. Or could have been. Instead, I manoeuvred the Fiesta so that it lay across the gates; no one could drive in or out. Shooing Griff back in, I dashed to the front door and put my thumb on the doorbell, which rang loud and long enough to waken the dead, thus confirming, of course, Aidan's belief that I was an inferior form of life with no manners. I was sure he'd tell me again when he flung open the door.

But it wasn't Aidan who responded in fury to the bell. It was Charles. He was wearing one of Aidan's dressing-gowns, which, given the difference in leg-length, revealed a very great deal of him.

'What the hell are you doing here?' he demanded.

'I could ask you the same,' I said mildly, hoping the effort not to choke with fury – or with laughter – wouldn't show. To think I'd been worried that Carwyn might be gay, and all the time someone I did once fancy, for all I'd denied to it to Griff, was here with Aidan. I'd never noticed any attraction between them at Richard's. Never.

'I'm here as Aidan's guest. What do you think you're doing?' As I stepped towards me he gave me a violent shove in the chest.

'Just stepping out of the rain. Lovely porch, isn't it, but not very effective when the wind's in this direction. Charles, I really need to speak to Aidan – you don't suppose I'd come out on a night like this if it really wasn't necessary, do you?'

'I'm afraid he's tied up at the moment,' he said with an unbecoming smirk, just to make sure I got the innuendo, which didn't sound any better in that lovely voice of his.

'I'll bet he is. I've heard the longer you're kept in suspense, as it were, the greater the sexual intensity.' His smirk deepened. 'So my guess is that he's been – er – tied up for some time while you've been casing the joint.'

'How dare you! You make me sound like a common thief.'

'Do I? I'm sorry. Aidan says I always betray my origins when I use cant expressions. I should have said "while you've been going from room to room looking at the wonderful objets d'art that Aidan has on display". I'm sure you haven't nicked anything – yet – because to be quite honest you really don't have anywhere to conceal anything, do you? Anything at all.' I permitted myself to lower my eyes a little and risked a sarcastic giggle – it was better than letting him realise how angry and upset I was. It was quite clear that he was not pleased to see me. At all. 'Charles, why don't you go and free Aidan, just so I can see he's all right? It'd be so embarrassing for him if Griff found him. Humiliating. Upsetting for Griff, too, which wouldn't be good for his heart. They've been together for over twenty years,' I added truthfully.

'Just get out.'

'Oh, I think not,' Griff declared, in a voice remarkably like Brian Blessed's – deep, loud, carrying. A foghorn of a voice. A very actorly voice. And Aidan would have heard it whichever room he was trapped in.

'For God's sake, just go and set the man free,' I hissed. 'Don't be so damned malicious! Or,' I added in the tone and accent I'd used as a no-hope kid in care, 'I'll forget that Griff's dragged me up from the gutter and remember how I used to make people do things they didn't want. Right?'

Right. With a huge sneer that didn't quite disguise a sudden rush of fear at the way the girl he'd taken dancing had metamorphosed into a particularly vicious worm, he turned as if to do as he was told. Griff was an inch behind him to make sure he did. Griff! What the hell did he think he was doing?

I set off hell for leather after him, but he didn't follow Charles into Aidan's room. What a dear, tactful man. I didn't go in either, but I did call out: 'Aidan, as soon as you're decent, come out, please.'

I didn't have to wait long. Eyes ablaze with fury, though I wasn't sure whom it was directed at – even himself, perhaps – he exploded on to the landing, sporting one of his more splendid dressing-gowns. 'What the hell do you think you're doing here?'

263

With an insolent shrug, I pulled my most irri-tating face. 'Several guesses, Aidan?' And then I remembered he was not just Griff's lover, but also his friend. If Griff cared enough to maintain the relationship, I would have to as well. 'Why don't I make a cup of tea and explain?'

With Aidan fully dressed, but Charles still in the skimpy robe, I went into a bizarre sort of hostess-mode, even though I was wondering what – and where – the hell Griff had got to. The kitchen was the room Aidan was least at home in, so I kept us there, putting the mugs of tea or coffee and a plate of biscuits – Griff's home-made ones, as it happened – on the expensive and rarely used table. The fact that we were in what had become more my territory than his unsettled Aidan even further. In fact, I was getting worried about him: he might be younger than Griff but he hadn't had me exercising him and looking after his diet, as Griff had. So a heart attack or even a stroke wasn't impossible.

'Aidan, I'm only here because Griff was worried about you. You didn't respond to his texts or answer either of your phones. Of course he was worried – he was afraid you'd be like Toby, unconscious, maybe dying. Do you think I'd have brought him out on a night like this if I hadn't thought he was right to worry? Neither of us was spying on you, or wanted to catch you with your trousers down.' Oh dear: I really hadn't meant to say that. I raised an apologetic hand, like tennis players when an awkward bounce of the net means they've scored a point they didn't deserve. 'Seriously, this is just a matter for the two of you to sort out.'

'So why are you still here? Why didn't you just go when you . . . when you realized . . . Heavens, did you think Charles was a burglar or something?'

This time I did manage to keep my face straight – yes, and serious too. 'Not a burglar. Because you'd invited him in.'

'Are you implying that he was trying to rob me?' he squeaked.

'Why not ask him? Yes, why not? Or check the good miniatures, not the ones in Griff's room. The ones you showed me.'

'This is outrageous and preposterous,' Aidan declared.

Still no Griff.

Charles leapt in. 'Of course it is. You warned me about her, remember?'

Did he indeed? I wondered when. Before or after we'd boogied the night away? And there was I thinking he fancied me and it was only my common sense and decency that had kept him out of my bed. Perhaps I should have said that aloud. Instead I said mildly, 'It would cost you nothing to check.'

'Of course it wouldn't,' Charles said. But his face seemed stiffer than usual, and his voice less resonant. What was he up to? 'And don't forget to check all the cupboards and in the safe.'

'Why don't you start with the safe,' I agreed, 'while Charles and I stay here? That way neither of us gets to see the combination. And I'll bet

265

that if you've got a masterpiece of a miniature, that's where it will be.'

Aidan stared furiously at me, but then got up and left us alone in the kitchen. I didn't feel it necessary to start a conversation. Neither did Charles, ruminating on the implications of what I'd said.

It was like being in a dentist's waiting room. The elegant kitchen clock, about the only time-piece in the house that wasn't two hundred years old, ticked irritatingly away: perhaps if he changed it he'd spend more time in the kitchen. Aidan was away so long that I thought he must have run into Griff. In fact he must have been checking the whole house, because he came back with a vicious smile on his face. 'Everything is where it should be. Now, get out of my house before I recommend that Charles takes legal action against you for unlawful detention and defamation.'

'And there I thought it was you that was unlaw-fully detained,' I said affably. 'I'd love to leave your house, but I can't without Griff, can I? Did you find him?'

'You can wait in the car.'

'Don't worry – I will.'

# Twenty-Six

Griff was in the passenger seat of the car, shaking. Shock? What should I do? Go back and, cramming humble pie down my throat, ask Aidan to call his tame doctor? But even as I dragged open the passenger door I realized that he was convulsed with laughter.

'Get in and let me shut the door, my love! We're both getting soaked!'

I didn't argue. He slammed the door and I ran. Collapsing in the driver's seat I gasped, 'Tell!'

'May I suggest you move the car first? In fact, I'd further suggest you put a good deal of road between us and Tenterden. You might even want to go the back way, if you can see well enough.'

'Via Leeds? Hell's bells. The Ashford road's bad enough . . .' But I wanted him to talk.

The wretched man kept mum until we were clear of the town, though still lapsing into occasional giggles.

'My darling, you are a heroine,' he said at last. 'That appalling drive, then bearding two monsters in one den. And now – can it actually be raining harder?'

'Probably. So what were you up to?'

'Listening in, some of the time. But when Aidan went walkabout, I beat a judicious retreat. Not empty handed.' He was off again, his chortles almost drowning the slap of the wipers.

'You didn't nick his best silver! No, you couldn't have done. He'd have noticed.'

'I did better. I nicked Charles's clothes. No, they're not in the car; you're not an accessory after the fact. You know that holly hedge, designed to keep would-be plunderers at bay? The one with particularly sharp points? That's where poor Charles will find his clothes. It's likely he won't be able to wear them again. I know, I know . . . But hell hath no fury like an old queen scorned. And in years to come I dare say Aidan and I will laugh about it.'

I gaped. If anyone had betrayed me like that I'd never want to see him again.

'My loved one, I can tell you're appalled. But neither of us would win medals for fidelity. We've remained friends because – well, who knows why?'

'You can forgive him – for that?'

'Without wishing to usurp dear Robin – and unless I'm much mistaken we still haven't heard from him – forgiveness is an excellent idea. Boiling with resentment hurts you more than it hurts the person you've got a grudge against – who probably doesn't know, anyway. My late and pretty much unlamented father – who died well into his nineties – spent his twilight years reliving all the battles he'd had during his long and colourful life. And this time round he won them all. By then his opponents had been dead thirty or forty years, of course. But he still got his blood pressure spiking away to horrific heights because of those real or imagined slights. Foolish old man. And, to be profoundly serious, my love, when I was awaiting my operation, I was getting flashbacks of all the awful things I'd ever done and deeply regretting them. And asking forgiveness. In fact, while I was waiting for the anaesthetic to kick in, I was reciting the Lord's Prayer. I got as far as "forgive us our trespasses as we forgive those who trespass against us". I had to wait till I woke up to finish it.' He chuckled. 'But, dear one, I'm no saint, and I did so enjoy tucking those Armani underpants into the hedge.'

Late as it was when we got back, I insisted he had a long hot bath: being soaked to the skin was bad enough, but having to sit in wet clothes was worse. He also had a medicinal glass of red wine, though I was anxious about mixing alcohol and his pills. I checked all the instructions and there was no explicit warning, so I let him have his own way.

'So long as you promise me you'll oversleep tomorrow,' I said threateningly, and headed to bed myself. My heart ached a little too – until I finally admitted that it was bruised pride, not unrequited love, it was suffering from. At least there was a text from Carwyn: progress was being made, he said, and he'd give me more info in the morning.

But he didn't, of course.

At least, apparently none the worse for his soaking, Griff insisted on taking the Internet business helm. He waved aside my half-hearted protests, saying truthfully that I had more than enough to do in my workroom. Apart from tea breaks and a lovely salad lunch – Griff at his best with smoked salmon, avocado pear and mixed leaves, and a large spoonful of capers, not to mention his special dressing and wholemeal bread – I worked without interruption, after leaving further messages for Freya and Robin. There was nothing else to worry about, after all, so long as I didn't think about Carwyn and his broken promise. I couldn't do anything about Toby Byrne, who was still unconscious, according to Richard, who'd evidently managed to contact the hospital without Charles's assistance; I needn't do anything about the dratted white horses, because I'd dumped them on Yorkshire Trading Standards and also because Carwyn would be getting his south-western colleagues to check out Totnes, and someone would be knocking on the door of the shop in Hastings Paul had identified; I needn't do anything about stolen miniatures, since the Thames Valley police were deeply involved with them too. Most of all, I found I needed to be worrying less and less about Griff. He really seemed perkier than he'd been for months – even perkier than before he'd admitted to being less than well.

'Lina! Come quickly!'

I was on my feet and down those stairs like a shot. It was only when I saw the phone in his hand and the smile on his face to realize I didn't need to panic.

'Robin!' he mouthed, handing it over.

'It's a girl, Lina,' Robin was saying. 'A beautiful girl. Perfect.'

'And Freya?'

'Fine. Now. They were both poorly to start with. Both in Intensive Care for a while – though they let Imogen stay with her in an incubator. Which is why I've not been in touch. But she's fine now. They both are. Oh, Freya wants a word.'

I could hear the phone being dropped and picked up. In the background were various muffled gurgles.

'Lina? I really could do with a hamper. You know how rubbish Robin is with food. No, hang on – take it to the rectory. Not here. They say I should be able to go home later this week. As soon as Imogen's well enough. Got it?'

'Got it,' I said.

'Good. Are you shagging Carwyn yet? Or are you still hanging out for bloody Morris?'

'I'll tell you everything when I see you,' I promised, fingers crossed tightly behind my back. On the other hand, she'd certainly enjoy the story of the confiscated underpants. 'In the meantime, all our love. Griff's putting the champagne on ice right now.'

'So long as he saves some for me . . .'

There was a muffled noise and Robin chimed in: 'No booze – she's breastfeeding.'

'And how long will she keep that up?' I asked Griff as the call ended. 'Freya's not really one for patience, is she?'

'Motherhood has been known to change a woman.'

'I still reckon Robin'll be mother. Well, the difference between their salaries for a start . . .'

\* \* \*

271

After *Today*, Griff's favourite news programme was *PM*. Feet up, he was listening to it when someone rang the front doorbell. Since I was involved with glue and paint, I let him open it, though I admit I called down to remind him to check who the visitor might be. He grumbled loudly that of course he would. Then I heard voices: whoever it was had been admitted. Brian and Helen? What were they doing here?

Though they were both seated and clutching cups of tea by the time I'd cleaned up and made myself respectable, I thought they looked embarrassed. But Griff kept general chatter going for a few minutes, before excusing himself to check something in the kitchen.

Helen led. 'We're after a favour, Lina. I know you don't do your divvying to order, but we . . . we really need some help. There's a lot riding on it. Tris's future, really.'

I must have looked aghast.

'No, he's not stolen anything, nothing like that. But it seems there's a chance of him getting what he insists on calling a proper job, and he needs a reference.'

'And you're not happy giving it?' I asked with a frown.

'Not exactly. Yes, a bit doubtful, I suppose.'

'But he's immensely knowledgeable. I mean, he knows far more than many dealers I know. Far more than me. What's the problem?'

They looked at each other. Brian said, 'We don't want to give him a bad reference without a reason. And to give him no reference at all – well, that'd scupper any chance he might have.'

272

'But you've not told me why you can't give him a good one,' I pointed out. 'I'd really hate to say the wrong thing. The trouble is, as Helen knows, he had a bit of a thing for me, and . . . it didn't end well. If he ever found out I'd had a hand in writing it, he'd go berserk. Rightly.'

Helen snapped her fingers and looked triumphant.

'He won't. But it's interesting,' Brian said, 'that you imply he's got a temper. He has. Not with us, not often, but with people he speaks to on the phone. His friends, not our clients. Which maybe doesn't count.'

Griff reappeared. 'It seems to me, Brian, if I might join you, that you like and would recommend this young man, but both of the women have – implied – reservations. What have you said to the young man?'

'Nothing yet.'

'And do you have any doubts of his honesty? Because if so I don't know why you're asking Lina about his reference.'

Brian and Helen exchanged another look. 'Actually, the police aren't happy with the way he checked the provenance of a couple of batches of miniatures we sold,' Helen said. 'Which reflects badly on us, of course.'

As did the fact they were paying him zilch.

I made rewinding gestures. 'The police have been round?'

'Didn't they tell you? Oh, yes. They wanted chapter and verse on every single one. Seems Tris had verified both the seller's details and the rest of the provenance. On both lots.'

273

'Yes, the Midlands . . . But surely someone else must have checked the payment details?'

'All valid as far as our accounts department were concerned. The payment was made and went through. All fine and dandy. One was something Estate, near Alcester. Can't recall the exact name. Or the one in Worcestershire. But there's something worrying the police, no doubt about it. They wanted to know who'd bought the lots so they can examine each and every item in them.' She added the question my headmistresses had always asked me when something bad had happened: 'What do you know about this, Lina?'

Too much by far? 'I know at least one valuable miniature has gone astray. From a private collection. Thames Valley police were on to it – thought I might have nicked it. I hadn't. But someone has. Perhaps they're checking all batches of miniatures sold recently.'

'All batches?' Brian repeated. 'Not just ours?'

'My theory would be,' I said, 'that the stolen item is being sold with a group of others, so it goes under the auctioneer's radar. You see, I bought a really good miniature the other week, but it was tucked away in a batch of uninteresting ones – just like the ones at your place cheek by jowl with the brilliant ones.'

'Which Tris was very dismissive about and you weren't.'

'I hadn't seen the paperwork, Brian, just the miniatures themselves. And I didn't – don't! – know anything about miniatures. So I was just reacting. Instinct. Intuition. Whatever.'

Brian looked as if he was sucking a rotten tooth,

but Helen said, 'So is Tris involved in this scam or not? And can we write him a reference?'

Griff stepped in. 'I don't think Lina's divvying powers extend that far, Helen. With all due respect, you have to make that judgement yourself. What I might, in your situation, be tempted to do is to give a fair evaluation of what he's done as an unpaid volunteer but say that until an ongoing police investigation is complete you are unable to comment on the honesty or otherwise of anyone at all in your organization. Anyone at all. That should cover it.'

My eyes rounded at the flow of official-sounding language.

'So it's a no, then,' Helen said. 'Poor Tris.'

'Poor Tris,' I echoed.

# Twenty-Seven

I was waving them off when I noticed a car parked opposite. It was Tris again, slumped as before behind the wheel of his battered Subaru. He wasn't looking in our direction. He wasn't looking anywhere. Just staring ahead.

What should I do? Finish locking up for a start, before nipping back inside to consult Griff.

'Ignore him,' he said, switching on the radio again.

'But what if he's . . .?' I made a throat-cutting gesture. What if he was after us?

For once Griff misunderstood me. 'At this time of day? Not the usual time to top oneself, my child.'

I hadn't even thought about that possibility, but it seemed more likely. Horribly likely. Nibbling a nail, I said, 'All he wanted was a real, paying job . . . Griff, what if he's had too much to drink, or has taken drugs? Or what if he's got a hose from his exhaust into the car and—?'

'With Brian's BMW parked right opposite? And our neighbours coming home from work? Really, Lina, I have to tell you that for once your imagination or your kind heart is working overtime.' He put his feet up again and reached for the radio. 'Very well, do you want me to go and ask him if he's trying to top himself?' Sighing, he made as if to get up. Half-heartedly.

'It'd better be me, hadn't it?'

\* \* \*

It all started well enough, with me asking Tris through the driver's window if he was all right.

And when he got out, he insisted all he wanted to do was talk about his future. 'Lina, it's all such a mess. I need to talk to someone—' Then he grabbed me. Really, his line in snogging was pretty poor. And I didn't even have any ice cubes handy.

As I tried to fend him off, the street was flooded with lights, a car skidded to a halt and suddenly I was staggering backwards and watching someone thump Tris so hard several times that he fell backwards, hitting his head on the car and slithering to the ground apparently unconscious. More than apparently. For real. Certainly there was a lot of real blood coming from his nose. But the other man was gathering me to him and demanding to know if I was all right.

Morris? Even, and possibly better still, Carwyn? But I knew that viciously expensive aftershave, and, come to think of it, I knew that viciously expensive car. Bloody Aidan and his bloody Merc. Not to mention his knuckles, which were also – but this time literally – bloody.

'What I can't understand, Aidan,' I said, not very graciously as an ambulance removed Tris, just in case the bang on the head had done anything serious, 'is how you came to be here. Before you explain, though, you'd better have some ice for that hand of yours.'

It wasn't just me eyeing at it: an embarrassed police community support officer, no doubt wondering if he should call in for his proper colleagues, was trying to make sense of the scene.

Naturally, Aidan ignored him. And my suggestion. 'It's a good job I was here. What would it have done to Griff to see you being raped in front of his very eyes?'

'What good will it do Griff seeing you here after what you were doing with Charles?' I countered.

He had the grace to look hangdog. 'That's why I'm here.'

But it wasn't. Not entirely. Or even not exactly. To do him justice, though, even as I unlocked the front door, he was calling to Griff in the most penitent of tones. I let them sort things out between them while I spoke to the PCSO, a man in his early forties with a very whiny Kent accent, in the warmth of the kitchen.

'I'm quite sure that Tris won't press charges if I don't press charges against him. I think he just wanted to . . . Something had upset him and he just turned to me . . .'

'For a bit of a hug, like?'

'Possibly. On the other hand, since I don't particularly want to hug him, I'd be really grateful if I could have a word with him and find out what was really going on inside his head. You know, since we used to be . . . Just in case Aidan was right and he meant to hurt me.' Maybe the sight of me might shock him into saying something.

The CSO looked embarrassed. 'I suppose if you want to . . . They're very big on reconciliation and arbitration and stuff these days. Cheaper than going to court and ASBOs and that. So if I could fix a meeting . . .'

* * *

It was almost as if Griff and Aidan had been waiting for the officer to leave, because Aidan erupted from the living room as soon as I closed the front door, only to hang back as if waiting for my permission to speak.

I gestured. It would be the living room for all of us. It would never do for Griff to have to eavesdrop in his own home. 'Let me get you that ice first.'

Wrapping the tea towel I produced, full of crushed ice cubes, round his hitting hand, he said, 'Lina, I owe you the most profound, my most sincere apology.' He really looked sorry too – which made me wonder why all those syllables weren't nearly as effective as the simple words, *I'm sorry*. Griff would be able to explain later. 'You were right; I was wrong.'

My next words weren't very long or very gracious. 'What about?' After all, I had a lot of grudges against him stored up, whatever Griff had said about forgiveness.

'About my miniature. Lina, I implore you, get it back for me!'

My little mental wheels worked overtime. 'You mean,' I said slowly, to give them the chance to catch up, 'that someone really has stolen a prize miniature?'

'Of course. I thought it was safe and sound with all the others, that no one would picked it out from the others hanging there. But Lina, someone's taken it and replaced it with a copy. The frame's still there, but not . . .' He was almost in tears. Was in tears.

No wonder he hated me. Because all I could

279

think of were brutal questions. 'It's been removed? Like Toby's? What do the police say?'

'Police? What do they know about such things?'

I thought of Carwyn. 'A very great deal, actually. And you know what, your insurance company won't think much of your talking to me before dialling nine-nine-nine.'

He wrung his hands. 'But – so awkward . . . Admitting . . .'

'If you're alleging that Charles replaced it while you were tied up,' Griff said, 'admit it you must. The police have heard and seen worse. Lina's right, Aidan. It's a job for people who can fully examine the scene of the crime, take DNA samples . . . That sort of thing,' he said, with an airy wave of the hand.

'Besides which,' I added, 'it's almost certainly part of a pretty big scam.' I repeated what I'd said to Helen and Brian. 'Whoever's involved must be stopped. From the people operating out of the Midlands, providing the selection of miniatures and their provenance, to the people taking the money via an authenticated bank account. And I can't do any of that.'

'But the gossip . . . my reputation . . .'

'Which always was that you were an old bugger who liked an occasional bit of bondage,' Griff said, softening the words with a ruefully affectionate smile. 'And spanking. Not that Charles is anything but a young gentleman, of course. But I bet you couldn't sit down for a bit. Do as Lina says: call the police. I bet you have the number of that darling young Welshman, don't you, dear one?'

280

'Would you phone?' Aidan whispered. He opened his mouth, looking first from me then to Griff. It was obvious he had something else to say but not while I was in the room.

Sure I'd slip out and make the call. But this time I couldn't help keeping my ears open.

'It isn't necessarily young Charles,' I heard him confess before he shut the door very firmly. I'd have given a great deal to hear more, but it wasn't my relationship, and in any case I really wanted to phone Carwyn, as at least one sane person in an otherwise crazy world and the one best suited to dealing with Aidan's antics. In any case, he owed me news about the emporium and Hastings. Didn't he?

Carwyn showed no irritation at being summoned to talk to Aidan, greeting me with a quick apology for not getting back to me earlier.

'Not much to report,' he said. 'Shall I fill you in when I've dealt with your friend?'

Aidan, never one to be kept waiting, recounted his goings on, though at this point he coyly told Carwyn he preferred not to name names. Names! I know it's just a cliché usually, but might he in fact mean there was more than one? Eventually, the admission inched its way out. I couldn't look at Griff, for whom this must be painfully embarrassing. As for Carwyn, I had a feeling that, though he was serious and still quite deferential, he'd have a wonderful time regaling his mate with the tale in the pub later.

'You've been very helpful, sir,' he said, when he'd put the last full-stop to his notes. 'You realize, of course, that you're making a very serious allegation against one at least of these . . . escorts. Did you ever give me the full names, sir? Or that of the agency?'

Nice, neat question. Of course he hadn't. Aidan blushed, and to my chagrin I found myself joining him, though I'd bet it was for a different reason. I'd never even asked Charles' full name. He'd always been just Charles, Richard's minion. Not a person in his own right.

'I'm afraid you'll just have to ask Charles' employer, Sir Richard Walker, of Warebank Court,' Aidan declared airily, trying to regain control of the situation. 'It's not far from Cirencester.'

Carwyn nodded, jotting. 'And for the other man?'

This time his face was crimson, and he looked furtively at me. 'His name's Collingwood.'

I don't think I've ever sat so hard on a sofa. 'Not Tris! So why, Aidan, did you hit him so hard?' I narrowed my eyes. 'I know. It wasn't anything to do with rescuing me, was it? It was because you suspected it was him that had nicked your miniature.'

The silence was crushing. It was filled with all the scathing words I didn't know well enough to use out loud, plus a few more I'd rather Carwyn didn't know I could use. 'Hit him hard enough to land him in A and E,' I prompted at last, to update Carwyn. Then I produced my brassiest smile, the sort that most irritated Aidan. 'I should imagine it's all recorded on our CCTV system, which is always attracted by brawls.'

Carwyn, bemused, fumbled for his mobile.

Griff, who seemed remarkably calm, perhaps courtesy of all those pills he had to pop, gestured elegantly. 'The mobile reception's terrible round here. Please feel free to use our office phone to make any calls.'

As much to escape the highly charged atmosphere in the living room as anything else, I led the way. He closed both the living room door and, once we were both inside, the office door.

His smile was cautious. 'What's your role in all this, Lina?'

'Aidan came to ask me for advice. God knows why. And my advice was to talk to you.'

He nodded. As he picked up the phone he asked, 'Heard from DCI Morris recently?'

I stared, very hard. 'Where's that coming from?' Bloody Freya, that was where, of course.

'Just wondered.'

'Weird thing to wonder about when you're supposed to be chasing criminals. Which is,' I added, as offhand as I could, 'what I suppose Morris is doing. Haven't heard from him for weeks. I'll leave you to it.' Whatever *it* was – which he clearly had no intention of telling me.

I wandered into the kitchen. Maybe my thinking processes would be helped by a coffee; on the other hand, even if Aidan would like one, Griff wouldn't sleep all night if he indulged. So though I filled the kettle I didn't switch it on.

Tris first. Was he truly gay? In which case why had he bothered to try and snog me? Gay men didn't need what Griff called beards these days, so he didn't need to pretend to be straight. Was

283

he trying to worm his way not into my knickers but into our cottage, with a view to arranging a few thefts from that? Or did he genuinely want a paying job with us? If he'd had one, perhaps he could have given up what I was sure Griff would discreetly call his agency work.

There were two rich collectors and two resentful young men – surely Charles' treatment as no more than Richard's minion must have rankled as much as Tris's unpaid status, assuming that was a major motivation? Were they possibly connected? The collectors were friends, of course: were they conspirators? Or did they even know each other? And what, for goodness' sake, might either of them have to do with white horses, one complete with fingerprint, and *sang de boeuf* Ruskin ware? Somehow I didn't see them as masterminds of criminal gangs, either. They were both too sure of themselves and their place in the order of things to need to change anything – unless, of course, they could get their mitts on a prize item without asking troublesome questions.

There was another question, too. Were the attempts to get through our security system in any way connected with all these goings on? That would have implied a degree of sophistication I really didn't like, but which Sir Richard might conceivably have. He wouldn't have soiled his hands himself, of course – he'd have got one of the workers to do it. And certainly the guy posing as an operative was genuinely working-class by his accent. But connection? I couldn't see one. Not even a hint of one to mention to Carwyn.

284

# Twenty-Eight

'Drinking alone?' Carwyn made me jump so much that I slopped a drop or two on the otherwise pristine tablecloth.

'Griff's got pills to take and I presume you and Aidan are driving,' I said, which didn't seem the answer to his question. I mopped up the wine with a J-cloth. What a good job I wasn't drinking red.

'All this is really getting to you, isn't it? On top of that nasty assault only a few weeks ago. And I'd guess that with Griff out of the loop you've been working all hours. With no support.' He sounded as kind as I imagined a favourite uncle might – I could imagine Paul saying his words, in exactly the same tone.

'Wrong there. Mary Walker and Paul Banner, her fiancé, have been saints. Speaking of which, is there any news about the antiques shop where he bought the little white horse?'

He checked his watch. 'We've got your friend Paul ID-ing a couple of people at this very moment.' He added, his smile hard to read, 'So we may not need to contact your ex in Devon.'

For some reason I needed to say, 'We were never an item, so he's hardly an ex. But it'd be good if you people could deal with it all, wouldn't it?' I think I said that, but my mind was suddenly groping after something it had forgotten.

'Lina?' he prompted.

'You'll think I'm an absolute idiot, but I've just recalled that one of the young men . . . involved . . . with Aidan knows a lot about Beswick horses. Our first conversation. I'm sorry. My memory's awful. Especially under stress. And Griff was still in intensive care or only just a day out of it when the conversation took place.'

'So are you trying to tie this young man – Tris Collingwood, I presume – in with the white horse scam?'

'No! Absolutely not!' My fingers crossed behind my back. 'The community support guy was hinting I'd save him a lot of trouble if I talked to Tris. About why he grabbed me and why Aidan socked him.' More or less true, anyway. 'Do you want me to?'

He shook his head, absent-mindedly helping himself to half an inch of the Sauvignon Blanc I'd not returned to the fridge. 'On what basis? You couldn't ask him if he stole Aidan's minia- tures – or any other miniatures. That's a job for us, Lina. All due respect but we do have proce- dures. I know we were slow picking up the case, but we're certainly running with it now.' He looked at the bottle and topped up my glass and his, emptying it.

'But . . . Can't you let me talk to him? As a mate? He was an unpaid intern, Carwyn. Humiliating. Had to ask me to buy meals and drinks. Begged me for a job. A paying job.' My eyes filled with tears. 'Isn't that what everyone wants? A fair day's work for a fair day's pay?' Hell, wasn't it usually the other way round? If it

286

was, Carwyn didn't pick me up on it. As something as an afterthought, we clinked glasses.

'Why didn't you give him a job, if you were sorry for him?' He sat almost but not quite opposite me, something that reminded me horribly of police interview rooms.

'No vacancies,' I told him.

'Would you have created a vacancy if you'd trusted him?'

'What gave you the idea I don't?' But I'd hesitated a second too long.

Even if he meant to reply, two phones rang – the office one and his mobile. 'Try out in the yard, by the washing whirligig,' I said, taking my glass of wine with me.

The call was from the security people. Should I panic?

'Geoff? Haven't heard from you for a bit,' I said doubtfully.

'Did you expect to?'

'Well, yes . . . That security impersonator. The one who scared me rigid.'

There was a pause. He'd obviously no idea what I was talking about. It was easy to forget, wasn't it, that I was only one of many clients to worry about. At last – and I could almost hear him slapping his forehead in irritation – he said, 'Ah! That bugger pretending to be one of us? Dennis, his real name. We picked him up doing the same with some other clients. Says he needs to check their system, disables it, and goes back later to help himself to the stuff he's checked out. He had a bit of an accident, so we called the police.'

'Accident?'

'Hurt his face a bit. Very sad,' he said, irony dripping from his voice. 'Anyway, no need to worry about him: he won't be hitting the town again for a bit. Though I must say, and this is why I called, if you carry on meeting all and sundry out in the street, you'll have plenty of other things to worry about.'

'Meeting all and—?'

'Recall that nice little kerfuffle there a while back?' His voice changed. 'What the hell were you doing going out on your own to talk to that little scrote? Nah, don't bother explaining. Got a teenage girl myself. Going to get five top A levels they say, but when it comes to *lurve* she's got no more idea than a flea. Any road, nice bit of work from that guy with the Merc.'

'I'll tell him.'

'Do that. But watch your back. That's my advice.'

'I might even take it. But why did you call him a scrote?'

'All the images of him we've got on file. What a tosser.'

'Anything specific?' I asked carefully.

'Babe, it's confidential, isn't it?'

'What if it affects my health and safety?'

'What if it doesn't though? Not yours.'

'Look, Geoff, there's a detective downstairs. Fraud and theft and I don't know what. Talk to him?'

'You talk to him,' he said, enigmatic as Titus, and cut the call.

It felt dead weird tapping on my own living

room door and waiting, instead of marching straight in. Weirder to have Carwyn emerge and close the door behind him, edging us towards the kitchen again.

I tried to take the ascendant, but couldn't quite manage an arms akimbo challenge. 'You know stuff about Tris you've not yet told me. Were you trying to find out if I was his accomplice?'

'The thought never once crossed my mind.'

I think I believed him. 'Good. So what do you know?'

He patted his phone. 'He's just been fingered, Lina – by the people who made your friend Paul give back the white horse. And since they show up on Ashford CCTV as having had a hand in wrecking your friend Rob Sampson's shop—'

'*A* hand? They weren't working on their own? Was an ex-security guy called Dennis involved?'

'Not as far as I know. They were working with a young man – very talented, by all accounts, with a degree in ceramics and goodness knows what else. Wayne Sergeant. Based in Rye, as it happens, not Totnes. Access to his own kiln, and knows the theory too. Unlike the others, a working class lad made good. Or not, in view of what he's been up to.'

'The others? So more than one posh young man?' My stomach clenched.

'The provenance part and finances were dealt with by a very clever young man, living in Warwickshire, with all sorts of diplomas and degrees in art and a gaga uncle who didn't know his estates (oh yes, two or three of them) – called Torquil Hart-Richards.'

'My God, what a moniker. As posh as . . . as posh as Tristam's. And possibly Charles's?'

He nodded, as if pleased that my guess spared him the trouble of having to break bad news. 'Charles Huddleston's.'

'So this posh gang – how did they come together? All Millfield School pupils?'

'Absolutely not. Charles was a model pupil, and an excellent student at uni. He seems to have gone bad later – there appears to be a polo connection, actually, with Collingwood. Hart-Richards knew Collingwood through his cousin, a lady you might know as a Mrs Fielding. What made them turn to crime, goodness knows.'

'Money? Or rather, in Tris's case, lack of?'

'Their families are loaded.' He gave a massive shrug. 'I'm sure they'll wheel out top counsel, who'll come out with all sorts of pseudo-psychological crap about why their poor clients suffered these temporary aberrations.' With one swig he downed the now lukewarm wine he'd left earlier. He stared at the glass as if blaming it for his outburst. Managing a smile, he added, 'I forgot to tell you. When I spoke to Sir Richard Walker, to find more about Charles, he said he wanted you to know that someone you made a promise to is on the mend after emergency surgery.'

'Toby Byrne. Just as posh, but a nice ordinary name,' I said, irrelevantly. 'I promised him I'd get him his stolen miniature back.'

He gave a bark of laughter. 'Will you be returning each stolen masterpiece to its owner, or just those to the collectors you know personally? Because it'll take quite a bit of your time to do that. We've got the Met's Fine Arts unit involved now. They and my colleagues are working their way through the records of all the auction houses in the country where mixed groups of miniatures were sold as single lots. And through all the known collectors who might have lost one. Some museums actually have so many in their vaults, they were robbed without even knowing it, apparently. Even some abroad. So Interpol may come into it,' he added, almost apologetically. After all, he knew that such a connection with Morris might touch a raw nerve.

It didn't. Not very hard, anyway. In any case, I was more interested in other things just now. 'My miniature – the one you took into protective custody – was stolen, of course?'

'I'm afraid so. From some collection in Germany.'

'The Tansey Collection,' I said. I wouldn't have known about it, of course, unless Titus had mentioned it. Titus had mentioned something else, hadn't he? It was time to tell him my theory. 'I don't suppose the miniatures had been smuggled out without frames and ended up in modern frames with fake hallmarks?' His face gave him away. 'Yes! I told you my friend Titus was kosher! It was he who put me on to it – tried to warn Freya Webb, you remember.'

'I think kosher might be going a bit far, Lina, but I'm prepared to say he was right on this occasion. Can we leave it at that?'

I twinkled at him under my lashes. 'No chance of a reward for him?'

'Not the smallest chance. Now, if you can stop

291

winding me up for a moment I ought to take a formal statement.'

'Do you still get involved with such mundane stuff? I thought it was farmed out to non-police personnel these days.'

'Perhaps I don't trust them to spell *miniature* correctly?'

I ventured a couple of alternative spellings.

He cackled.

'All the same,' I said at last, 'I really don't think I could give a full and accurate statement tonight. Not with that wine on an empty stomach.' Which he'd had too. In the best tradition of Tripp hospitality I turned to and made sandwiches – Griff's own bread, of course. He made a willing scullion.

By the time we carried the trays – Aidan and Griff would no doubt want refreshments too – the conversation in the living room involved, of all things, laughter. Both the old dears sported Cheshire cat grins. Bridges were under repair, if not quite rebuilt.

Griff saw me first, getting up to pull out a couple of occasional tables. 'My darling child, we were just talking about my night nurse.'

Carwyn raised an eyebrow but didn't ask why. He poured wine – red – for Griff, and then for Aidan, but a mite less willingly, I thought.

I frowned. 'The invisible one? The one who didn't give you your pills? Smoked salmon or low-fat cheese,' I added, pointing.

'Exactly. The invisible one. But not the inaudible one. My love, the reason you never saw

292

her was that she lasted precisely one night. God knows how much Aidan paid for her to care for me—'

'But care for him she did not,' Aidan concluded, waving away the expense with his beautifully manicured hand.

'In fact, she required Aidan to care for her. The bedroom with the en suite bathroom; the baby-alarm. We weren't exactly happy, but didn't know what to expect. What we did know was that she wasn't supposed to sleep through the night, snoring so loudly that she kept Aidan awake, and then demand tea in bed in the morning.'

Aidan added darkly, provoking further laughter from the others, 'And other favours.'

As if!

'We didn't want to worry you by telling you the truth,' Aidan added, 'since you seemed to have enough on your plate already.'

I could hardly argue with that. In any case, there'd been plenty of bad feeling without my adding to it. So I just picked up on one word. 'The truth! All I wanted – all! – was to know the truth about what's been going on. That's all. And now I almost wish I didn't know. All those young lives ruined. I ought to sneer and somehow say it'll do such spoilt young men good to see what life behind bars is like. But I can't. All I can see is the waste of all their talents. Would it have saved Tris if I'd spotted early on that he really needed paid work – if I'd taken him on for the day Paul isn't with us? Like Griff saved me?'

Griff took my hand and squeezed it, but left it to Carwyn to reply.

'He was in way too deep for that, Lina. He might have been born with a canteen of silver cutlery but it was well and truly tarnished within twelve months of his leaving uni. And you know what, he might just have responded to your generosity as he did to the Bakers' – robbing you if not directly, certainly indirectly. DCI Webb tells me you value your reputation for probity above anything.' He looked from me to Griff, who nodded.

'I could quote *Othello* at you if you wanted,' Griff said.

'I could do it myself,' Carwyn said, grinning. '*I have lost the immortal part of myself, and what remains is bestial.*'

# EPILOGUE

There had been no argument: Griff had lost so much weight that he had to consign his best suit to the clothing bank, and he enjoyed himself enormously in the best men's outfitters in Canterbury – he still didn't fancy a trip to London – shopping for a replacement. He had almost outraged the flower ladies who were decorating the church by importing far more flowers than Mary had ordered, but since he messed in with them, and supplied coffee and cakes to sustain them, he became a part of their team. In straight mode. Not a hint of campness to outrage their village souls. When the organist went sick with a whitlow, Griff conjured one whose face I'd only seen on CD covers.

On the Big Day itself, he kept his promise to apply Mary's slap, and mine, of course. Mary, giggling with the nip of pink champagne he pressed on her, fumbled her way through the long row of tiny buttons up my back and stroked the tippet's fur the right way. Then she sat down, quite silent. At first I was worried I ought to jolly her along, but then I saw her face, so full of joy that it was clear she couldn't find words to express it. As I slipped her dress over her head and helped her into the long flowing top, which she'd insisted on to cover what she claimed were bingo wings, I realized how lovely she must have looked when she was young – and how beautiful she was today.

Aidan, who I'd thought wouldn't be seen dead at such a rustic event, instituted himself as a sidesman; not for anything would I have passed on a whispered question from one of the choir-boys hanging round outside – was he what they call an undertaker?

The three of us walked with unconventional speed up the aisle: clearly, she didn't want to waste another moment of her life away from Paul's side. The distinguished organist, not used to such cavalier treatment, insisted on playing the rest of the piece although it was clearly redundant.

Paul looked handsome, supported by one of his equally handsome sons, whose presence had Griff nudging and winking at me encouragingly. Robin, officiating in his favourite church, looked his usual divine self and preached an appropriate but blessedly short sermon. Little Imogen, in Freya's suddenly maternal arms, slept soundly throughout.

Even the sun, which had lurked behind clouds long enough to make the day seem cold, emerged for the photos. Smiling at Carwyn, who'd somehow wangled an invitation from Mary, I remembered another quotation. Byron? No . . . Browning! Griff always said it was always taken out of context, and was in fact deeply ironic, since the poem involved regicide and betrayal. But it seemed to fit today:

*God's in His heaven—*
*All's right with the world!*